She was his prisoner n...

"Listen to me." It was i...

kind of peace between t...

Upon my oath as a Viking, you will be safe upon this ship."

Her eyes met his and she could read the truth of his promise within their depths. She relaxed and breathed a sigh, then looked towards the wide expanse of ocean. "Take me back." The words held no pleading but were instead a command.

"I can't!"

"You can!" She searched his expression for any sign that he would relent and saw none. "You can not think to take me with you!"

"I don't want to cause you further unhappiness but I cannot turn back." The words were spoken as gently as Selig could manage. "You have no choice but to be a Viking now, at least for a while."

"A Viking . . . ?" She looked around her. The other Vikings surveyed her with curiosity but there did not seem to be blood lust in their eyes. They also seemed to acknowledge that she belonged to their leader. Would she? "No . . . never . . ."

"You must . . ."

"I'll never act, speak, or be like a Viking!" she spat at him.

The hatred in her eyes was more than he could bear. He could remember another time when there had been softness in those violet eyes, and yes, love. He had not been blind to her childhood fondness for him. Now he longed for her to love him again.

"What a woman you have become. I was right . . ." he whispered. She was his greatest treasure yet she was untouchable for he did not want her to hate him any more than she already did.

There has to be a way to overcome her anger and make her love me again, he thought.

The question that plagued him as the ship skimmed through the waters.

Dear Readers,

In July of 1999, we launched the Ballad line with four new series, and each month since then we've presented both new and continuing stories set everywhere from medieval England to the American West—the kind of passionate, romantic stories you love best, written by the most gifted authors. At the back of each book, we'll tell you when you can find subsequent books in the series that have captured your heart.

This month, the fabulous Willa Hix returns to historical romance with her new series, *The Golden Door,* which follows the adventures of a pair of half siblings new to America during its lush Gilded Age. In **Cheek to Cheek,** a young woman fleeing an arranged marriage finds herself faced with the possibility of real love—with the man who has hired her as his aging mother's companion. Next up, ever-talented Linda Lea Castle continues the triumphant saga of *The Vaudrys* with **Surrender the Stars,** as King Henry III commands a loyal subject to wed a mysterious woman who may be his doom—or his heart's destiny.

Reader favorite Kathryn Hockett sweeps us back to the turbulent era of *The Vikings* with the **Conqueror,** a warrior sworn to vengeance . . . but tempted by desire. Finally, Cherie Claire concludes the lushly atmospheric story of *The Acadians* with **Delphine,** as fate reunites a dashing smuggler with the girl who once professed to love him—but who has become a woman with wealth, obligations—and desires—of her own. Enjoy!

Kate Duffy
Editorial Director

THE VIKINGS

CONQUEROR

KATHRYN HOCKETT

ZEBRA BOOKS
Kensington Publishing Corp.
http://www.kensingtonbooks.com

AUTHOR'S NOTE

Like a bolt of lightning, the Vikings burst upon Europe at the end of the eighth century. The age of the longships, which carried Viking raiders from northern England to North Africa, had begun. These raids were prompted by a desire to acquire wealth, a reputation, and to attract an armed following that would support ambitions at home. Trade and land hunger were also factors in the Viking phenomenon.

The Anglo-Saxon Chronicle makes many references to the "sea-borne pagans" who attacked the south coast. The glimpse of a square sail and dragon-headed prow on the horizon struck fear into the hearts of the inhabitants of Britain. To the Anglo-Saxons the first Viking raids seemed to be a divine judgment on their sins. The irony of it all, however, is that there was an obvious similarity between the Viking attacks on England and those which the Anglo-Saxons had made on Roman Britain over three hundred years earlier.

The first of the raiders were the Danes, who attacked the monasteries and abbeys. After a reign of terror they came to conquer and later to settle the territory in England later called Danelaw. For the promise of peace the people of Britain often paid the Vikings money but were rewarded with treachery.

Before the Vikings came, England was a scene of perpetual conflict among its kingdoms. Under the weight of the Viking assault the English kingdoms of Northumbria, East Anglis, and Mercia collapsed one by one, their strength drained, their royal lineages extinguished. Despite the fact that the Danes penetrated into much of their territory, Wessex was the only part of England that resisted the Danes.

The Danish invasion was just the first breath of a storm that was to sweep away all rivals to the house of Wessex and with them some of the best achievements of English civilization. During this turmoil, Norwegians also came. Swarming out of their longships in an ever-growing host, they sought not just to plunder but to conquer and carve out vast territories to rule. The word "Viking," which means pirate, was coined by their victims and refers to both the light-haired Norwegians and dark-haired Danish invaders. Anglo-Saxons were frequently confused as to the distinction between the two because they spoke the same language.

Amidst this turmoil a search is under way to find the sons of Ragnar Longsword, the daring Viking jarl whose bold raids and conquests of the heart were already legend. To each of his lovers he has given a jewel from his Viking sword to hang around his child's neck when each is born. Now those pendants are the only key to the quest.

In Wessex the quest continues, linking a Viking, once sold as a slave, with the greatest prize of all, the English daughter of his greatest enemy.

NOTE: Newfs, the "canine seamen." There are many legends about the Newfoundland dog (Baugi in *Conqueror*) saving drowning victims by carrying lifelines to those who had fallen overboard. Vikings and fishermen made use of these dogs and their skills in the water. The breed as we know it today was developed in England during the Viking Age but was nearly legislated to extinction in 1780. Though the dog takes its name from Canada's maritime province, the origin of the dog is disputed. Vikings and Basque fishermen gave accounts of natives working side by side with the sweet-tempered, giant, web-footed, thick-furred dog.

PART ONE

Damsels, Deceit, and Dragon Ships

Wessex and the Western Coast of England—858

ONE

The soft glow of the early morning sun lit up the rocky shoreline and cast a glow upon the petite, dark-haired woman who sat upon a cold, damp rock gazing into the swirling waters of the ocean. Hugging her arms around her knees, she breathed deeply of the sea air, trying to calm her nervousness. It was her wedding day. From this day forward, her freedom would be curtailed and she would have a husband.

"Husband . . ." Gwyneth whispered, not liking the sound of the word at all when it applied to her. But there was little that she could do about her upcoming nuptials. It was a man's world and a daughter had to obey her father's dictates no matter how much it uprooted her life or how disappointed she might be that she was marrying for the sake of an alliance and not for love.

Gwyneth's father and Alfred, the man she was to marry, were two of the greatest landowners in the west part of Wessex. Long ago they had discussed joining their lands by marriage, and since her older sister, Ethelin, was already spoken for, Gwyneth was the daughter who was betrothed.

"It is a marriage made in heaven," her father had proclaimed, but Gwyneth felt otherwise. Since she had seldom seen Alfred, she would be marrying a man she didn't even know. That thought was unsettling to her even though such an arrangement was common.

After tonight I will no longer be a maiden, she thought, feeling a stab of fear for what was going to happen. Would he be gentle with her? Or would he be forceful in claiming his husbandly rights? Though her sister Ethelin insisted that "it wasn't so bad," Gwyneth wanted something more. She wanted the wondrous joy of love that the bards sang about, a feeling she had felt briefly for a young Viking slave a long time ago.

Closing her eyes, she remembered the first time she had seen the handsome young man with hazel eyes as stormy as a thundercloud. Her father had dragged him to the hall with his hands tied behind his back with thick ropes.

"We have a slave," he had announced triumphantly. "Now we can make this one pay for all the suffering they have brought to our shores."

Curious, she had pushed through the crowd to take a look at this fierce pagan, expecting him to look like the devil himself. She had been stunned to see that except for his fair coloring, the young Viking didn't look much different from the youths of Wessex.

Gwyneth had been struck by his youth. He was no more than five or six years older than she, yet his still-beardless face bore the mark of strength and stubborn pride. Looking straight at her, his head held high, he appeared to be the conqueror, not the conquered. She had read pain and disillusionment, however, in those eyes, and had felt sorrow and compassion.

"He insists that he is not our enemy. He says that he is half English and that his father was Norwegian and not Dane," her father continued, "but I say that a Viking is a Viking!" With a curse her father had roughly nudged the young man, sending the captive sprawling.

With an aggressiveness foreign to her nature, Gwyneth had rushed forward, feeling protective even then. "Leave him alone! He has done us no harm." Clasping the Viking's strong hand, she helped him to his feet. His touch stirred her deeply. This time, when the Viking had looked at her, his gaze was bright with gratitude.

From that moment on she had brought him food whenever she could because of her fear that the gruel and water he was fed would not be enough. She had stolen food from the table or more often than not, given him her own portion. His thankful smile had been reward enough. Looking forward to seeing him, she had visited him every day and every night, selfishly treasuring those visits in the depths of her heart. As long as he was near and she could love him, she felt that everything was all right.

Then one day while she was watching the Viking work from a distance she was shaken out of her dreamworld. When the young Viking stubbornly refused to be humiliated by one of her brothers, he had been whipped. Though she had placed herself between the two young men, begging for him to be spared, she was shoved away, helpless, as the Viking suffered a beating.

"And you say *they* are barbaric, Beorhtric! If so, then what are you?" she had asked angrily. In that moment she had known that despite the consequences she had to set the Viking free.

Later that night when the moon was hidden by clouds she had come to him, bringing more than just food and healing salve. She brought the key to his dungeon and the promise of escape.

The wind swirled about her, whipping thick strands of long, black hair into her face. Gwyneth brushed the silken threads away and was not surprised to find tears on her cheeks as she remembered. Tears for the captive, tears as she remembered their goodbye.

She remembered how she had stared at his bare chest and back as she had rubbed ointment on his injuries, how she had wondered what it would be like to hold him close. For a moment she had selfishly tried to tell herself that she couldn't let him go, that freeing him might endanger his life if he were caught. But such rationalization was wrong and she knew it. Reaching into the folds of her cloak, she had taken out a knife and sawed at his bonds. She would face her punishment bravely, knowing that at least her beloved was given a chance to be free.

It had taken several minutes to work through the ropes and all the while the young Viking had stared at her with an unfathomable look in his eyes. Then he was free.

Gathering her into his arms with words she knew to be of gratitude, he had hugged her for a long, long time. In that moment she had known that he would be in her thoughts and her heart forever. Then, as if wanting to give her some token of his appreciation, he had bent down, picked up a rock, and exposed a hiding place. From that hiding place he had brought forth some kind of necklace, holding it towards her with a smile that told her it was for her.

Gwyneth reached for that necklace now, looking lovingly at the silver dragon decorated with a sapphire. The sapphire was set below the dragon's eye so it appeared to be the dragon's tear. Each time she looked at the amulet, she thought of him and warmth filled her heart.

"Still dreaming about your Viking?" a voice scolded. Gwyneth turned to see the familiar face of her sister, Ethelin.

"I was just wondering where he is . . ." She sighed.

"It doesn't matter. Even were you to meet again, you will be a married woman. Best then to put the necklace away with other childhood toys." Ethelin held out her hand as if to take the necklace, but Gwyneth shook her head. She would never take the necklace off. Never! Somehow she sensed that the Viking had given it to her for protection.

"Have it your way then." Taking her arm, Ethelin had insisted that she come back with her to the hall. "There is so much yet to do for the wedding."

At first Gwyneth refused, then she turned away from the ocean. Walking arm in arm with her sister, she headed towards the stone building that was her fiancé's house and which soon would be her own. She did not see the red-and-white-striped sails upon the horizon coming closer and closer to shore.

The Viking ships looked like monsters from the sea, flashing their overlapping shields like a dragon's scales in the cold glint of the sun. The carved dragon heads looked ominous but not nearly as frightening as the raiders aboard.

"Let us hope that the traitorous Englishman will not betray us and that we will take them unaware," murmured the Viking leader, a tall blond-haired man. Selig the Bold was his name, a half-English, half-Norse Viking whose courage and exploits were already legendary.

Selig watched as the land's rocky shoreline came into view. For seven years he had raided these shores in retaliation for the humiliation and pain he had suffered in his younger days. Now he felt a sense of exhilaration that was unsurpassed, for today he would avenge himself on the man who had sold him into slavery.

Selig lifted his eyes towards the sky. "Odin," he called out. "Odin, be with us this day."

Hearing him, the other Vikings took up the chant, their voices blending with the wind. "Odin. Odin. Odin."

TWO

The voices of the wedding guests sounded like bees buzz-buzzing as they meandered into the church. Gwyneth, her mother, and sister stood together in a small room as Ethelin hurriedly combed her sister's shining, dark-brown hair. She entwined the soft, waist-length strands with flowers and ribbons and plaited the crown into braids.

"Relax, child, you are standing as stiff as a board," their mother entreated, putting her hand in the small of her younger daughter's back.

"I'm frightened," Gwyneth said softly, admitting the truth. "I know naught of men."

Ethelin laughed. "When they are not thinking of warfare they want one thing. Give your husband what he wants when he wants it and he will be moldable clay in your hands."

Gwyneth frowned. "But that will make me feel like a whore. What about me and my feelings?"

"There are certain duties you must perform, child—cooking, cleaning, giving your husband children, and pleasing him when he is in the mood for bed sport." Her mother shrugged. "I fear that I have let you have your way too much because you are my baby, but you will soon learn that the man of the hall is like a rooster. He rules the roost."

"And crows to let everyone know it," Ethelin added.

Ethelin stood back to appraise her sister's beauty. She had a fine-chiseled nose, high cheekbones, and large, dark-fringed eyes. "Alfred will be pleased, for you possess a beauty that is rare and a body that is healthy and curved in just the right places." She ran her hands over her own ample hips. "Alas, how sad it is that after five or six children you will look like this."

"You're beautiful!" Gwyneth was quick to say. "Much prettier than I."

Ethelin grinned at the compliment, then tugged at her sister's hair. "You lie, but I thank you for it."

Gwyneth felt the cool linen of her gown as her mother slipped it over her head. It touched the ground and covered her thin chemise, its long split sleeve showing the fair skin of her naked arms. The white material was a striking contrast to the darkness of her hair.

"I want everything to be perfect—your hair, your dress, the words the priest says, and the wedding feast. I want this to be a day you will long remember." Gwyneth's mother gave her a quick kiss on the cheek. "It will give you something to dream of in days to come."

"Something to dream of." Pulling the dragon's tear pendant from beneath her gown, Gwyneth gazed down at it. She had dreamed so many times that she would find her Viking again, that he would fall in love with her, and that she would marry *him*. Now all those dreams were lost. He would be only a memory that she would hide from her husband so as not to anger him.

"For the love of God, put that thing away!" Though she was not easily angered, Aenella gripped her daughter's shoulder. "You should be wearing a cross, not some pagan's amulet. If your husband sees it he will question you and you will begin your marriage amiss."

"I can't help it. I cared for him and wonder where he is and if he is safe. Surely Alfred can not be concerned because I was rewarded for an act of kindness."

"An act of stupidity!" Ethelin countered. "You freed an enemy of your own father. Had it been anyone else you would have been put to death." As it was, Gwyneth had been locked in a room without food or water and lashed with a belt across her back until she was bruised and bleeding. Even now there were traces of those scars, yet they did not severely mar her slim form.

Not wishing to fight, Gwyneth slipped the pendant under her gown and between her breasts, then belted her fur-lined robe around her waist. Bending down, she pulled on her fur-lined leather shoes.

"Are you ready?" Ethelin and Aenella gave her one last inspection. Deciding that she met their approval, they gently pushed her out the door and went to join her father.

"For the love of God, don't frown so, Gwyn," her father scolded as they rounded a corner. She felt his hand on her arm and winced. "Do you want all the guests to think that I have beaten you?"

"I'm sorry." Gwyneth tried hard to smile but the expression she affected was more of a grimace.

"Leave the girl alone, Cedd. I remember how nervous I was on my wedding day and you and I had known each other all our lives." Reaching out, she took the bouquet of magenta corn roses, white shepherd's purse, and violet delphiniums out of his hand and placed them in Gwyneth's. "Go on, child. Alfred awaits you . . ."

Fighting against nervous tears, fearful that she would embarrass herself in front of the wedding guests, Gwyneth stumbled towards the portico where the gray-haired priest stood in his somber robes of the church—a white tunic and a Romanesque embroidered cloak.

Feeling as if she were sleepwalking, Gwyneth joined Alfred.

Dressed plainly in a tunic of white with a fur-lined cloak, Alfred took the hand of his bride. The tall, thin man would soon be her husband, Gwyneth thought as she looked at his face. Like his body, his face was elongated; his nose was a bit long but he had nice brown eyes.

"You look beautiful," he complimented as his eyes swept over her.

Gwyneth wondered if while he was looking at her he was adding up the lands marrying her would bring him, then decided that was unfair. Perhaps in truth Alfred was just as nervous as she was.

Though the priest spoke, she barely heard his words. She only knew that her hands were cold and her heart was beating wildly. She couldn't help but wonder what it would be like to spend her life with this man.

The sound of wood splintering shattered Gwyneth's contemplation. Her instincts warned her of danger as the fearful words sounded in her ears from behind her.

"God help us, it's the Vikings!"

"No, it's not possible . . ."

"To arms," cried out her father, struggling to retrieve his sword. He did not unsheathe it quickly enough before the nightmare descended upon them.

A scream tore from Gwyneth's mouth as she saw the gleam of upraised swords shining in the torchlight. Her heart instantly filled with terror, not only for herself but for all her loved ones.

"It can't be happening! It can't!" she cried, yet as she spoke she could see the fearsome warriors break into the hall, their long hair flying wildly about as they ran, shouting their harsh battle cry.

"Oddddddin!"

Gwyneth wanted to flee but her feet froze and her voice became paralyzed with fear. Her eyes met those of one of the Vikings, a tall, blond-haired, bearded man whose brows arched above piercing hazel eyes. What was it about those eyes that stirred her and drew her to him with a rush of emotion? Was it because he reminded her of *him?*

As the Viking struck out at one of the wedding guests, she pushed such thoughts away. This heathen wasn't anything like the Viking she had known. Her Viking had been kind, this one was cruel. He seemed to enjoy moving about the room, bringing carnage in his wake. Looking at her, he grinned; she shivered as she realized he must be thinking that he could conquer her as easily as he was conquering her people.

Gwyneth was in the midst of a nightmare but she couldn't wake up no matter how hard she tried. Screaming as she was forcefully separated from her mother, she fought like a wildcat. From out of the corner of her eye she saw both her father and brothers fighting and she feared that they would be killed. Worse yet, she could see that her sister had been cornered by a hulking Norseman.

"No!" At last finding her voice, she ran forward to save her sister, but her father pushed her back.

"Get out of here, Gwyn. Run for your life!"

She started to obey him, then paused in midstride as she watched two Vikings grab him from behind, keeping him immobile. No matter what happened, she couldn't think only of herself. Either they all fought together or together they would die! So thinking, Gwyneth hurled herself forward, lashing out wildly. Grabbing a candlestick, she swung it like a club, hitting first one Viking then another.

"Alfred!" Infuriated to see her betrothed standing by while her family suffered, she yelled at him over and over.

Gwyneth screamed as she saw her father fall but no one came to his aid. Instead her shrieks caught the attention of the broad-shouldered, blond Viking leader who moved slowly towards her. Her eyes pleaded with him to end the fighting but his fierce scowl indicated that it was just the beginning.

"Stay back!" Calling upon God to aid her, Gwyneth made one last lunge against her captors, kicking her foot, catching one of the Vikings in the leg. He cursed at her and started to strike her down when a loud, masculine voice told him to halt. Gwyneth waited in terror for the end to come but instead found herself face-to-face with the Viking leader.

She felt his strength, his authority in every pore as he bent down, picked her up in his arms, and then, as if she weighed little more than a child, walked across the church with her. Finding a small chamber, he brought her inside with him and shut the door.

The noise of battle was so loud that it could be heard through the thickness of the door. The battle was nearly over; the English would be subdued and the treasures of the church taken.

"And I have another prize of battle," Selig exclaimed as he looked down at the lovely young woman with long, dark hair and blue eyes.

"Your prize? Never," Gwyneth answered, staring him right in the eye. Digging her fingernails into her palms, she forced herself to be brave.

Stunned that she could speak his language, Selig set her down. "We will see," he said, his eyes wandering over her like a caress. She was small and barely came to his shoulders, yet she raised her chin in defiance. He reached out, touching her arm, but she shrank back. Her eyes searched for a way of escape but there was only the door and he stood in the way.

I should let her go, Selig thought. *I don't make war on women.* Why didn't he, then? What was it about this woman that had obsessed him the moment he laid eyes on her? Was it the dark hair? The eyes? Or was it because she was to be a bride and the thought of taking her from her English husband gave him a sense of retribution?

"Bah, the Englishman was a coward," he whispered. He had just stood by as the sky had fallen around his people's heads. He had not even lifted a finger to save his future bride. Selig knew that if the woman had been promised to him he would have fought long and hard to keep another man from possessing her.

"I will never let you touch me," Gwyneth rasped, her eyes riveted on the door.

" 'Never' is a strong word. I have learned never to say never." Toying with her, he stepped away from the door.

Seeing her chance, Gwyneth made a mad dash for the thick wooden portal, struggling to open it before he could react. Anticipating her reaction, Selig caught up to her before she could open it. Grasping first one wrist and then the other, he held her tightly while she kicked and clawed at him, trying to break free.

He laughed, watching as she struggled against him in vain. "I like a woman with spirit."

"And I like a man who knows when to show mercy," she countered.

"Mercy?"

Selig reached up and touched the gold collar around his neck. Once he had worn an iron collar similar to this, only instead of decoration it had been a slave collar. When he had at last become a free man he had replaced that collar with the gold one as a reminder of those days and the cruelty of his one-time English masters.

"The English don't know the meaning of the word. They fight each other like dogs over a bone, exhibiting a meanness that is unequaled." Releasing her wrists, he touched her face with his fingers, tracing the curve of her cheek and neck.

"Don't touch me again." She looked at the sword that he had stuck in the wood of the door. "If you do I . . . I will kill myself."

"They all say that," Selig whispered, "and not a one has actually carried out her threat. Instead they are soon begging me to touch them."

"Not I!"

Selig reacted to her reply as if it were a challenge. Pulling her up against the hardness of his chest, he bent to kiss her. His lips were soft yet firm, taking her breath away. Gently his mouth moved against hers, his tongue parting her lips to explore the softness of her mouth.

His nearness made her dizzy. For a long moment she enjoyed kissing him, until she remembered what he had done. Angered more at herself and her reaction to his kiss than at him, she pulled back her hand and slapped him.

The blow stung but it injured his pride more than it hurt. Still, Selig lost all patience with her. He had been determined to be gentle, yet suddenly he was obsessed with possessing her. She was his by right of conquest.

"I did not want to have to force you but by Odin's beard I will!" He put his hand on the neck of her gown and tugged with all his might, ripping it all the way to her waist.

"No!" She put her hand in front of her breasts, trying to maintain some semblance of modesty.

Selig reached out for her again, his fingers wrapping tightly in her long, dark hair with the intent of bringing her face closer to his. His eyes traveled downward, looking at the soft mounds of her breasts. Suddenly he gasped as he noticed something sparkling in the torchlight. No, not just something. It was the dragon's tear pendant.

Pulling back his hand abruptly, Selig stared at her. "Loki take me!" His face was grim as he ran his fingers through his long, blond hair. His heart beat fiercely as memories assailed him of a sweet-tempered, beautiful young woman, little more than a child, who had shown him kindness and given him his freedom. Without her he would have been lost.

The last time he had seen her she was a lovely waif with dark hair hanging down into her eyes, skinny and gawky, with breasts just starting to bud. "What a woman you have become . . ." he breathed, regretting with all his heart that their reunion had taken place amidst violence.

Gwyneth was confused as she saw myriad emotions flit over his face. "What is it?"

Turning his back on her, Selig strode to the door. "Go. I won't stop you, nor will I let anyone harm you."

Surprised yet confused, she stammered her gratitude.

"Stay within view so that I can protect you from the others," he announced.

"Protect me?" She was confused. One moment he was lusting after her and the next he acted as if he had been appointed her guardian.

He wouldn't look at her. She could sense a deep sadness in him and wondered what had happened to cause such pain. He had spared her. Why? It was a question she kept asking herself as she pushed through the door and went in search of her family.

THREE

Cursing aloud, Selig strode up and down, back and forth in front of the doors of the church. What ill luck! What terrible fortune to meet *her* under these circumstances.

For the last few years he had fantasized about meeting her again, it was true, but in his dreams he had been prosperous, a man of renown, and he had led her up the pathway to his fine house. He had wanted her to admire the man he had become so she would never regret, even for a moment, setting him free. Now that fantasy had been shattered because fate had set her in the path of his pillaging and violence.

Selig cursed again. Little had he known when he embarked on this raid that he would find her in a church in Chester. Her family's lands were farther up the coast. Though he had hated her father all these years, though he had sought revenge on all the others who had harmed him he had never raided her kinsmen for fear of somehow causing the pretty, dark-haired child harm. Now, without meaning to, he had unwittingly repaid her kindness by harming those she loved.

Though he assumed that his emotions had been dulled over the past few years of raiding, he was wrong. Knowing he had inadvertently harmed her tore at his heart. He remembered how she had given him water when he was thirsty, brought him food to ease his hunger, and stepped in front of the whip to try and stop his punishment. She had always been kind and gentle to him, ignoring his status as a slave. She had respected him! She had given him a reason to go on living in spite of the cruelty and depravity of his surroundings.

He remembered the night she had freed him as if it were only yesterday. For just a moment he had been tempted to turn back, fearful of the punishment she would receive for helping him, but she had insisted that he go.

For a time he had wandered—lost, alone, and hungry—in a hostile land, but he had the will to survive and indeed he had. Living on wild animals and any edible vegetation he could find, he had slowly made his way across the land to a Viking settlement hundreds of miles up the coast, where he had made his home. For a time he had been wary, even of other Vikings, knowing that one of his own had betrayed him, but at last he had gone on a raid with the others and from that moment on had spent his life seeking revenge by pillaging and plundering the English. Now, after seeing her, he deeply regretted his way of life.

Damn that traitorous Englishman! He had not told him that *she* was to be the bride at the ceremony today, though he had known. Selig could only wonder if some sinister plot had been hatched in the Englishman's mind when he had given the Vikings a drawing of the church's floor plan. Had he intended for Selig to kill all the guests, including the young woman's father? Had he hoped he would carry the bride away? What evil had lurked in his mind?

Selig stared at a statue of a young woman holding a baby whose peaceful expression belied the carnage that had been left in the wake of the raid.

Suddenly he longed to put everything back the way it had been before they came crashing in. There were other churches, monasteries, and castles all along the coast just waiting to be plundered. If he had it to do all over again, he would choose one of those.

"Curses on the Englishman!"

How he loathed the kind of man who brought death and violence to his own! He should be repaid in kind. Perhaps he would be, Selig thought as a scheme flitted through his mind. The Englishman would be given his share of the spoils according to their agreement but Selig had a surprise in store for him as well. And why not? He who betrayed one man had no loyalty and could be counted on to betray again and again until he came full circle.

"It would only be a matter of time until he betrayed me. But I will not give him the chance." Selig would give the Englishman to Roland to do with as he pleased.

At least if I cannot have her now he will not touch her either, he thought, feeling smugly satisfied. She deserved a better man for a husband than the coward who had been her betrothed. At least he could take some comfort in the knowledge that the raid had put an end to her wedding! At that thought he laughed aloud, yet the sound was hollow. After what had happened he could never come back into her life the way he had planned. Better for her to remember him the way he was than to know that he had brought death and destruction to her people.

"She will never know . . ." And perhaps it was just as well. He was a Viking and she was one of them. Even under the best of circumstances, there would have been turmoil in such a union. And yet how could he ever forget her?

He closed his eyes and could see the face of the

lovely child looking at him with her dark-fringed blue eyes. It was a face that had haunted him all these years. She had been so young that Selig had fought against any feelings he had for her while he was a captive. Nevertheless he had envisioned the beauty she would be when she blossomed into a woman. That expectation now paled when compared to the reality of the lovely woman she had become.

"The pendant!" If not for the necklace, what might he have done to her? Would he have forced her and earned her hatred forever?

Selig remembered the carved figure of the dragon with its sapphire tear. His mother had given it to him when he was just old enough to walk, making sure he understood to never take it off. She had insisted that it would protect him all the days of his life. It had been precious to him, yet he had given it to another. Why? Because at that moment she had been more precious to him than his own well-being.

"It did protect her!" And in turn protected the others, for the moment he had recognized her he had put an end to all of the pillaging and violence. "But she did not even have a flicker of recognition towards me."

He tugged at his beard, thankful that it had hidden his identity. Perhaps that was not so surprising. He had changed a great deal. He was taller now, battle-scarred, more muscular and, most importantly, he now wore a beard.

"Selig . . . !" Turning towards the church doors, he saw Roland coming towards him. "What are you doing out here? You should be inside making certain that you get your share."

"I don't care about the spoils."

"Don't care?" Roland squinted as he looked at him. Reaching out, he felt his head for sign of a fever. "Are you ill?"

"No!"

Roland cocked his head. "Are you sure?"

"Yes!" Selig yelled so loud that Roland covered his ears. Realizing that he should not take his foul mood out on his friend, he grabbed him by the arm and led him over to a stone bench.

With few embellishments, Selig told Roland the facts about his days as a slave and the girl who had set him free.

"She was my only link with sanity. If not for her I would have died one way or another. And now she is here and I have done her the gravest wrong! A wrong that can not be repaid."

"Take her with us!"

"What?"

Roland repeated it louder this time. "Take her with us! I can tell by the way you talk about her that you have feelings for her, that a part of you hoped you would meet again. So, claim her as yours and then spend the rest of your life making it up to her."

"No!" He didn't think he could make Roland understand that if he forced her to go with him the precious feelings that had been between them long ago would die. She would be with him but it would be in the flesh and not in the heart. He didn't want that. Better to leave and never see her again than to see hatred in her eyes every time she looked at him.

Roland was exasperated. "Did anyone ever dare to tell you that you are a stubborn man?"

Selig nodded. "You have, again and again."

"Oh." Roland laughed. "Well, I'm saying it again, and pleading with you to change your mind."

"And make a captive out of her?" He was adamant. "No. Never! I'll leave and ask the goddess Freyja to watch over her and bring her happiness."

He was silent, then he said, "Gather up the men. Tell them we are leaving at once."

"Leaving so soon?" Roland put up his hand. "Sorry . . . I will not question." He bounded up from the stone bench. "I'll tell them."

Long after Roland had left him, Selig sat with his head bent and his face in his hands. He felt desolate. Though he knew it was the only thing he could do, he felt miserable at the thought of leaving and never seeing *her* again.

It seemed as if the church were filled with Satan's devils, stuffing large sacks with anything that was valuable. Oh, how Gwyneth abhorred them. Doing her best to avoid them, she ran down the hall towards the chapel, searching for her family.

She found her mother first, hiding behind the altar, still trembling with fear. Calling out her name, she collapsed in Gwyneth's arms, mingling her tears with her daughter's.

"Father?"

"I don't know what has befallen him. He has just disappeared."

"Ethelin?"

Aenella shuddered. "I heard her kicking and screaming as she was carried off." She stepped away and gripped Gwyneth by her wrists. "What of your three brothers?"

She fought against her tears. "I saw Pengwyrn fall beneath a Viking sword. The last glimpse I had of Edwin he was holding his own but his arm was bloodied and he looked dazed. But I saw naught of Aidan."

"Come, we have to find them." Fighting against her own fear, Aenella walked arm in arm with her daughter down the long hall, seeking their loved ones among the wounded and the dead.

Gwyneth located two of her brothers lying on the floor, bleeding but alive. Kneeling down, she helped her mother bind their wounds.

"God has turned his back on us, Mother," her oldest brother croaked. "Why?"

"Perhaps to punish us for all our sins," Aenella whispered, crossing herself.

"No." Gwyneth shook her head. "I can not believe that God had anything to do with what has befallen us. 'Tis the Vikings and they alone who are responsible for this atrocity. And I swear to God that they will pay."

Roaming the church grounds, Gwyneth searched everywhere for Alfred, her brothers, and her father while her mother stayed behind, tending the wounded.

"Aidan! Edwin! Father!"

She shouted out their names until she was hoarse, but there was no answer. Stopping by the well for a drink of cool water to soothe her parched throat, she heard a faint sobbing sound that echoed over and over. Looking down, she gasped as she saw young Aidan hiding in the well. Sitting on the bucket, his hands desperately gripping the rope to keep it from plunging into the water below, he was crying.

"Aidan?"

She grabbed the rope with both hands and pulled the bucket to the side, then struggled to pull him out. She watched as he brushed off his wet garments, then swiped at his eyes with his hand.

"What are you doing in there? You could have fallen into the water and drowned!"

"When the Vikings came it was the only place I could think of to hide." Between sobs, he told her of his humiliation at being such a coward. "I ran,

Gwyn! When the Vikings came, I fled. I . . . I didn't want to die so I hid!"

Reaching up, she dried his tears. "You were afraid. We all were."

"But *you* didn't run."

"That's because my legs were shaking so badly that I couldn't move." Putting her arm around his waist, she walked with him to a large rock and sat down beside him. "You have naught to be ashamed of. Even Mother, who is always so brave and wise, hid behind the altar."

"Is she . . . ?"

"She is unharmed."

"I should have protected her." He hung his head. "Father always says the men of the family are supposed to guard you, Ethelin, and Mother. Instead I ran away and left you to *them*."

She patted his shoulder with sisterly concern. "You are young, with no experience at fighting the Norsemen. Why, even Alfred lost his head. I saw him just standing there like a statue. He didn't lift one finger to help Father or Pengwyrn."

"I saw Alfred when I peeked over the rim of the well. Alfred and a big, ugly Viking with a missing eye. They were talking together."

"Talking?"

"I saw the Viking hand him a sack." It was damning evidence.

"Alfred and the Vikings?" She didn't want to believe that any Englishman would betray his own. Giving him the benefit of the doubt, she shrugged off her misgivings.

Determined to find her father, Gwyneth looked everywhere, but he was nowhere to be found. At least on the church grounds, that is. But what about the Viking ships? Having heard that sometimes the Vikings took captives as slaves, she was determined to find them before the Viking ships sailed away.

Still, she had to be careful and not bring more trouble crashing down on her head.

Hurrying back inside the church, she yanked a hooded cloak from a peg on the wall and put it over her head and shoulders. If she was careful and kept to the shadows, she would not attract attention.

FOUR

There were two Viking ships, a dragon ship and a longship, beached in a cove hidden by tall trees. Going to and from those ships were Vikings, swarming the shore like ants, loading sacks, barrels, boxes of relics, chalices, and artifacts that Gwyneth knew were from the church.

"Thieves," she said under her breath. "They strip us of everything that is precious!" She hated them more each moment! Would these cursed heathens never leave?

Keeping to the shadows, she inched closer, her eyes quickly scanning the area for any sign of her father or brother. Though she did not see either of them, she did see the Viking leader. Standing with his legs straddled, he looked like a pillar of strength as he shouted out orders. Seeing him reminded Gwyneth of their kiss; she reached up to scrub at her mouth as if she could wipe it away.

"If only I were a man and had a sword right now I would aim it straight at his heart!" More than anything she wanted to avenge her family.

"Selig . . . !"

Turning her head, she saw several Vikings walking down the rocky hillside toward their dragon ship. Quickly she ducked out of sight, but craned her neck just enough to watch as they strode up to their leader.

"He wants to talk with you. He says that you have cheated him." Grumbling beneath his breath, a balding Viking pushed a black-hooded man towards the Viking leader.

"Cheated?" Folding his arms across his massive chest, the Viking leader looked just as ominous as she remembered.

"You struck too soon. There was not enough time for the vows to be spoken."

Though she could not see the man's face, Gwyneth recognized the voice. Still she was not ready to believe her ears. She had to be mistaken!

"There was plenty of time! Had I been you I would have urged the priest to talk faster."

"I told you not to attack until I signaled."

"And I told you that I am the one in charge of these men, not you." The Viking leader took a step forward. Bending his head towards the hooded man, he stood nose to nose with him.

"All my plotting and planning is for naught. I wanted the men in the family killed so that I alone would inherit but you only wounded them."

Gwyneth knew the identity of the traitor. His words had given him away. Even so, she moved closer, hoping that her eyes would be witness to her ears.

"We are Vikings, not assassins! I agreed to raid the church because it would be profitable for us. What deaths occurred . . ." he shrugged, "so be it. I did not agree to murder men for you."

"I want a larger share to atone for your blundered attack."

The Viking raised his fist. "You will get only what *I* say!" With a loud curse, the Viking leader stormed off, heading towards his ship.

The dark-hooded traitor turned around. Had Gwyneth not already known his identity, she knew now. She whispered his name: "Alfred!"

She didn't need to hear any more to understand what he had plotted. He had wanted to marry her so that her father's lands and his would be joined. Then, conveniently, he had schemed to have the Vikings attack and kill her father and brothers so that he would have total control of all the land west of the sea.

"Thank God there was not enough time to marry!" she whispered. In some ways she could thank the Vikings for that. Involuntarily her eyes moved in the direction of the dragon ship as he climbed aboard. Though she still hated him there was someone else whom she hated more at the moment.

Alfred will rue the day he plotted with the Vikings against my father, she thought as she slowly turned and walked back up the hill. She would raise the whole kingdom of Wessex against him if need be! Everyone hated a traitor! Alfred would be lucky if he wasn't drawn and quartered.

Cautiously listening for every sound, Gwyneth headed towards the church. Suddenly she thought she heard footsteps behind her. Stopping in her tracks, she listened again. Someone was following. When she walked, he walked; when she halted he did likewise. Trying to outsmart him, she dodged in and out among the rocks and trees, but it did no good. He had caught up with her.

"Out for a walk?" Alfred inquired. His features seemed to be carved in stone. He looked stronger than she remembered and dangerous.

"Yes . . . a walk." She knew that he knew that she had heard his conversation with the Viking. Worse yet, she knew that because she had overheard him her life would be forfeit. Alfred could not risk having her tattle on him.

She spun around, intending to put as much distance as she could between them, but in a few strides he had caught up to her again, his hand curving brutally around her arm, jerking her to face him.

"Let me go!" Futilely, Gwyneth clawed at his imprisoning hand.

"Alas, I can not! You pose a problem." His dark eyes narrowed and she suddenly realized how feral he was. With a snarl he was upon her, shoving her so hard that she tumbled to the ground. The impact with the hard earth winded her. She fought to catch her breath.

Alfred didn't wait for her to recuperate. Wrapping his hands around her throat, he squeezed. "There is nothing else to be done except choke the life out of you!"

She couldn't breathe. She couldn't think. All she knew was that the man to whom she was nearly married was going to murder her.

"No!" she cried out, coughing as the burning in her throat blocked out all air.

"Beg me for mercy!" Alfred was enjoying her helplessness.

"Please . . ."

"Again . . ."

It pained her to talk, but still she forced the words from her mouth. "Please . . . please don't kill me."

He thrust his face only a few inches from hers and she knew suddenly that he meant to do more than just strangle her.

She stiffened, her mind refusing to accept what was inevitable. Taking a deep breath, she let it out in a scream hoping that either her father or brothers might hear and come to her rescue, but instead a tall man wearing a conical helmet interrupted.

"By Odin's whiskers, there is more treasure over here."

Alfred loosened his grip. "Go away! You heathens

have gotten what you came for. Let me attend to her."

"No. I want her!"

Looking into the Viking's scarred face, Gwyneth knew at that moment she would rather die. More so, as four other Vikings formed a circle around her, each man leering at her.

Alfred knew better than to fight. "Go ahead, take her with you far away from here . . ."

With a grunt the Viking picked her up and slung her over his shoulder. Struggling, Gwyneth beat at his back with her hands and kicked him in the chest. Swearing at her, the Viking paused as they came to a large tree and without a second thought swung her in such a manner that her head struck the wood. Though she fought the swirls of blackness that danced before her eyes, Gwyneth sank into the cold darkness of unconsciousness.

The men aboard the dragon ship bent to the oars. Since some had been lost in battle there were fewer than the usual seventy-two oarsmen. Several oars were in place without men to pull them.

Selig could see the smaller ship, the longship, being pushed clear of the land by several of the men who sailed on her. The longship was finely built, ninety feet long and fourteen feet wide with fifty oars to move it through the ocean's waters, but the dragon ship was even larger. It measured a full one hundred sixty feet long and twenty-five feet wide.

As they pulled away from the shore under oar power, Selig looked back to the mist-shrouded land of Wessex and thought of the blue-eyed beauty he was leaving behind. How he secretly longed to take her with him, but he had brought her enough pain. He had left her alone to tend the wounded and try to get on with her life.

The wind gusted from the northwest, blowing Selig's blond hair into his eyes. He could taste the salt and smiled. It was good to be on the sea again. Perhaps now he could forget what had happened here on this shore.

"We have made the sacrifice to Thor," Roland shouted, waving his sword in salute to his leader from the next ship. "We will be assured a safe journey."

The helmsman swung the prow around to face the open ocean. The ship dipped and pitched in the blue-green waters, then Selig himself took the steerboard.

"Hoist sail!" he commanded. The oars were run in and stowed as the sail was unfurled. Each man sat on a sea chest or large barrel as he worked with the oars.

The *Sea Dragon* glided over the waves as Selig left his post and walked to the prow. Looking at the carved dragon, he felt fierce pride in this ship of his. Watching the dragon as it nosed its way through the sea spray, he thought that its open mouth made it look as if it were gobbling up its prey.

Selig felt a hand on his shoulder and looked into Roland's smiling face. "I still think you should have brought the woman with you."

Selig shook his head. "No. I did what was right, for her and for me."

The ship sailed on through the rolling ocean. Selig had insisted, as always, that his men have clear heads as they sailed, lest some severe storm take them unawares. When they pulled ashore during the night to eat, they would be free to indulge in merrymaking and mead. They had taken plenty of wine from the storehouses of the church.

"I don't think these Christians are so bad," Roland joked. "From what I have heard they drink wine when they give praise to their gods."

"Aye, they drink but they abstain from women," exclaimed one of his comrades.

"Abstain?" Roland scratched his head quizzically.

"They are not allowed to come near women. No bed sport."

"No bed sport?" Roland rolled his eyes in mock horror. "It is no wonder then that they are always frowning." The Vikings standing around him guffawed.

Suddenly, without warning, a fight broke out. There was shouting, fisticuffs, and shoulder-butting.

"She is mine."

"We can share her!"

"No, I claim her as my share of the spoils!"

Selig raised his hand, signaling silence, then strode toward the quarreling men. "What's wrong?"

"I brought her aboard!"

"I'll fight you for her!" There was a pause in the arguing.

"Her?" Selig questioned.

For a moment he thought he heard a faint moan, but the moment the squabbling began again, the sound was lost. Selig's interest, however, had been piqued. Quickly moving toward where the boxes, barrels, and crates were stored, he peered down at the figure sprawled on the deck. To his amazement he saw a face that was instantly recognizable despite the fact that her eyes were closed.

"It can't be!" But it was. The lovely, dark-haired English girl. He could hear her deep breathing and knew she was alive. Even so, he was infuriated. "Someone's head will roll for this!" His angry gaze searched out and found the guilty party.

"It was Gorm! He admitted to the deed."

Selig stared the man down, at last saying, "I told you that the woman and her family were to be left alone and that no more harm was to come to them! Is this how my orders are obeyed?"

As if hearing the arguing, Gwyneth opened her eyes for just a fleeting minute, then closed them again.

Gently, Selig lifted her in his arms, smiling when she snuggled close to his warmth. For a long time he just held her, then he laid her on one of the warm furs on the deck. Stroking her hair, he waited for her to wake up.

Selig did not foresee her reaction as her eyes flittered open, nor did he anticipate the way her eyes would stare into his own with such intensity. Every muscle of her body stiffened as her eyes wandered over the deck of the ship, then took focus on the Vikings surrounding her. An ear-shattering scream tore from her throat as she realized what had happened.

FIVE

"No!" Gwyneth gasped. She felt numb. Confused. It couldn't be true. She had thought she was in the midst of a nightmare but as she looked up at the Viking chieftain she realized it was all too real. In that moment it was as if all the blood suddenly drained from her body. She screamed again.

"Silence her!" shouted one of the Vikings. "She will anger Aegir, God of the Sea."

"Throw her overboard," said another.

Selig signaled for silence. "No one will harm you," he said quickly, taking notice of how her face had paled as she stared at him. "I won't let them."

As her eyes moved from one Viking to another, as she saw the glint in their eyes and the grins on their heathen faces, Gwyneth didn't believe that for a moment. Reason fled her mind. All she knew was that she had to escape. Ignoring the pounding in her head and the whirling of her senses, she stood up. Stumbling as she walked, she somehow made it to the ship's stern.

"I'm surrounded by enemies . . . !" Hateful ogres who had no mercy.

Looking down at the foaming waters, she hesitated for just a moment; then, as she looked back, a sense of desperation surged through her. She had no choice. Closing her eyes, she said a prayer as she prepared herself to plunge into the ocean.

"Don't!"

She had moved so quickly. Selig hadn't been expecting that. Now, as she stood poised to jump into the waters, he realized he was too far away to stop her. Worse yet, if he moved towards her it would hasten her act of desperation. There seemed to be only one thing he could do.

"Baugi!"

Gwyneth hesitated. Her eyes bored into the Viking's with myriad emotions; then she crossed herself. Let *my* death be upon his conscience, if he has one!

With a gasp she threw herself forward but she did not fall. She felt something tug at her from behind, holding her tightly, keeping her from falling. Looking over her shoulder, she shuddered as she realized that a bear held her firmly in his jaws.

Selig's strong arms encircled Gwyneth's waist as he pulled her backwards. The force of his pursuit sent them both sprawling to the wooden deck. Gwyneth's fall was broken by the girth and thick fur of the big dog that still held her clamped in its jaws.

"Baugi! Let go!" Obeying the Viking's command, the "bear" released her.

Gwyneth wept and fought the arms that held her. "Let me go. Let me go!"

All that had happened to her family came back to haunt her—the blood, the destruction, and worst of all, Alfred's betrayal. Her father had trusted him, had been willing to welcome him into their family. She, too, had trusted him but what he had planned was more treacherous than words could ever convey. Worse by far than what the Vikings had done because he had turned against his own kind.

"I hate you all!" She was determined that was the last thing she was going to say. Once she had been proud of herself for learning the Vikings' language;

now she hated the sound of the words on her tongue.

"Hate me if you want, but my dog and I just saved your life." What else could he say? He couldn't find the words to tell her of the remorse he felt for all that had happened, although he felt it to the depths of his very being.

Gwyneth remained silent. She tried to get up but the weight of the Viking kept her from moving. He and the big animal he called a dog.

Dog. Ha, she thought. Her father had dogs. Hunting dogs. He often boasted that he owned the finest pair of lymers in the land. But even her father's bloodhounds weren't as huge as the big, shaggy, black animal now sitting on her legs.

Selig saw her looking uneasily at Baugi. "He's a sweet-tempered and gentle giant, thus his name. He's great on the ship. He can retrieve objects or people who fall into the sea."

He loosened his hold on her just long enough to give Baugi an affectionate pat on the head. He truly loved the dog and felt pride in owning such a magnificent animal.

Selig had come across the dog in Wessex where he was being worked near to death by a cruel English fisherman. The dog had been put to work hauling fishing nets out to sea, then at the end of the day's fishing he had been hitched up to a cart to haul the load of fish into town with little or no chance to rest. Something about the dog's plight had reminded Selig of his own ill treatment; thus he had stolen the dog and taken the hundred-and-fifty-pound animal with him. He had called him Baugi after one of the giants in Norse mythology.

"I've lost count of the men whose lives he has saved." He could see that she was looking at the dog with new respect so he smiled. She did not smile back. "If you jump into the ocean a hundred times, Baugi will bring you back and all you will do is get wet. I don't intend to let you die!"

Now that she thought about it, Gwyneth was glad that the dog had kept her from plunging into the ocean. Even so, she was not going to soften her heart against the dog or his owner. Whether he had abducted her or not she was virtually his prisoner now.

"Listen to me." It was important to him to make some kind of peace between them. "We will not harm you. Upon my oath as a Viking, you will be safe upon this ship."

Her eyes met his and she could read the truth of his promise in the depths of his eyes. She relaxed and breathed a sigh.

"If you promise not to do anything foolish I will let you up. Do you promise?"

She nodded.

"I did not seek to take you with us but it seems the gods will it to be so."

"No God of mine . . ." she choked, breaking her oath of silence. She wanted to be angry but she knew that the Viking leader was not the one to blame—in this instance, at least. The blame was on Alfred's head. And the danger was not over. Her father did not know of Alfred's treachery. She had to tell him. But how, when she was far out at sea?

Selig loosened his grip on her. "So, I have your word that you will not try to end your life?"

"Yes . . ." She looked towards the wide expanse of ocean. "Take me back." The words held no pleading but were instead a command.

"I can't!" Selig couldn't take the chance of doing as she asked. Undoubtedly the word had spread throughout Wessex of the raid he had led. He and his men would be met with swords and axes if they dared put into land. He couldn't endanger the life of his men, even for her. Besides, now that she was with him he realized that a part of him had wanted this very thing to happen.

"You can!" She searched his expression for any sign that he would relent and saw none. "You can not think to take me with you!" The thought of such a fate made her blood feel as if it had turned cold again.

"I don't want to cause you further unhappiness but I cannot turn back." The words were spoken as gently as Selig could manage.

"My father would give you a great reward for my return!" She fought the panic rising up inside her.

"Your father would no doubt take great delight in seeing us all killed." He shook his head. "You have no choice but to be a Viking now, at least for a while."

"A Viking . . . ?" She looked around her. The eyes of the other Vikings surveyed her with curiosity but there did not seem to be blood lust in their eyes. They also seemed to acknowledge that she belonged to their leader. Would she? "No . . . never . . ."

"You must . . ."

"I'll never act, speak, or be like a Viking!" She spat her defiance at him.

For one so petite, so lovely, so feminine, she was capable of such a great anger and hatred that he felt as if she had scalded him. The hatred in her eyes was more than he could bear. He turned and walked to the opposite end of the ship.

He could remember another time when there had been softness in those violet depths and yes, love. He had not been blind to her childhood fondness for him. Now he longed for her to love him again.

Selig remembered the night she had set him free as vividly as if it had been yesterday. He remembered looking up and seeing the loving look in her eyes as she bent down to soothe him with her soft hands. Though the wounds on his skin had hurt, her touch had seemed to heal him. Then, before he could even react, she had cut through his bonds and set him free.

He had gathered her into his arms in a gesture that he had meant as a show of affection and gratitude but as he had looked into her eyes he had felt another emotion. Something that had touched his heart to the very core. He had thought then that he would give anything in the world to be able to take her with him, but she had been so young! Too young! Little more than a child, though a beautiful one to be sure.

Selig had bent his head to kiss her forehead, knowing that had she been just a bit older it would have been her mouth. In that moment he wished with all his heart that he could bide his time and wait for her to blossom into a woman, but he did not have the luxury of time. He had had to leave and leave quickly.

"What a woman you have become. I was right . . ." he whispered. She was his greatest treasure yet she was untouchable for he did not want her to hate him any more than she already did.

Looking down he saw that Baugi had followed him.

There has to be a way to overcome her anger and make her love me again. But how? It was a question that plagued him as the ship skimmed through the waters.

SIX

The setting sun looked like a huge golden coin as it hung suspended from the sky over the dark blue ocean. Gwyneth sat curled up on a thick pile of furs near the sternpost, watching as the ship swayed up and down. Trembling, she pulled one of the furs up around her chin, enjoying the feel of its warmth and softness against her skin. She could hear the rhythmic thrashing of the long oars as they swept through the sea in time to the melodic chant the Vikings were singing. Push. Pull. Up. Down. The Vikings maneuvered the ship through the waves, each stroke of the oars taking her farther and farther away from her mother, her father, her sister, her brothers, and the familiar shores of her youth.

She brushed a strand of hair from her eyes. It was sticky from the sea spray, a strong reminder that this was not a dream. When she awakened on the morrow she would find that she was still on this ship among the very men who had raided her kinsmen.

"Oh, God, please be with me," she said softly, making the sign of the cross. "Protect me from the Vikings . . ."

Her eyes were drawn to the tall form of the Viking leader, so powerful as he stood near the mast. What kind of man was he? What would be her fate when they reached the Viking settlement? Was she to be his woman? His slave? His captive? Whatever her fate was to be, it sent shivers of apprehension down her back.

"Do I hate him?" She did, and then again at times she did not! Her feelings were at war and her emotions ever-wavering. She had seen firsthand his brutality and yet there were times when he had seemed strangely gentle. Certainly he was an enigma! Besides, it was not he who had brought her aboard the pagan ship.

As she thought about Alfred and his treachery, her heart hardened. He had betrayed them all. Someday she would return to her home and denounce him before everyone. Only when he had been punished would she be able to feel peace in her soul again.

"Are you hungry?" The Viking chieftain startled her as he came up behind her.

"No," she replied stubbornly, though her stomach rumbled constantly.

"You aren't seasick?" He gave vent to his concern by touching her on the shoulder.

"No. I am just not ready to accept food from my captors," she replied tartly, pulling away from his touch. The memory of his hands upon her after the Viking attack was still too fresh in her mind. Perhaps that was why his presence beside her was so unnerving. She shivered as a cold gust of air whipped the fur from her shoulders.

Selig bent to pick it up, his hand brushing hers as he did so. For a moment their eyes met and held, then Selig looked away. "This fur is from a bear as white as the snow. I traded for it in Kaupang," he mumbled, placing it back upon her shoulders.

Her skin was so soft. He longed to reach out and caress her trembling body, but he held himself in check. He didn't want to frighten her. His intent was to woo her slowly, gently, until she felt for him what he did for her. There was all the time in the world.

"A white bear?" Gwyneth pulled the fur cloak tightly against her body.

"I have heard all the bears are white far to the north."

Gwyneth didn't answer. She was suddenly tongue-tied, like a schoolgirl learning to read from the kindly nuns of the monastery. The silence between them made her all the more conscious of his male-ness and set her heart to beating rapidly. At last she asked, "How long will our journey be?"

"Several days," he answered softly. He looked down at the English beauty. Her dark hair nearly blended with the night. She held her chin up with pride like a true Viking woman. It seemed that she had accepted her fate with dignity and grace and that intrigued him even more. In that moment he made a silent vow to protect her always.

"Several days?" she repeated. She remembered the few ships made of rawhide stretched over wicker frames which belonged to her people. They were nothing like these great ships. Nonetheless a sudden fear stabbed through her. "What if we sail over the edge of the world?"

Selig laughed. "Haven't your Christian monks taught you that the world is gently curved and not flat? If there was any danger of falling over the edge I would have done so many, many times by now . . ."

She blushed at his amusement, then turned her back in anger. How dare he act as if she were igno-rant! She could read and write and had been taught history by Father Aiden himself. She doubted that this big lout could even read the Holy Book. Fight-ing was all he could boast about.

Sensing her irritation at his laughter, Selig laid a hand on her shoulder again. "You have a lot to learn about the world, little one," he said gently. "But soon you will understand our Viking ways."

"I hope not! I don't ever want to understand thieving and murdering!" Once again she pulled away from him.

This time Selig was angered by her reaction. She acted as if the English never stole or killed and yet he knew that to be false. Grabbing her shoulders, he forced her to face him. "Your people have preyed upon others. I know. I have seen their cruelty with my own eyes. My mother was killed when your King Egbert attacked the Mercians . . ." He started to say more but fearing to reveal too much, he quieted.

Gwyneth could not deny what he said. England seemed a confused scene of perpetual conflict. Father Aiden chided the English as being one huge battlefield, fighting among themselves, fighting the Welsh, or battling the Danish and their invasions.

"It's true, but there are many of us that want peace . . ."

She looked into his eyes and could see a pain there that she did not understand. Before she had time to ask him about it, however, he had turned and left her alone.

Gwyneth sighed as she closed her eyes. She was hungry. Famished. As her stomach grumbled, she chided herself for refusing food. Father Aiden said that she was much too stubborn and proud and she suspected that in this instance he was right.

Like a lost child fighting against her tears, she gazed at the churning waters, deep in thought. What would be her fate when they arrived in the Vikings' land? Would she ever see Wessex again?

Sensing a presence beside her, she turned, expecting the Viking. She was surprised to see that it was the Viking leader's big, black dog. As if sensing her sorrow and uneasiness, he nuzzled her hand. She knew in that moment that she had made at least one friend.

Thick clouds billowed across the sky like smoke, hiding the setting sun. "I do not like the look of those clouds, Selig!" Roland exclaimed, his eyes focused upward as he appraised the sky. "Those formations mean a coming storm."

For the moment Selig was preoccupied, staring at the dark-haired English woman as she sat curled up with Baugi. The black bear dog had never shown interest in anyone but him until now. Perhaps the animal sensed his master's feelings for her, he mused.

"Selig, did you hear me?" Roland nudged him in the ribs. "Stop pining for the woman and listen to me. A storm is brewing."

Selig shrugged. "A storm doesn't frighten me. It will not be the first one I have faced." He was experienced in dealing with the sea. "My ships will hold."

"But the wind . . . it's starting to blow fiercely . . . and the waves . . ." Roland was uneasy. He did not make a secret of his fear of storms. He was one of the few survivors of a Viking ship that had capsized off the coast of Alba.

"You worry too much!" Selig patted his friend on the arm.

"And you don't worry enough. I know that you do not believe it to be your destiny to be killed yet, but what about the rest of us?"

Selig believed, as did other Vikings, that no one could change his destiny. That was ordained only by the Norns, who wove the fate of the gods and men alike. It was believed that the way in which a man lived his life was strictly up to him. If there were problems they must depend on their bravery and battle skill to rise above them.

Roland looked up at the sky again. All the signs were there. Attuning his ears, he said. "Listen."

Selig did, but didn't hear anything out of the ordinary. If anything, it was even quieter than usual. Then, from far off, he seemed to hear a gentle roar moving closer and closer. The wind groaned a warning that could not go unheeded.

Selig shouted his commands as his crew hustled about with poles and rope. "Get busy rigging and tacking spar." That would prepare the ship and strengthen it to hold out against the storm. Each Viking quickly and expertly hurried to do his particular task.

There was no better seaman than Selig. For that reason many men had been willing to leave their homes to follow him, even though he had been born of an Englishwoman. Nevertheless, there were rumors that his father was a great Viking, though Selig would never speak about it.

The ship dipped and pitched, nosing its way through the sea, shaking free of the thick waves. All too soon, Roland's words had come to pass. Both men had been through storms before, but this one promised to be devastating.

Gwyneth tried to stand up, but the movement of the ship made her dizzy. Instinctively she looked towards the Viking leader, fearing that he had forgotten her in the turmoil of the moment, but he hadn't. He was coming towards her with purposeful strides. How could he stand, much less walk, when the deck plunged and dipped so beneath his feet?

Selig bent down to help her stand but a giant wave lashed out like a hand, throwing their bodies together with such force that they both lost their footing. His strong arms and sense of balance, however, kept them from tumbling to the deck. Then, before she could say a word, another wave drenched them. Clinging desperately to the Viking leader, Gwyneth was certain she was going to be swept overboard.

The Englishwoman's breasts were pressed into his chest. Through the water-soaked linen of her gown he could feel every curve of her body as if nothing separated them. In spite of his resolve and the danger, Selig was engulfed by his desire and reacted physically. He knew it and as the woman looked up, he knew that she knew it, too.

With an oath he pulled away. Reaching for a length of rope, he sheltered her in his arms as he strode towards the nearest ship's T-shaped crutch, a rising beam of wood. Without a word he tied a rope around her waist, leaving her hands free to clutch at the wood.

"No!" She was on the verge of panic.

"It must be done to keep you from being swept overboard." He could see her struggling against the rope, trying to untie it, and he choked on his swear words. "Don't. I know what I'm doing!"

In spite of her fears something in the way he looked at her seemed to calm her. She sensed that he was trying to protect her. Though the rope bit into her soft flesh, she stopped struggling. In fascination she watched as he prepared for his fight with the ocean as if going into battle. As she watched him tie a rope around the big, black dog's neck, she thought to herself that it seemed even Baugi had a role in the forthcoming struggle.

Loose rigging snapped and slashed in the savage winds. As the huge Viking ship dipped dangerously low, the Viking crew struggled to keep it afloat in the raging storm. Foaming spray sprang high in the air, splashing into the ship. Giant waves lashed out like hands, spewing water over the ship's side. The entire ship's company was faced with a desperate struggle to keep the ship afloat, some even using buckets to clear the water that flooded the deck.

Gwyneth was certain that at any moment the ship would turn facedown into the churning water; she clung to the pole until her hands were numb, thankful that the Viking leader had been wise enough to secure her with the ropes. They had become her umbilical cord to keep her on board the *Sea Dragon*.

She watched as the Viking leader took his place at the stern, heaving on the tiller to keep the ship from broaching to in the fearsome waves. At the moment the ship looked like little more than a leaf in the wind as it battled with the ocean. Then the rains came, pouring down upon the ship like water from a barrel. Those aboard the *Sea Dragon* and the other ship, the *Sea Serpent*, fought for their very survival.

As Gwyneth fought her terror, she could not seem to take her eyes off the handsome blond Viking. He showed no fear as he moved about the ship. In fact, at the moment he seemed to be the bravest man she had ever laid eyes on.

"Look out, Selig, the mast is beginning to creak," Roland called out just as the mast spun around, nearly hitting Selig in the back. The force of such a blow would have sent him over the side into the dark, swirling water.

"A timely warning, Rol." Selig turned towards his friend to vent his appreciation just as a giant wave lashed out to crush another beam, sending it tumbling. "Roland, watch out!"

It was too late. With a resounding crash the beam swerved, landing upon Roland's skull with a force that sent him hurtling over the edge.

Gwyneth heard a mournful cry and looked up in time to see one of the Vikings fall into the ocean. Though he was a Viking and a pagan, she closed her eyes as she whispered a prayer for his soul.

SEVEN

Selig had seen the beam land on Roland's skull with brute force. His loyal friend and follower, who had saved his life a hundred times over, was now in danger of being swallowed by the sea. Worse yet, Roland had never been a very good swimmer.

"Baugi!" The dog was large enough to pull in a drowning man. His lung capacity allowed him to swim great distances and fight the ocean's currents. But Baugi had never been tested in such turbulent waters. Even so, Selig had to risk the dog's life to save his friend.

Selig tied one end of a long rope around the dog's neck and put the other end in his mouth so that Roland could hang on as the dog pulled him close to the ship and his rescuers. It was a process that had been tried before and had been successful.

"Go get Roland!"

With a grace that belied his size, the black dog obeyed, jumping into the icy waters.

Selig watched the dog maneuver through the choppy waters, feeling a sense of awe at the strength, power, and skill of the animal. Baugi had a stiff, oily outer coat and a fleecy undercoat so he could adapt to the harsh, cold water. The dog had skin around his feet that made it look as if they were webbed which enabled him to swim with a kind of breast stroke instead of a dog paddle; thus it did not take him long to reach the fallen Viking.

"Roland, grab the rope and Baugi will tow you in . . . !" Selig cried out. "Roland!"

It was no use. The blow to the head had rendered his friend unconscious. Without thought to his own safety, Selig quickly stripped off his leather corselet and ornamented belt and dove into the swirling waters.

"Mother of God, no!" Gwyneth gasped, seeing his act of self-sacrifice. The very thought of his death caused her more grief than she could ever have imagined.

The ice-cold sea took Selig's breath away as he hit the waters. He heard a roaring in his ears as the ocean closed about his head. He felt as if his lungs would burst. The burning in his chest was unbearable. Don't let the seawater fill your lungs, he thought. If he did he wouldn't have any hope of surviving, much less helping Roland.

Pushing with all his might against the waters, Selig broke the surface. Air filled his lungs. Though the salt water stung his eyes, he opened them wide, scanning the waters. It was then that he saw his friend facedown in the water with Baugi beside him, nudging him, trying to get the Viking to take the rope.

"Roland!" Selig sputtered desperately.

Though he struggled, he felt the strong currents of the ocean carrying him farther and farther away from his ship. It was a helpless feeling. He who had always been so strong was powerless even to help himself, but he fought against the ocean with every bit of strength left in him. Struggling against the waves, he somehow miraculously made it back to where Roland and Baugi were floating. He reached out, grasped the free end of the rope, and tied it around Roland's inert form.

"Haul him in, Baugi!" The dog instantly obeyed. Selig swam directly behind the man and the animal.

Selig was exhausted. Breathless. His battle with the currents had taken their toll. Flecks of black danced before his eyes but he was determined to make it to the ship so he could help the others get Roland safely back on deck.

"God be merciful to him," Gwyneth prayed, hoping that her God would take this Viking, heathen though he be, to his bosom. "And God be with me," she added, looking about her at the other Vikings. What was to become of her now? At least she had felt as if the Viking leader wanted to protect her, but she had no such trust in the others. Fear seeped through at the realization of her plight.

"There!" She heard one of Vikings cry out. Then there was a loud cheer.

For a moment she was nearly afraid to hope. Struggling to untie the ropes that held her to the beam, she hurried to the side of the ship. Looking over the side, she could see the dark form of the Viking's dog and beside him she could see the other Viking bobbing up and down. She squinted, hoping against hope.

"Please . . . God . . . !"

As if in answer to her plea, she saw him braving the icy waves, moving closer and closer to the figure of the other Viking as if to offer the dog help in the rescue. Reaching him, he gripped him around the neck with one arm as he grabbed hold of the steering oar with the other.

"He's alive!"

Amid cheers and shouts, the fallen Viking was dragged back on board the *Sea Dragon*; then the dog was hauled aboard, and lastly Selig was helped back on the ship.

Gwyneth looked in the direction of the cheering men. What kind of men were these Vikings? What kind of a man was their leader? Was it possible that he was not as loathsome as she had insisted?

Looking up, she saw him and she could not deny the quickening in her breast. He was clad only in his *braccae,* the trousers he always wore. They clung to his powerful body, making him look at that moment like some kind of heathen god.

Selig ran to her side, leaving behind him a coughing Roland, who was being carefully tended by his shipmates. He gathered her into his arms, pushing her hair back from her face. Without even thinking, Gwyneth clung to him.

"Hold me close!" she cried, overwhelmed by the feelings which stirred within her at his touch. For the moment she had forgotten all about her parents, her family, and her homeland as she gave herself to the precious ecstasy of his embrace.

"It is over," he said then, looking down at her with a reassuring smile. It felt so good to hold her in his arms. He had the strong feeling it was where she belonged. "The storm is abating. All will be calm."

His words cut through the fog in Gwyneth's brain and she struggled in his arms. How could she have so easily forgotten what he had done? He was a Viking who had ruthlessly attacked her family and her homeland. Worse yet, he was a heathen. An enemy! She had been foolish to let the rescue of the Viking and the emotions of the moment cloud her thoughts and emotions.

"Take your hands off me!" she said angrily, as if he were somehow to blame for her emotional turmoil.

Stung by her attitude, he quickly complied, turning his attention to Baugi, who was eagerly awaiting his master's praise. "Good dog! Odin himself could not have a better champion." Though all the glory was being heaped upon him, Selig knew that it was the dog who was the real hero.

Gwyneth watched the affection the Viking gave to the thick-furred black dog, once again confused by her feelings. The storm that raged within her was far more dangerous than the storm which had blown around them. The question was, how was she to fight the tempest in her heart?

Lying on her back on her warm bed of furs, Gwyneth looked up at the stars, studying the night sky intently. She had heard that the Vikings relied on the glittering sky lights to navigate their ships but to her they were wishing stars.

"I want to go home . . ." That was her greatest wish, but as she heard the gentle swish of the water against the side of the Viking ship she doubted that it would be fulfilled. They were traveling farther and farther away.

How long she stared at the stars she didn't know. She was as still as stone yet the world seemed to quake around her. She remembered the Viking leader's body touching hers as she had clung to him and a sweet ache coiled in her stomach. His touch had ignited a host of sensations she wanted to deny but could not. The truth was she was attracted to him even though she didn't want to feel that way.

"No . . ." Somehow the feelings stirring within her made her feel as if she were betraying her memories of the other Viking she had loved so long ago.

Closing her eyes, she fought against sleep, tossing and turning as she pictured every detail of her tumultuous day. For several long, tormented hours she lay awake, trying to exert her will over her emotions, but then at last exhaustion overcame her.

Gwyneth was surrounded by the mists of a fog.

Faces hovered before her eyes. She glimpsed her mother and father, her brothers, but though she tried to touch them the faces eluded her, fading away in a cloud of light.

"No . . . come back . . . please . . ."

Two entwined silhouettes hovered in the distance, coming closer and closer. She recognized herself as one of the figures, but who was the other?

It was he! Her young, handsome, golden Viking. He was smiling at her, beckoning her to join him. She stretched out her arms and he came to her, kissing her, caressing her, stroking her hair. Together they rolled about, locked in an embrace as they made love.

"No one will ever harm you again," he was whispering . . .

"Don't ever leave me . . ." she mumbled. "Stay . . ." She felt safe, secure, and deeply loved.

Suddenly another silhouette intruded on her serenity, the features indistinguishable at first. Who was it? Who would dare intrude?

"No!" It was the bearded Viking. He was tugging on her, trying to pull her away from her lover.

She reached out to the man she loved, seeking the safe shelter of his arms, but he turned away, moving through a translucent cloud of people. Running, she tried to catch up with him but he hovered just out of reach. Come back, she thought. Please don't leave me.

She tossed her head from side to side as visions swirled madly through her mind. Terrible visions of the bearded Viking chasing after the man she loved, his sword raised, anger twisted his face. He was going to kill him! Why? Why would he want to destroy her happiness?

"No . . . Don't . . ."

With a start, Gwyneth opened her eyes. She had been dreaming, yet it had all been so real.

Trembling, she covered her face with her hands. What did the dream mean? And why did the images she had seen seem less like a dream than a premonition?

EIGHT

After much-needed repair of the damaged masts, the Viking ships glided through the ocean waves as smoothly as if there had never been a storm. It seemed that the danger was forgotten and the crew's major goal was to reach land.

Though she feared them, Gwyneth could not help but admire their skill. They were masterful navigators and seemed to be at home upon the fearsome waters. Moreover, the ships they had built showed a craftsman's skill and care.

The ship's captain also drew Gwyneth's admiration, though she was cautious not to show it. Her dream troubled her. She worried about what might happen if she somehow found her girlhood love when they reached shore only to thus target him for the Viking leader's wrath. Though the Viking the others called "Selig" had shown her kindness, she could not forget how ruthless and violent he could be in battle.

And yet he had a gentle side, she mused, her eyes raking over his well-muscled body. She remembered the look on his face the day he had led the attack on her people. Was it regret she had seen in his eyes? He had sworn to force himself upon her yet he had left her untouched. Why? And then yesterday, during the storm, he had risked his own life to save the life of his friend. Surely he had been heroic.

As if sensing her appraisal Selig looked at her and their eyes met. Once more, Gwyneth was taken aback by the intensity of her feelings. It made her feel disloyal to the memory of the young Viking who had given her the amulet. As if trying to force herself to remember him, she reached down the front of her gown and touched the Dragon's Tear pendant with reverence. Closing her eyes, she tried to conjure up memories of days long past. She could remember the young Viking's smile, his eyes, and a small indentation in his chin that she had sometimes traced with her finger. But though she sought to recall details of *her* Viking's face, she realized that his visage was fading from her memory.

"Because of him!" Her gaze turned to an angry glare as she placed the blame squarely on the Viking leader's shoulders.

A crude tent had been erected in the stern of the boat where she could have some privacy. Turning her back on Selig, she sought the haven of that tent now. She would never forgive him for what he had done. Never! Not even the ocean could wipe the blood from his hands.

In frustration she brushed at her red gown. The Viking had found it among the sacks and barrels plundered from the church and had given it to her after the storm. It was one of Gwyneth's own dresses that she had brought for the wedding celebrations that would have followed her nuptials.

"He gifted me with my own gown. Did he expect gratitude?" she thought wryly to herself.

That Selig was trying to make amends was obvious. He had not only brought her food—bread, salted fish, and mead—he had tried repeatedly to engage her in conversation. Why? Because he hoped that she would be a willing concubine when they landed? Gwyneth vowed she would never give in to him.

Selig watched Gwyneth return to the tent and smiled. He had seen her staring at him. Though she tried to pretend otherwise, her anger was softening. Once they passed the Isle of Man and reached the Viking settlement in Northumbria he would make her his wife. And what a Viking wife she would be! Knowing that her arms awaited him after a long journey would bring him home much sooner.

"Are you going to tell her who you are?" Roland's voice cut into his thoughts.

Selig was adamant. "No!"

"Why?"

"Because I have changed."

A hundred memories assailed him, bringing old hatreds to the surface again. He had been beaten, humiliated, and spat upon by those who were English like the lovely, dark-haired young woman. But it had strengthened him and turned him from a boy into a man.

"I want her to fall in love with the man I am now, not care for me because of some past attachment to an untried lad."

With that hope in mind, Selig set about to win her affection, watching her closely to take advantage of those times when her guard was down. He told her of his travels which had taken him all the way to the Baltic Sea and upriver into Russia.

"And did you plunder those lands, too?" she asked tersely.

"No!" He wanted to make her understand that he was not a violent man by nature. "I only raid when I seek vengeance on those who have done me a great wrong." Such as murdering his mother in cold blood and selling a young man into slavery.

Remembering all too vividly the attack on the church, she whispered, "I can not imagine why you would want to harm a holy man."

"I did not. That was one of your Englishman's ideas. The man you nearly married."

Though she wanted to deny it, Gwyneth could not. She had heard Alfred's confession. Still she bristled. "How many times have you brought death and destruction to the people of Wessex?"

"Twice!" he answered. "Once to avenge my mother's murder and the next time to avenge . . ." He looked at her face and was reminded once again of the wide-eyed child who had shown him kindness. "It is a long story. I'll tell you about it one day."

Curiosity got the better of her. "Tell me now?"

"I trusted someone who then betrayed me . . ."

There was silence between them as each was deep in thought, a quiet broken by the sound of the waves splashing against the side of the ship. For just a moment it was as if they were caught up in a world of their own.

"Who killed your mother?" she asked at last. She read the answer in his eyes. "An Englishman!"

Selig thought to himself that there were really two men to blame. His mother's brother and Selig's father, who should have been there to protect her. Instead he had left her at the mercy of her treacherous family. It was a betrayal he had never been able to forgive.

"The bold Ragnar!" he swore beneath his breath.

"What did you say?" She was taken aback by the pain she read in his eyes. *There is something about his eyes* . . . something that seemed familiar. She shook the thought away.

"We'll be reaching land soon," he said, changing the subject.

"And what then?" she asked fearfully. She asked a question, uneasy about the answer. "What will happen to me?" The appraising expression on many of the Vikings' faces prompted her query.

"That depends on you!"

"On me?"

He reached for her hand. It was cold. Her fingers were trembling. "I want you . . ."

She pulled her hand away. "No!"

She hadn't let him finish. He was going to say that he wanted her to decide her future but as usual she had been quick to anger. It prompted him to goad her.

"Then perhaps you would prefer one of the others. Gorm!" He pointed towards the big, hulking Viking who had been responsible for Gwyneth's abduction. She gasped in outrage. "Or Einar?" He nodded his head in the direction of a Viking who was equally revolting. "Or Thorbjorn?"

"I will never choose any of you. I belong only to myself!" Without realizing it, she gently stroked the bulge of the pendant beneath the bodice of her red gown. Once she had wanted to belong to someone. But that Viking had been as different from this Viking as the moon was different from the stars. Her Viking had suffered; this Viking inflicted suffering. The only thing they had in common was their name. Selig. *And the color of their eyes,* she thought.

So she still treasured the pendant, Selig thought, both pleased and disturbed at the same time. "The necklace that you wear. I've seen you looking at it. Who gave it to you?"

She stiffened. Her dream made her wary of revealing anything about her memories to him. "No one!"

"No one?" He smiled. "I was able to see it briefly. A dragon shedding a tear. Unusual. It looks like a Viking pendant. Perhaps you do not hate us after all."

He longed to take her in his arms, tell her that he loved her, that he was that same man she had once idolized, but as she backed away and looked at him with apprehension, he held to his vow.

"You would never understand . . ." she whispered.

"No, I don't think I would," he replied. He thought differently about things now. A change had been wrought in his heart and his soul.

A horn sounded at the opposite end of the ship, signaling the men to assemble.

"We will soon be upon dry land again," he announced.

And now my problems begin, she thought. On the ship they had been surrounded by Vikings with no privacy; thus Selig had not made any advances towards her, but what would he do when they were upon land?

I will not let him touch me, she thought with resolve. *If I do, all is lost.* She could not lie to herself. Being near him brought forth a primitive kind of feeling deep within her. If she were alone with him for any length of time she might give in to temptation. She might be swayed by her passions to stay with him. But she couldn't! Alfred had betrayed her father. He might yet harm him. She had to go back. She had to warn them all about what had happened.

"Don't be afraid . . ." He had not spoken her name since the night she had freed him but he said it now. "Gwyneth . . ."

Her name on his lips was like a caress, warming her, making her wish . . .

"Gwyneth . . ." he said again. Always before, a woman merely warmed his bed; he had never loved anyone. Until now. With her it would be different.

She took a deep breath, trying to steady the hammering of her heart. In that moment Gwyneth knew that it was not the bold Viking leader whom she had to fear in the days to come. It was herself.

NINE

Gwyneth stood all alone on the deck looking east towards the cliffs of the Isle of Man. Though she had scoffed at the fascination some men had with the sea and had scorned the Vikings, she was coming to understand how a man could soon have sea water in his blood. There was something about the smell of fresh sea air and the sting of salt spray that made a person feel alive.

"You're looking in the wrong direction," Selig exclaimed, gently laying his hand on her shoulder. "We are going to put in over there . . ." He pointed west to an area across from the large Isle bordered by low dunes and grassland.

Gwyneth felt apprehensive as the ships touched the shore. The helmsman guided it to the land, bumping into the rocks. She was told that the Vikings preferred to run the ship aground so it was not a gentle end to the voyage. When the ships were safely at anchor the men began to unload the cargo.

Selig was the last to leave the ship. Lifting Gwyneth up in his arms, he carried her to shore with him. There were times when he was so gentle that it was hard to imagine him as the fearsome Viking she had seen the day in the church. Even with his kindness to her the past few days, however, she was apprehensive about the days to come. Worse yet, she was unfamiliar with the territory so there would be little chance of escape.

As they walked, Gwyneth found it hard to maneuver her legs because she had been on the ship for a while. Her knees threatened to buckle beneath her, but still she trudged along, trying to keep up with the long strides of the Viking leader. At last they reached the small settlement and she could see the dwellings of timber and wattle and daub. The huts seemed to have no windows, and the doors were so low that even Gwyneth had to stoop to enter.

Even my father's peasants live in better hovels than this, she thought with alarm. She could see that several cows were sheltered at the other end of the building. The animals were separated from the house by only a thin partition.

"Modest, but home," Selig announced with a smile.

"Where will my sleeping quarters be?" she asked, her fingers twisting together nervously.

"Over there," he answered, gesturing to a pile of furs which Gwyneth guessed to be the bed. "You and I will share this house," he said, putting his hands on his hips in the gesture she was now well accustomed to.

"Share this . . . this . . . hut, perhaps, but not the bed," she responded tartly. Going over to the furs, she picked up what she thought must be a bear skin and dragged it to the opposite side of the room, then looked back at him defiantly. Baugi followed her, lying down on the fur as if to claim ownership.

"Sleep where you will . . ." Selig answered, walking over to a large wooden chest which held his belongings. Rummaging through the trunk, he pulled out leather shoes, tan trousers, a red tunic embroidered with animals, and a leather belt.

He said he would not force me, she thought to herself, but wondered if he would keep his word.

Gwyneth glanced at him out of the corner of her eye, then surveyed her surroundings. In the center of the room, she could see a cooking pot hanging over a simple stone hearth. It was suspended from the roof by ropes. Looking upward, she noticed the hole in the roof above the fire and imagined that the small dwelling would be full of smoke whenever a fire was burning.

"No doubt you will want me to cook for you," she muttered with annoyance. At home there had been slaves to do such chores, but she had watched them often enough to know how to do the tasks. After all, how difficult could it be?

"Here everyone must do his part in order to survive," Selig answered matter-of-factly.

"There are no jarls or thralls among us, only men and women." He felt the necessity to add, "Nor is there any treachery here. Not a one of us would side with an enemy against our own for profit."

Gwyneth thought about Alfred as Selig had intended. "I curse the coward and traitor who led you on your raid," she said. "If it is any consolation, I hate him even more than you Vikings."

Moving towards her, Selig took hold of her hand, drawing her into his arms. "It is my hope that I can change your feelings towards us," he whispered, then kissed her.

His lips were firm and strong as if to somehow assert his claim. Gwyneth neither resisted nor did she respond. At last he stepped away.

"I won't force you. When I take you it will be because you long for me as much as I long for you . . ."

Though she was inwardly shaken by her response to him she refused to show it. "That time will never come. I will never forgive what you and the others did."

" 'Never' is a long, long time . . ." he answered, then left her to return to the ship and help the others unload. Baugi followed.

Walking to the doorway, Gwyneth could see the tan linen smocks of several of the women of the settlement. She wanted to go to them and offer her hand in friendship but felt somehow awkward in doing so; thus she busied herself with tidying up the small house that would be hers, at least until she thought of a way to get home.

Soon the floor of the dwelling was clean and the room neat. Rummaging around for food, she found a sack filled with dried peas and pine bark, one with a few onions and another filled with cabbages. There were also dried berries and some kind of dried meat. It appeared that someone, whom she suspected to be a woman, had made certain that Selig would find provisions when he returned.

Gwyneth didn't have any idea how to start a fire so she satisfied her hunger with the berries and dried meat. Outside the door she found a large tub, most likely for bathing. Beside it was a barrel of rainwater. Running her hands over her bare arms, she felt the urge to cleanse herself from the voyage's dirt. On the ship she had not been able to wash her hair.

Eyeing the large tub, she was tempted to bathe, but also afraid to be caught in the nude by the Viking. Instead she had to make do with sponging her body clean with cold water, then washing her long hair in the tub. Shivering, she found a length of wool in Selig's trunk, a cloak perhaps, and dried her damp hair as well as she could. Stepping outside, she finished drying it in the waning sunlight.

She went back inside, opened the trunk, and explored its contents. Perhaps she could find a comb or a brush. The chest was filled with silver and gold plates, chalices, knives and spoons, and fine linens. It seemed that life as a Viking was prosperous, she thought scornfully.

"Finding anything of interest?"

She could sense that he was standing right behind her, moving closer and closer. It made her tingle all over with a feeling of expectancy, though he did not touch her.

"I wanted to cook something but . . ."

"But you never learned how to go about it, is that it?" He laughed softly. "Don't worry, little one. I'll show you."

Though he was bone weary from unloading the ship, he started a small fire, then as she stood bedside him he put water in the cooking cauldron, cut up cabbage and onions and dried beef, and started it boiling over the fire. The smell made Gwyneth realize just how hungry she was, though she thought with dismay that the odor would not be pleasant to have in the house at bedtime.

Spreading one of the large linens on the small table, she set earthenware plates and bowls from a large sack near the fire on top of it. Near each plate she laid a silver knife and spoon and stepped back to view her handiwork. Selig filled two silver chalices from a keg of mead he had brought with him from the ship; then, sitting down on one of the small benches near the table, he motioned for her to sit opposite him.

When the food was ready, they ate in silence, Gwyneth looking down at her plate all the while, afraid of meeting his eyes. Even though she did not look at him, however, she felt the tension of his presence. At last he broke the quietude.

"I have something for you."

Pushing his plate aside, rising from the table, and stepping outside the low-slung door, he returned with something in his hand. He beckoned to her and held out a garment made of the smoothest and softest fabric she had ever touched.

"What is it?" He held it near the fire. It seemed to glisten in the firelight. "Silk. From lands far to the East. Many Vikings treasure it." It was blue silk, a color that matched the sapphire in the pendant he had given her long ago. He had traded for it in Kaupang, hoping that someday he would find her again and be able to give it to her.

"It's beautiful!" She held the bright blue dress in front of her, imagining what she would look like in it.

"Put it on." His voice was low and husky.

"No . . . I . . . I . . . couldn't . . ." She blushed at the thought of him watching her as she disrobed. On the ship she had the tent for privacy.

As if reading her thoughts, he took a step forward. "It is time that you got used to me looking at you, for I intend to do so many times from now on. You are beautiful. There is no shame in my seeing your body."

Viking women were not hindered by the strict restraints of Christian women, he thought. They could explore their sexuality freely without it being seen as a sin.

He repeated, "Put it on . . ."

She stood still, unable to move away from him, yet unable to do as he asked. She felt as if his eyes had already stripped her linen garment from her slim form.

The minutes passed slowly as Selig stood looking at her; then he reached out and brushed her left breast with his right hand, tracing the peak of its perfection. His hand moved lower to the smooth curve of her waist then to the tautness of her stomach. Gwyneth shivered as a flame seemed to course through her veins.

"No . . ." she breathed, intrigued and yet at the same time terrified of the feelings he unleashed in her. Lust, she thought. Not love. The priest had often talked about such sinful feelings with the admonition not to give in to eroticism.

"You say no and yet I can tell that there is a part of you that really means yes. Yes, please hold me, Selig. Touch me, Selig. Make love to me with such passion that we both touch the stars." As if intending to do just that, he put his arms around her and held her tightly against him.

Gwyneth stepped backwards with a gasp and tripped over the wooden chest. She would have fallen had he not caught her in his arms.

"You promised!" she admonished.

He was disappointed but he was not going to go against his word. "I did not promise not to kiss you or touch you," he whispered. Bending his head, he kissed her with a passion that overwhelmed her and took her breath away.

He was right. Her body had become a traitor to her mind. Although she kept telling him "no," there was a lustful part of her that wanted him to pick her up in his arms and carry her to the bed of furs and touch her all over until this tension inside her burst into the stars that he spoke about.

Selig could sense her response to him and knew what a quandary she was in. Taking advantage of the moment he moved his lips to her neck.

"Tell me that you want me and I promise you such pleasure that you will take me willingly to your bed tonight, tomorrow night, and . . ."

"Never . . . !" Her breath caught in her throat. She had to do something to stop this assault to her very soul. "And if you do not take your bloody hands off me I will loathe you forever."

A frown creased his forehead as he let her go. He made no further move to touch her. Instead he stood staring at her. Then he turned and walked away, leaving her all alone.

Gwyneth collapsed on her bed of furs, drowning it seemed in her own tears. Somehow she had to get away from him. Away from the temptation. Away from the feelings he inspired. She closed her eyes and sobbed softly.

Something wet and warm touched her ear. She reached up, fearing she would have to fight for her honor, but it wasn't the Viking kissing her ear; it was Baugi. As if sensing her anguish, he had stayed behind. Lying down beside her, he snuggled close, giving her comfort.

Feeling betrayed by Baugi, Selig cursed the dog beneath his breath as he peeked inside. The animal was lying beside her where he longed to be.

Grumbling, he walked away from the hut until it was little more than a speck in the distance. All the while his eyes caressed this wild and unspoiled region of long, sandy beaches spattered with outcrops of rocks and split by river estuaries that ran far inland. Reaching a large lake, he stripped off his garments and plunged into the cold water in an effort to cool his ardor. Why had he made such a promise? Could he wait much longer to have her?

It had been a long time since he had bedded a woman and Gwyneth's beauty tempted him beyond all endurance. He remembered her small waist, her slim hips, her long legs, the breasts which had felt so smooth under his exploring fingers.

"And her eyes!" He was certain that he could drown in the sea of blue, he thought as he swam back and forth in the water. He also knew that any other man wouldn't have hesitated to take her to bed with or without her agreement. Why then was he being such a fool?

"Because I don't want her hatred! I don't want her to look at me again the way she looked at me after the raid when I touched her." More than anything, he feared her hatred for he did not want to take a chance on destroying forever the bond he had felt for the gentle child who had helped him and shown him mercy. Deeper than his desire for her was his love.

Rising out of the lake and donning his clothing, Selig spent the next hours wandering by the ocean, gazing out at the Viking ships. Far away, to the north, was the land that his father had come from.

"I will prove that I am a better man than you, Ragnar. If I win Gwyneth's love I will bind myself to her forever. I won't leave her. And I won't desert any child that is born of our union."

If he won her love! Selig knew that he must! Somehow.

Returning to the hut, he found Gwyneth lying on the bed of furs, Baugi beside her. Her hair was spread out around her like a dark cloak. Her eyelashes shadowed her face. She looked lovely and strangely peaceful. Though she had not put the blue silk dress on, she clutched the hem of it in her fist as if she feared losing it.

"At least she approves of my taste in garments," he whispered to himself.

Lying down on his own bed, he swore silently. "Freyja, goddess of fertility, help me for I do not know how long I can keep this vow of mine not to claim her." With that thought in mind he closed his eyes, determined to claim at least a little solace and slumber before morning came.

TEN

Boisterous conversation and drunken laughter awakened Gwyneth from her fitful sleep. The Viking men were celebrating their return to the settlement with the mead and wine that they had been denied on the voyage. Selig had insisted that they be sober while navigating the ship and it seemed that they were making up for their abstinence now. She could also hear giggles from the women and suspected that these men were enjoying more than just their drink.

"Well, if Selig takes it into his mind that I will be like them, he has a lot to learn . . ." Perhaps Viking women were free with their favors but English-women were not.

Selig! She remembered the way he had caressed her and felt her face flush. Where was he? Was he with the other Vikings taking part in their revelry? The soft sound of his snoring told her otherwise. Sometime during the night he had come back and now lay much too close to her for her liking.

Her heart beat wildly as she remembered the look of desire that had sparked in his eyes, his bold caress, his searching fingers, and worst of all, her reactions to his touch. If he kept after her, and he would, she would capitulate for she was, after all, only human. If she responded to his lust with a lust of her own, what then? Did she want to be his concubine? No! His wife? Marry a Viking? Never!

"I have to escape!" There was no other alternative. By his own words he had said that he would not vow not to touch her or tease her or assault her senses. How long could she hold out against the sensations he unleashed? A day? A week?

For just a moment she cursed her own healthy body for its response to his virility and herself for her cowardice in remaining within his clutches. On the ship she had been surrounded by water but now that they were on dry land she had no more excuses for remaining. She must leave and leave quickly before he sensed her intentions and made provisions to keep her within his grasp.

Escape! The word pounded in her brain. She was on the western coast of Northumbria where the people at least shared a common Anglo-Saxon ancestry. Though the Northumbrians had fought with her own people of Wessex, at least they were united in their hatred of the Vikings. Surely she would be able to find someone who would help her and take her back to her home. A fisherman perhaps? She would promise a reward.

"And if I can't find a fisherman, I'll even walk all the way back if I have to!" she muttered, forgetful of the danger such a venture would bring. In her mind she had no alternative.

Her mind made up, Gwyneth tried to sit up but was held bound by the weight upon her long hair. Baugi! In frustration she sank back down upon the bed. How was she going to escape without the dog sounding the alarm?

Gently she prodded him as she sought to free herself of his weight. "Go back to your master . . ." she whispered. "He's right over there."

She stiffened and held her breath in expectation as Selig moaned in his sleep. Fearing that he was going to awaken, Gwyneth remained as still as a statue, but he merely rolled over on his side. She had learned that Selig was a sound sleeper.

Gwyneth rose and peered out into the darkness of the early morning. Many of the Viking men and women were distracted by their lovemaking, or they were in a drunken stupor, and had finally sought their beds. If she were careful she could leave without being seen but she had to hurry before the sun began to rise and before Selig awoke.

Fumbling around in the dark, she assembled what supplies she could for the journey, thankful that she had familiarized herself with the room while it was daylight. Even as careful as she was, however, she did not keep from dropping something. As it clunked to the floor she held her breath, expecting Selig to wake, but his heavy breathing encouraged her to continue.

As she ran her hand over the silk dress, Gwyneth had a fleeting moment of misgiving, then quickly hardened her heart. She would leave the dress behind for she did not want any reminders of the Viking.

She filled a sack with as much food as she could comfortably carry, then stepped out into the brisk early morning air. The dog followed.

"Go back, Baugi! Go back!" When he didn't obey she pointed. This time the dog obeyed.

The moon was shrouded by dark clouds thus her only guide was the light of the fading stars. She had noticed the Vikings navigating by their map of the star-covered heavens. She could only hope that these same stars would guide her too.

Gwyneth looked back several times to make certain she had not been seen leaving and was not being followed; then she walked until her legs ached and her feet were bruised and bleeding from the rocks on the pathway. She was driven only by the

fear of her desire for the blond Viking leader. If
only she could put a great distance between herself
and Selig, she would survive somehow. She was
young and she was strong.

Gwyneth followed the coastline, heading south,
all the while looking for any sign of a fishing village
but saw none. Though she refused to let it worry
her, she did have to re-evaluate her plan. She started
to walk farther inland towards the low dunes and
grassland, hoping she would see at least some sign
of a village. At times she nearly crawled along and
at times she found herself running wildly as an unfamiliar sound shattered the stillness. Was she imagining it, or was she being watched?

She cursed herself for being foolish. Why had she
left the safety of the settlement? Perhaps she had
made a big mistake. Doubts flooded her mind as
she contemplated what she had done. There was
more than just the danger of wild animals and
rough terrain. What if she encountered Vikings who
were not from Selig's settlement? What then? Her
fate might well be worse than the one she had fled
for there would be no bold Viking arm to steady
her, no sword to protect her, no one who really
cared if she lived or died.

She wanted to go back but instead pushed onward, driven by her fears. Her breath came in
ragged gasps, her heart beat within her breast like
the waves upon the shore. As a muscle spasm
cramped her ankle with pain, she sank to the
ground.

From far off she could hear a howling sound.
Wolves? The thought of becoming some animal's
breakfast filled her with terror.

"Selig . . . !" Suddenly she longed to feel his
strong arms around her. At least with him she had
been safe. She wondered what he would do when
he awoke and found her missing. Would he order

his men to search for her? Even if he did was there any hope that he would guess what direction she had taken?

She was so tired, so exhausted that she could do little more than lie upon the ground, resting on her side. Should she go back? It would be humiliating and yet what good was her pride when weighed against her well-being? But which direction should she take?

Gwyneth looked out at the horizon. It was pink and orange as the sun peeked over the horizon. Although the sun was a welcoming sight it also was a source of confusion for she could not retrace her steps by remembering the pattern of the stars.

"I'm lost!" It was an agonizing reality.

Putting her hands up to her face, she brushed her eyes, as if willing them to see the right pathway. She wouldn't lose heart. She wouldn't give up. She had to keep her wits about her.

Was she imagining it or did she hear the sound of a barking dog?

"Gwyneth . . ."

The voice sounded in the distance. Was she imagining it or was it real?

"Gwyneth . . . !"

Shading her eyes against the sun, Gwyneth saw Baugi first, then Selig's muscular form as he made his way towards her. What would he do to her for running away?

Her apprehension was put to rest as he knelt beside her, then reached out to her. "Are you hurt?"

"No!"

"Odin's teeth, don't ever do such a foolish thing again!" He held her tightly against his chest, stroking her hair. "Don't you realize what might have happened? If not for Baugi I never would have been able to find you!"

"Are you angry?" she whispered.

"Yes, very much so."

"Are you . . . ?"

"Going to punish you? I should, but I won't." His arms tightened around her. "What is it going to take for you to realize how very much you mean to me?"

Her heart soared. She clung to him, forgetful now that she had sought to flee from him.

"Promise me by the God you hold so dear that you will never run away from me again. Swear it!" he exclaimed.

"I so swear," she answered, knowing that she would never be that foolhardy again. She had learned a lesson. There was a big difference between being brave and being impulsive.

Selig kissed her then, a gentle kiss. Picking her up in his arms, he carried her all the way back to the settlement with Baugi leading the way.

It was strange how the very place that had seemed like a prison now seemed like home. Thankful to Selig for having come after her, Gwyneth viewed her surroundings with a less prejudiced eye, seeing how with a few changes here and there she could transform this man's dwelling into a comfortable place to live.

She poured water in a large bowl, splashing it on her face. Her hair was matted from her morning's excursion so she picked up a large bone comb she found in the trunk and combed her long, dark-brown tresses and fashioned them into the braids she had noticed the other women wearing. It would keep it out of her eyes.

She appraised the damage done to her dress by her escape attempt. Between the ocean voyage and the snags and tears from her misadventure, she could see that the garment was beyond repair. She would have to find something else.

Searching through the large chest, she found a chemise of lightweight wool and a long gown of the same cloth. As she held them up to her, she realized that they would fit. Moreover, the same could be said for a pair of leather shoes that were also in the trunk. She also realized that it was no coincidence that they were the right size. Selig had undoubtedly put them in the trunk for her use.

She donned the garments, fastening the overdress by the use of the two brooches, one above each breast. "Now I look like a Viking," she murmured, remembering her vow never to become like them. Perhaps they really weren't so bad.

She could hear their guttural chatter as they worked. If she did not want to be a hermit she would have to make friends with them. Gwyneth strode outside.

At first they simply stared at her, then at each other, then they giggled. One of them was even so brazen as to tug at her dark braids, but it was not long before she was working beside them.

While the women worked they sang and Gwyneth was soon tapping her feet and humming the tune. After so many days on board the ship among only men, it was good to be among women again. The only thing that marred her happiness was the gaze of one overbold Viking, a short, stocky man with powerful arms and a straggly beard. His beady, ice-blue eyes seemed to follow her everywhere.

Gwyneth realized that she was very lucky that it had been Selig who claimed her that night and not a Viking such as this one. This one revolted her and she wondered who he was. He had not been on Selig's ship. She would have remembered.

Never be alone with him, a voice inside her head seemed to say. It was the kind of warning her mother would have given.

Though Gwyneth had never had to do women's

work before, she found that she really didn't mind it. If a person had the right frame of mind, in fact, it could really be fun. She tried to think of creative ways to cook and found that by using garlic, onions, certain spices, and combinations of herbs she could improve the taste of what was being boiled or broiled.

It was a day of learning, in fact. Gwyneth found out that the fire in the hearth was kept burning a long time for cooking and all day long to heat the small houses when it was cold. Wealthy households had baking ovens in separate rooms, heated by placing hot stones inside them. In the settlement there were designated "communal" ovens.

Food had to be preserved so it would keep. Fish and meat were hung in the wind to dry, then smoked or pickled in saltwater. Salt was collected by boiling seawater, a boring job that had been given to her father's churls.

Since they were living by the ocean and not near a forest, the major portion of their food was from the sea. Though Gwyneth had never been particularly fond of fish she could tell that cod, herring, and haddock would quickly become her staple diet. An occasional duck or rabbit was thought of as a rare treat.

This time when Selig returned home, his meal was already cooking, the house was clean, and the table was set for supper. "Woman, you are a marvel!"

Having heard from the Viking women that Selig was fond of horseradish she had used it in preparing the fish. Best of all, she had found a nest of gulls' eggs and had roasted them as a special treat.

"Thank you, Gwyneth . . ." he whispered.

This time when they ate there was more conversation than previously. Gwyneth questioned him about the various pieces of furniture and tools. She learned that most of them were wood-working tools and that Selig had a talent for carving.

"I had a hand in carving the dragon head on my ship," he said proudly. He knew exactly what wood to use for what purpose and how to cut timber to give maximum strength and flexibility. His artistic flair extended to painting and he showed her some of the designs he had painted in bright colors.

"They're beautiful!" She was amazed. The thought of him as a heathen or a pagan had forever been pushed from her mind.

"I treasure beautiful things," he said, explaining that the large chest was a collection of treasures he had gathered during his raids or had traded for in Kaupang. "But you are my greatest treasure . . ."

"Selig . . ." He spoke the words with such passion that for a moment she was tempted to go to him put her arms around him and forget everything but his touch.

"I wanted you the moment I laid eyes upon you."

It was a compliment and she knew it; still in order to control her own emotions, she asked, "To add to your collection?"

"You know better than that . . ."

For a moment there was something in his voice, his tone, his words that made her feel drawn to him as if he were an old friend and not an enemy. It was as if she knew him from another time, another place. But that was ridiculous. The first time she had ever laid eyes on him was when he had come bursting into the church, a sword clutched in his hand. And yet . . .

Gwyneth tried to understand her longing for the Viking. He was handsome, yes, but it was something more. Something she could not fully understand.

ELEVEN

The next few days passed in peace and tranquility and with each day that passed, Gwyneth felt more and more at home in the Viking settlement. One by one she was befriending the women, whom she was coming to understand. Though the man was the head of the family, when the men went out on raids, it was the wife's responsibility to take care of her husband's holdings and to handle all the things that the man would do when he was there. As a result the Viking women were more independent and attained more status and authority than women did in Wessex, where the man held sway over nearly everything a woman did.

Had Gwyneth married Alfred, she would have been under his control and would have become part of his family. When a Viking girl married she did not become a part of her husband's family, but continued to belong to her own family and thus kept her own surname. In Viking society marriage was an agreement between two families. It was also common for a man of wealth to have more than one wife.

"Polygamy, as in the days of Solomon," Gwyneth had said when Ingunn had told her that she was one of two wives. "But don't you get jealous?"

"Jealous?" Ingunn had laughed. "We help each other in the household and protect each other when Gardi is quarrelsome. Besides, it means less time in his bed."

"But what of the children?"

"I have none but when I do they will be of equal value to Kadlin's two sons and will have the same right of inheritance."

For just a moment suspicion and jealousy gnawed at Gwyneth. She had to know. "Is . . . is Selig married?"

"Selig?" Ingunn smiled. "No. Until you came along Selig was always too preoccupied with his ships, though not because there weren't any women trying to attract him."

Though she told herself that such personal information shouldn't matter, Gwyneth smiled. She would never have been able to share Selig with anyone.

Mealtimes were always boisterous and happy affairs, especially *nattveror*, or supper. Gwyneth was learning more about women's work every day. She learned that tonight at sunset the Vikings were going to gather around the large outside cooking area to observe the feast meant to insure fertility in the soil of the fields.

"A pagan celebration," Gwyneth mumbled, wondering what her mother would think if she knew. And what would she think if she caught sight of Selig?

In a brown tunic bordered with blue and white embroidery at the sleeves and hem, a brown leather corselet with shoulder straps fastened at the chest with buckles, dun-colored leggings, and silver and gold bracelets arraying his arms, Selig looked handsome.

As usual, the men sat at one end and the women at the other, but Gwyneth was close enough to him to take in the details of his attire.

Selig seemed more content than usual. He even

exhibited his sense of humor by telling amusing stories and tales of his gods, of frost giants and dwarfs. Stories that she knew he was telling for her benefit.

"Gwyneth . . ." He beckoned her over and for a moment she thought he had caught her staring. "This is Oddbjorg. He has the distinction of being one of the few men left behind when we go a-Viking."

Oddbjorg whispered something to Selig, laughed, and slapped him on the shoulder. Gwyneth looked at him with questioning eyes.

"He said that Freyja herself could not be more beautiful than you. You have hair like hers, as dark as a raven's wing, eyes as wide as the seas, and skin as perfect as a flower. And he says that he envies me my place in your bed."

Gwyneth tried hard not to blush but she was unsuccessful.

Selig introduced her to more of the Vikings who had either stayed behind or been on the other ship. She met Aki, Frodi, Harek, and Thorne and his wife Hildegard, a much older woman with a round face and skin weathered by the sun. Gwyneth noticed that the men outnumbered the women three to one and wondered if it was like that in all the Viking lands. Perhaps that was why they found the need to abduct women from their own homelands, she thought.

As the platters heaped with fish, small game birds, boiled meat, and vegetables were passed around, Selig made it a point to show Gwyneth every courtesy. He thought of her as special and he made no secret of it.

The food was similar to that which Gwyneth's family prepared for their feasts except that the Vikings seemed to prefer boiling meat to roasting it on a spit. At home there would have been cheese, butter and dark bread in the center of the table but here there was only bread made out of barley and dried peas. Even so, it looked delicious and she felt pride in knowing that she had helped bake it.

Beside each plate was a goblet filled with wine, a rare treat and one saved for feasts such as this one. Like the English, the Vikings were fond of their drink. They raised the mugs and goblets to toast each other and drained the dregs dry.

Gwyneth had partaken of more of the strong drink than she ever had before and felt lighthearted and happily at ease. The flames from the fire fanned bright, casting a warm glow about her as she turned her eyes towards Selig. For one hypnotic moment their eyes met and held. She could feel his closeness, even though he was across the table, and she could see the desire in his eyes.

Selig's senses soared as he looked at her. He could see the deep emotion in her eyes. Did he dare hope that her look spoke of longing?

A shout broke out among the Vikings, breaking the spell. "To Selig. Long may he sail the seas!"

Gwyneth ate in silence. Sensing that she was being watched, she looked up and was alarmed to find the short, stocky Viking with the cold, ice-blue eyes staring at her. Something in his manner told her that he did not consider her to be Selig's property. The lust in his eyes made her shiver in revulsion. She wanted to go to Selig and tell him of her fears but at that moment Roland stood up and began telling a tale about the creation of the world.

"Flaming fire, burning ice, that is how it all began," Roland exclaimed. "In the south the realm called Muspell flickers with dancing flames. No one can endure the fire except those born to that land. In the north is the realm of Niflheim. It is packed with ice and covered with a vast drift of snow. In the center of the world was a fountain from which two rivers poured forth into a large abyss. These rivers became frost, but the fiery clouds of Muspell turned the ice to mists and caused clouds to form. Life quickened in the drops of water from this ice and formed the first frost giant called Ymir."

"Ymir," Gwyneth repeated, fascinated by the tale. It was so different from the story of creation in the Holy Book, but then, coming from a land of ice and snow as these Vikings did, it was not surprising that they should believe that the world had been created out of its frozen depths.

"Also out of the clouds came Audhumla the cow, who discovered a man's head while nourishing itself from licking the frost and salt in the ice. This new being married the daughter of the race of Ymir and brought forth the gods Odin, Vili, and Ve," Roland continued.

Gwyneth looked up to find Roland's eyes upon her as he talked. She smiled at him and he smiled back. Feeling a sharp pinch to her arm, she looked behind her to see the frowning face of Signe. Her jealous glance warned Gwyneth not to show too much interest in Roland.

As the young Viking continued his tale, Gwyneth sat with downcast eyes. The strange tale was one of giants and violence, of how Ymir the frost giant was killed and his body made into the earth, his blood made into the seas, his bones the mountains, his hair the trees, his skull the heavens, and his brain the clouds.

"Pagan," she whispered to herself. "But this is what Selig believes." At the moment it seemed to be a huge barrier between them.

"They took the sparks from Muspell and placed them in the sky as the sun, moon, and stars to encircle the round earth and the sea."

Another man rose to tell another tale and another man another and so on. Gwyneth found the stories interesting, particularly the exploits of Odin and Thor, but even so she was continually reminded of the differences between her religion and Selig's.

At last the Viking men rose and walked to the fire, forming a ring around it. Gwyneth followed, but was pulled back by Ingunn to stand with the women. Gone was the relaxed atmosphere, replaced by a sense of excitement. Each Viking was now wearing a helmet with horns sprouting out each side. Gwyneth had not seen this kind of helmet before. During the raid and upon the journey over the sea, the Vikings had worn conical helmets. She reasoned that these horned helmets must be for ceremonies and thought to herself that they did look like devils.

The men sang and chanted as if in a drunken frenzy. Upon the ledge of one of the rocks in the middle of the fire was placed the statue of a male figure with a conical helmet on his head. Gwyneth blushed as she realized that the statue was endowed with a very large manhood, huge in proportion to the small, ugly figure.

The men took turns pouring wine over this ugly statue, chanting all the while, and Gwyneth knew that this ceremony had something to do with fertility and the planting season. Was the wine supposed to signify blood? She felt a stab of revulsion as she realized that perhaps long ago it had been blood which had been sacrificed and not red wine.

"I must get away from this pagan ritual," she thought in alarm, "lest I be damned by God." Thinking not to escape but to get away from the furies of the festival, she turned and fled into the darkness of the night, heedless of where she was going.

After the smoke from the fire, the air was cool upon her cheeks as she breathed in its freshness. It soothed her lungs, but nothing could soothe the pain in her heart. Watching Selig participate in this chanting and dancing only magnified the differences between them, differences that could never be changed. He was a pagan. A Viking. How could she have allowed herself to forget that, even for a moment.

The wine she had partaken of earlier made her unsteady on her feet and lightheaded. It was as if the world were suffused with a hazy glow. She tried to relax, to forget about her doubts and fears.

The sound of a snapping twig alerted her to danger. Was it animal or man behind her? It didn't matter. Slowly, turning around, she started to run but a hand reached out and grabbed her.

"Let me go!"

The hand only held her tighter, imprisoning her against a rock-like chest. Feeling the brush of exhaled breath near her cheek, Gwyneth looked around, struggling to see in the darkness of the night. She gasped—it was the cold-eyed Viking staring down at her in the moonlight! His cruel eyes glinted at her. Thrusting his hands to invade her gown, his fingers began kneading her breasts.

Gwyneth let out a shriek as the Viking grunted and pulled her down to the ground. He ignored her pleading as he came closer and closer, lifting the hem of her gown.

"No! No!" she screamed. The horror of this hulking giant forcing himself upon her was terrifying. Fighting with all her might against this sacrilege, Gwyneth broke away from his grasp with a surge of strength. Stumbling around in the darkness, crawling behind a large tree, she prepared to fight against her fate.

TWELVE

Selig thought he heard a scream. He held up his hand for silence. He heard the shriek again, louder this time. "Roland, where is Gwyneth?"

"I don't know." The Viking looked around. "She's gone."

Fearful of what might have happened, Selig left the chanting Viking throng, picked up his sword, and ran as fast as his legs could carry him towards the direction of the sound.

"Gwyneth!" There was no answer. Again he called her name and this time he thought he could hear her calling to him from the bushes. Coming closer, he saw the form of Jokul Haraldsson hovering over her, clinging to her arm as she tried to fend him off. Kicking and lashing out with her arms, she was fighting like a cat to guard her virtue.

A cry of outrage tore through the silence of the night as Selig lunged for the hefty Viking. Jokul, seeing Selig bearing down on him, sword in hand, loosened his hold on Gwyneth and reached for his own sword.

Years of fighting battles had attuned Selig's ears to the sounds of danger. Hearing the whoosh of Jokul's sword, he ducked just in time. The sound of splintering wood told him that the blade had found a tree trunk instead of his neck and for that he thanked the gods.

Undaunted by his foe's attempt to behead him,
Selig swung his own sword. There was the clash of
metal upon metal as his weapon connected with that
of the hulking Viking. Jokul growled in anger,
throwing himself forward, swinging furiously, striking in every direction. Selig thrust with his sword
and felt it connect with the man's flesh. A howl of
pain rent the air.

Again and again the two Vikings collided, weapon
against weapon in the dance of battle. Selig stumbled over a tree branch and fell to earth with such
a thud that he was immobilized by the shock of pain
for just a moment. Just in time, his sword arm swung
forward, blocking his adversary's death blow.

In the semi-darkness, from her place upon the
hard ground, Gwyneth could hardly distinguish one
man from the other as she watched the confrontation in horror. She rose to her feet, watching the
shadowy forms, praying all the while.

"Please, God, be with Selig . . ." The thought of
his death was somehow unimaginable.

Straining his eyes, Selig looked up for just a moment and saw her standing there. The pause gave
Jokul just the chance he needed. Knocking the
sword from Selig's hand, he bore down upon him
to finish him off.

"Selig . . . watch out!" Gwyneth shouted. She
made her way to the spot where the sword lay upon
the ground, picked it up, and held it with both
hands.

A thin trickle of blood seeped from Selig's throat
as Jokul pressed his sword against his enemy's flesh.
His eyes locked with the other Viking's eyes. "Don't
send me to death without a sword in my hand. Give
me the chance to enter Valhalla," Selig rasped.

In that moment Gwyneth moved forward, holding
Selig's sword with both of her hands despite its

weight. Moving as if in a daze, she raised the sword and struck out with all her might.

For one so small her strength was fierce and her aim true. She wounded Jokul in his sword arm.

"Aaaaah . . ." Jokul yelled, dropping his own sword.

Selig took advantage of the moment to pick up his enemy's sword. He held it to his throat. "Get out of here. Don't let me see your face again. If I do, I'll kill you!"

"Where am I to go?"

"Loki take you, for all I care!" Though he had an uneasy feeling that it was a mistake to let the man go free, he did it for Gwyneth's sake. He did not want to strike the other Viking down in front of her. Picking Gwyneth up in his arms, he watched as Jokul Haraldsson walked away, holding his wounded arm.

"I thought I had killed him," Gwyneth whispered, still shaken.

"Perhaps it would have been better if you had," Selig answered, regretting his decision to spare the man.

They stood molded together for several moments, their bodies touching, their hearts pounding. His lips found the hollow of her throat and he gently traced a path upward.

"Let me make love to you, Gwyneth," he breathed. He ran his hands over her body, fanning the flames of her desire. "I love the smoothness of your skin, the taste of your lips, and the fragrance of your hair . . ."

He kissed her gently at first but as she opened her mouth to him his kiss became more insistent.

Gwyneth gave herself up to the kiss, reaching out to touch him as he touched her. She ran her fingers over his powerful chest, his flat stomach. She could feel the swell of his manhood pressing against her stomach and wondered what it would be like to have him deep within her. Would he make her cry out in passion the way the other Vikings had made their women cry out? So wondering, she snuggled against him, treasuring the warmth of his arms.

Whispering words of love, Selig slid his hand down to lift the hem of her gown. She gasped in pleasure as his fingers nestled in the silken curls of her womanhood, stroking gently, bringing ripples of fire to the core of her being. At that moment she wanted him just as much as he wanted her.

Selig pulled her down to the soft grass. The stars twinkled like sparkling jewels, making it a perfect setting.

He tugged at his garments in a flurry of passion, moving away for just a moment, then joining her again, his *braccae* gone. Clothed in just his tunic, he worked at her gown, pulling it down around her waist. It was then that reality came flooding back and she thought about the consequences of letting him make love to her. Lovemaking brought forth babies. Children conceived in such a manner were considered illegitimate and looked down upon by the Church. She rolled away from him.

"Gwyneth . . . ?" He reached out for her but she eluded him, pulling her gown back up in a gesture of modesty, then standing up. "I love you, Gwyn. Don't deny me now. Not now when we are so close to becoming one."

He rose to his feet and put his arms around her waist, bringing her close to him once more.

Gwyneth fought against her own desires as well as his. "I can't do this!"

"Do what? Something as natural as breathing?"

"I don't want . . ." She touched the pendant, willing it to give her the strength to refuse him even though there was a part of her that still wanted him to make love to her.

"Then what do you want?" Seeing her fingers fondling the dragon's tear, he felt a seething jealousy, knowing her thoughts, her heart were with someone else. The irony of it all was that he was jealous of himself and her great affection for a youth who no longer existed.

"My heart belongs . . ." She started to tell him, then remembered her dream and how Selig had tried to retaliate against her childhood love.

"Your heart belongs to me. Say it." He reached for her but Gwyneth escaped. She fled back to the hut. Throwing herself down upon the pile of furs, she wept her heart out. She *did* want him and the longing made her desperately unhappy.

Selig did not come home that night and she knew that she had angered him. How would she feel if he sought out another woman to quench his desires. What then? The very thought of Selig with another woman was unthinkable.

Gwyneth spent a miserable night tossing and turning; then, with the first light of dawn, she awakened to find that she was not alone. Some time during the night Selig had come back! He looked younger in his sleep and Gwyneth was overwhelmed with the feeling that there was something very familiar about him.

"Tell me about the man who gave you the pendant."

She was startled by the request, for she had assumed that Selig was asleep.

"He was a Viking like yourself, but much younger. Not more than a boy, really . . ." She paused. Did she dare tell him all? She decided that she had to. "I was but a child of thirteen, all legs and arms and awkward as a young colt."

"Was he a slave?"

She felt her heart skip a beat as their eyes met. "Yes. How did you know?"

"I guessed as much. How did you meet him?"

She sighed. "My . . . my father . . ." She was suddenly ashamed to tell him any more. "When I found out what he was suffering it was more than I could bear. I brought him food and did what I could to see that he fared well. Then one night I couldn't stand seeing him in bondage any longer and I set him free!"

"With dire consequences, I would suppose . . ."

"My father whipped me. I still carry the scars, though you can barely see them now."

"You were whipped?" Her admission tore at his heart. He had feared as much.

She nodded, then looked up into his flashing hazel eyes. "Who are you, Selig? Why do I feel as if . . . as if . . ."

"Perhaps it is time that you know!"

He picked up his dagger so he could shave his whiskers. From time to time she heard him utter an oath and supposed that he had nicked himself. Her mother had once joked that shaving was nearly as dangerous as going into battle.

"Turn around. Do you recognize me now?" he asked.

Slowly she turned, lifting her blue eyes to his face, tracing every line and curve as if it were a map. "It can't be!" Surely her eyes were deceiving her. Why hadn't she guessed before? She answered her own question, because the beard had covered so much of his face that she had been deceived. But the shape of his jaw and the cleft of his chin left no doubt now as to his identity. "You have changed." There was a hardness in his eyes sometimes that hadn't been there before. He was taller, more muscular.

"So have you. That's why I didn't recognize you

until I saw the dragon's tear. I could not force myself upon you, Gwyneth. I knew that you were the child who had been so kind to me."

Without knowing exactly why, she started to cry. In a way the dream had come true. Though he had not physically killed the boy that she had adored, he had killed her dream of him.

"I love you, Gwyneth. I did then, though in a different way. I do now."

"It's too late," she sobbed.

"It's never too late . . ." He reached out to take her face in his hands but Gwyneth pulled free of his touch.

"I have to have some time. I want to think . . . about . . . all of this."

"I'll give you time." With that he was gone, leaving Gwyneth alone.

THIRTEEN

Her thoughts and emotions tormented Gwyneth. The two Seligs, the boy and the man, were one and the same. Had she known that somewhere deep inside her heart? Perhaps.

She thought about the young slave whom she had loved the moment she had looked into his eyes. He was brave and strong and pleasing to the eyes. She had lived only for those moments when she could see him, then when she did, when he gifted her with one of his rare smiles, she had shyly looked down at her hands. Just the sight of him had made her stomach dance with butterflies.

The young man had been an enigma to her. Hard and strong one moment, yet gentle whenever she was near. His strength seemed so great but it had not been great enough to break the bonds that held him. That helplessness had tormented him but endeared him to Gwyneth's heart. If he could not protect himself, then she would be the one to protect him.

At first they had communicated with a strange blending of their languages; then, hoping to please him, she had learned the Viking tongue. Little did she know then that one day it would enable her to communicate with him in his own world.

"I loved him . . ." There could be no doubt of that. She had loved and idolized him with all the innocence of first love. But what of the man Selig? How did she feel about him? He was much stronger now, and just as handsome as he had been when he was a captive. He was, in fact, the embodiment of all that a woman looked for in a man. Handsome, bold, strong yet gentle, and he had a keen mind.

Suddenly there was no question or doubt in her mind. Her senses were filled with wanting him. Only her pride, her fears, and the difference in their beliefs had kept her from saying what he so wanted to hear, that she wanted him and that she loved him. Though she waited for a chance to tell him her feelings, the opportunity did not come.

As if determined to keep his distance from her, Selig did not return to the hut. Though she spotted his tall, muscular frame as he worked in the fields or walked by the shoreline, he did not come near the wattle and daub house nor seek out her company. The pain of his absence made her understand the meaning of true loneliness.

If he does not come to you, go to him, her mother would have advised. *If you do not and you lose him, you have no one to blame but yourself.*

"Lose him . . ." she whispered, trembling as she realized what it would mean to find him again only to lose him again. He had so quickly become her strength.

Days turned into weeks, however, and Selig continued to avoid Gwyneth. During the days she busied herself helping the other women dry or salt food and hang the various herbs to dry. She made bread, kneading it in the wooden trough, and she even helped brew beer and mead, watching the other women so she could learn how it was done.

The tasks helped her endure the loneliness of the days but the nights were unbearable. She would lie on her fur bed and think of Selig—his smile, his courage, and his boldness. He was everything she could desire in a man. What's more, he had been patient with her. "And how have I rewarded him for his patience?" By refusing to grant to him that which they both so desired.

Selig was every bit as miserable without Gwyneth as she was without him. He watched her from afar but refused to allow himself to come near her. His desire was much too strong to control and he feared lest he break his vow not to use force. His pride, too, had been wounded by her constant refusal.

Bending his back at the plow during the day, he slept aboard his Viking ship at night. But he always kept watch over Gwyneth or knew that others were nearby to protect her.

"So, this is where you hide yourself," Roland chided, finding him on the Viking ship late one night. "Is it that the Englishwoman snores?"

"You know it is not!" Selig was in no mood for jokes. Jumping up from the hard deck, he returned Roland's jibes with a scowl. "You know very well why I am here." He revealed Gwyneth's reaction to her discovery of his identity. "She told me she needs time. She said it was too late."

Roland cocked one eyebrow. "Selig, my friend, I always knew that you were a stubborn Northman, but I did not think you were stupid."

"Stupid?"

Roland laughed. "You of all men should know that women do not always say what they mean. Women have a different language all their own."

"Perhaps, but in this case I think she made her feelings—or lack of them—quite clear." He folded his hands across his chest. "She keeps telling me 'no'."

"Because she wants you to beg her, woo her, and sweep her off her feet."

"I am not the wooing kind!"

Roland shrugged. "Any man can be when the

need arises." He rested his hand on Selig's shoulder. "Life is too short to let it slip by without living it to the fullest. As a Viking, you know how soon we may die."

"Too soon."

"Go . . . and do what you must to win this woman of yours." When Selig hesitated, he poked him in the ribs. "Go!"

Gwyneth stood before the hearth fire in the small hut, warming water for her bath. Today she had worked herself into exhaustion. Her back ached and every muscle in her body was sore. Ingunn had given her a present, a small flagon of perfumed oil, which her husband had brought back from raids in the lands far to the south.

After filling the tub, Gwyneth undressed, laid aside her garments, and stepped inside the perfumed warmth. She enjoyed this peculiar Viking custom of submerging one's entire body in water rather than bathing with a washing cloth. It was relaxing and took away any aches and pains she had felt earlier.

Selig had told her that his people had learned the custom from those of the land to the east, the island off the coast of China. She had tried it several times now and had not caught the dread chill that her kinsmen always feared. When she got back to Wessex she would urge her mother and sister to try it.

But the water must be warm . . . That seemed to make all the difference.

Gwyneth stayed in the tub until the water turned cold, then stepped out and draped herself in a thick linen cloth. Standing before the fire, she rubbed her skin until it glowed, then sank down upon her bed. The soft furs tickled her bare skin as she pulled them up around her body to shield her from the night air. Enjoying the soft warmth, she closed her eyes and fell into a deep sleep.

Selig stood paused at the door of the small dwelling for a long while, contemplating all that Roland had said. Then, he opened the door and went in.

The embers of the fire glowed like bright red stars—by the light of their glow he could see Gwyneth's face reposed in slumber. He was struck by how much he loved her.

"What if Roland is wrong? What if her fear of me sends her out into the night and to her doom . . . ?" For a moment he was about to ignore Roland's advice, turn around and leave but her soft moaning detained him. She was murmuring his name!

Thinking that she was awake, he went to her side, but her eyes were closed. He gave in to a whim and brushed her dark hair from her eyes. Then he bent down and gently kissed her forehead.

Somehow through her slumber Gwyneth felt that kiss and opened her eyes. "Selig?"

"I'll leave if you want me to," he said quickly, searching her face for her reaction to his nearness.

"No, don't leave," she whispered. "I've missed you."

"And I've missed you! So very much . . ."

It was torture, wanting her so; still, he satisfied himself just by touching her hair, entwining his fingers in the thick, dark softness. But when she sat up, revealing her bare shoulder, he couldn't keep from gathering her into his arms.

"I love you, Gwyneth! Forgive me for bringing you any harm. I never meant to . . ."

"I know . . ."

He buried his face in the softness of her breasts. She didn't pull away. Instead she reached out and clasped him to her, knowing that nothing else mattered at this moment except his nearness.

Selig ran his fingers over the softness of her skin

and she sighed as waves of sensations swelled and surged within her. There was only the feel of his lips and tongue and hands.

"You are so beautiful. So very beautiful," he murmured against her ear.

He kissed her then, molding his lips to hers. His tongue explored the recesses of her mouth with great tenderness. Gwyneth's lips parted to his probing tongue, enjoying the taste of him, the feel of him, and the very smell of him. It was as if they had been fashioned, each for the other. As if somehow they were meant to be together. It seemed as if somehow this moment had been destined since she had first set eyes upon him so long ago.

Selig's hands moved upon her body, stroking lightly as if she were a cherished treasure, and indeed she was. He touched her mouth, her throat, her stomach, her thighs with both fingers and tongue until Gwyneth felt her limbs grow weak and her yearning for him reach an intensity that left her breathless. Arching her back, she sought to mold her body to his, pressing against him with a soft groan.

"Make love to me . . ." she murmured, stunned by her daring.

He left her side only for a moment to shed his garments, fumbling impatiently with his clothing, swearing beneath his breath as he yanked and tugged at his lacings and leggings. Then he was beside her again.

For a moment he feared that she would reject him as she had done so many times before, but Gwyneth merely reached out to touch him.

Kissing her mouth, he put his arms around her to draw her close against him. Every part of their bodies touched, blending them into one.

Gwyneth felt the warmth, the maleness of him. His body was so strong and muscular, his mouth so firm yet gentle. She wanted to give him the pleasure he was giving to her; she reached up and ran her fingers through his thick blond hair.

"I've never . . ." she breathed.

"I'm glad."

"But how do I? What do I . . . ?"

Selig brushed her hair back from her face again. "Just let me love you. What we do will come as naturally to you as breathing, my love."

He wanted to be gentle with her, not to hurt her, and yet he knew that this first time would bring her some pain. He would do everything in his power to minimize her discomfort for he wanted her to enjoy lovemaking.

Selig's mouth strayed down her body, his lips searing her skin until she was moaning with pleasure. A warmth, a fire, coursed through her body, causing it to respond with a will of its own. Suddenly all her shyness was forgotten. She returned his touches, exploring his body, feeling a sense of triumph when she heard him moan with desire at her inexperienced touch.

"Yes . . . yes . . ." he urged, as she reached down and ran her hand over his stiffened manhood. His flesh was warm to her touch, pulsating with the strength of his being.

Gwyneth thought of the times she had been so afraid of a man's proof of manhood. Now she was no longer afraid. She knew that Selig would never cause her injury. Instead she longed to feel him deep within her.

Selig slid his hands across her stomach and tenderly stroked the silken softness of her womanhood. Gwyneth felt the waves of pleasure flow through her like the ocean's tide and moved her body toward his questing fingers. He felt her shiver and knew that she felt the same ecstasy that he felt, a rapture that seemed to entwine their souls as well as their bodies.

"I love you," he whispered. "Please know that I

love you and do not wish to bring you any hurt
but . . ."

"My sister told me what to expect the first
time . . ." She braced herself for pain.

Selig covered her body with his own, gently parting her legs. He teased the petals of her womanhood, entering her easily, covering her mouth with
his own as he thrust.

Gwyneth welcomed him with a cry of joy, seized
by a surge of pleasure that was only stilled by the
sudden discomfort she felt as he broke through her
maidenhead.

She cried out, but her body relaxed as Selig
soothed her with kisses and gentle caresses. Then,
once that brief pain was over, only pleasure remained. They were no longer two beings, but one.
She welcomed his thrusts, moving with him until
they were both engulfed by the flames which consumed them.

Selig, ever the gentle lover, brought her such joy
as she had never even imagined possible. It was as
if the stars themselves had come down from the sky
to burst within them both, just as he had promised.
She called out his name over and over again as the
world seemed to quake beneath them and explode
into light. Then, with a shudder, he was still, buried
deep within her.

In the hazy afterglow of their lovemaking, they
held each other close, knowing that each had found
that elusive rarity: love.

"You belong to me, Gwyneth," Selig said softly.
"Only to me." And in the saying it was so, a spoken
vow between them that she hoped with all her heart
could never be broken.

FOURTEEN

The first rays of dawn awoke Gwyneth and she stirred, stretching her arms and legs in slow, easy motions. There was something different about the morning; she sensed it but didn't remember what had happened until she opened her eyes and saw Selig sitting cross-legged on the floor next to her. His look was intense as he concentrated on something he held in his hand.

"What are you doing?" In the bright sunlight she studied his face. He looked younger this morning and strangely vulnerable.

"Carving an image of you as you sleep so I will always have you with me." At the moment he was more gratified than he had ever been in his life but he had learned that happiness could be fleeting. He wanted to make a physical reminder of Gwyneth so he would always remember last night.

"Can I see . . . ?"

He nodded. "I'm nearly finished."

Wrapping the fur around her naked body, she got up and came to sit beside him. "Wood is important to you Vikings, isn't it."

"A tree supports the world, or so we believe," he explained.

The imagine conjured up in her mind made her smile. "Like a nest?"

He shook his head. "Someday I'll explain." He

held the small, carved figure out to her. "According to Viking legend, Odin made the man from an ash tree and the woman from an elm tree."

Gwyneth thought about the Holy Book and how it said that Eve, the first woman, was brought forth from Adam's rib. For the first time in her life she wondered if it were true, but quickly put her misgivings aside.

As she took the sculpture from his hand, he flushed. "It doesn't do you justice."

Gwyneth looked at the wooden figure in awe, admiring his talent. He had captured the contour of her face, the shape of her nose, the outline of her breasts, waist, and hips to perfection. Even the eyes were detailed to look just like her own. "I would say that you have flattered me."

She stared at the carving for a long time, sensing all the love that had gone into its making.

"I love you, Gwyneth. Never leave me."

She wanted to make that promise and she hoped with all her heart that they would be together for a long, long while, but reality could shatter dreams. "I'll be with you as long as you love me." Her eyes met his as she handed the statue back to him.

They sat side by side for a long while, basking in the warmth of each other's presence. All the while she felt a fierce surge of desire to feel his hand on her body again. But how could she convey her feelings without seeming brazen?

Out of the corner of her eye, she looked Selig's body up and down—from the powerful chest, flat stomach, and trim waist to the well-formed legs. She was even so bold as to glance at the mystery of his manhood, that which had given her so much pleasure. It had seemed to have a life of its own when aroused. The thought made her smile.

"What are you thinking?"

She snuggled in his arms, her head against his

chest, wishing that life could always be as peaceful as it was at this moment. If only she could remain in the safety of his arms forever. "I'm thinking how happy I am here with you."

With longing she reached down and touched his manhood, smiling again as it roused to her touch. In his turn, Selig outlined the swell of her breasts. Gwyneth felt the same desire she had felt the night before as his mouth covered hers.

Picking her up in his arms, Selig carried her over to the fur bed. His hard body was molded against her softness as he kissed her again. His hands moved over her back, sending a tingling sensation along her spine.

He caught her lips, gently nibbling with his teeth. His tongue touched hers, her mouth opening to allow him entrance at the same moment his maleness was poised between her thighs.

Then he made love to her, slowly, gently. He did not rush his pleasure but held himself back so that Gwyneth could experience the full joy of her newfound womanhood. He was amply rewarded for his patience as she met his raging fire with a blaze of her own. An aching sweetness became a shattering explosion of pleasure.

Afterwards she cuddled happily in his arms, her head against his chest, her legs entwined with his. Her hair tickled his chest as it flowed between them. It was with the greatest reluctance that they parted later that morning. As he walked to the door, she ran to him and wound her arms around his neck.

"Don't tempt me, little one. Tonight. We will have tonight."

Tonight seemed so far away as he stepped out the door.

* * *

Gwyneth had never felt more alive, so filled with happiness. Never had the days seemed so precious, yet there were times when that very happiness made her feel guilty. Despite the fact that Selig was so very dear to her heart, his beliefs were pagan. He believed, like other Vikings, in nine worlds and several gods, not one. And his gods and goddesses were warriors, not at all forgiving or loving.

The most important was Odin, the god of battle. Terrible, arrogant, and changeable, he was a formidable presence who inspired victory and determined defeat and required animal sacrifice. The one-eyed god could survey all that happened in the nine worlds. He was terrifying, a god to be respected but not a god to be loved.

To the common man his son, Thor, was favored even more than his father. He was strong and dependable. The huge, red-bearded god possessed a vast appetite, was quick to lose his temper and quick to regain it.

Most disturbing of all, however, was the god Freyr, a fertility god represented by a statue that flaunted his manhood. He decided when the sun should shine or the rain come down, and governed the fruitfulness of the earth. His sister was Freyja, a goddess that Selig referred to from time to time when speaking of Gwyneth. He had told her innumerable times that she was even more lovely than Freyja.

There was Frigg, Odin's wife, who shared a knowledge of men's destinies. She was invoked by women in labor. Gwyneth listened to the men and women talk about so many gods and goddesses that she couldn't keep track of them all. The Christians talked about eternal goodness of your soul but the Vikings talked about the good things in life. Their heaven, Valhalla, was a place of frolic where there was drinking and fighting all day long, while she and her people believed that heaven was a quiet place.

To reach Valhalla, a man had to die in battle; other actions in life did not affect his prospects of getting there. Gwyneth had been taught to believe that a peaceful and sinless life would take you to heaven.

"Sinless . . ." she murmured, wondering what Father Bede, her mother, or father would think of her living in sin with Selig. But what else could she do? She loved him and the alternative of being married in a pagan ceremony was unthinkable. But she could not live without him.

Gwyneth saw very little of Selig during the day while he was busy working with the men and she was performing her household chores with the women. But at night when she was alone with him, she gave of herself freely, putting all misgivings from her mind.

I will not think about it, she thought stubbornly, closing her eyes to block out the rest of the world. She breathed a sigh as Selig's lips traveled over her stomach, then returned to seize and explore the peaks of her breasts. She entwined her fingers in his hair as his hands and lips sent shivers of yearning through her. Still, at the back of her mind she knew that her contentment could not last forever.

FIFTEEN

Household tasks were fitted around the meal preparation twice daily, morning and night. In the settlement, fish and small game were the mainstays of the diet, eaten in some form at every meal. Grinding and baking were daily chores, for unleavened barley or wheat bread needed to be eaten while it was hot or it would soon turn hard and stale. Flour was ground from a rotary hand quern, dough kneaded in a wooden trough and baked on the long-handled iron plates among the embers of an open fire.

Gwyneth bent over the trough, forming the large roll of dough into small, flat loaves to be baked for the evening meal. Behind her several other women stood beside the large soapstone cauldrons, boiling seawater to obtain salt. The steam from the pots made the air moist and muggy; she brushed the perspiration from her temples with a flour-smudged hand, leaving a white streak on her dark hair.

"Are you and Selig going to disappear again tonight after supper?" Kadlin teased.

"I wonder what it is that is taking up their time," Ingunn said with a giggle.

"Whatever it is that keeps them occupied, it means that poor Baugi has been kicked outside their house." Kadlin brushed the flour out of Gwyneth's hair. "Oh, we shouldn't tease you so."

She sighed. "I can remember what it is like in the first year of love. Freyja herself couldn't have been more blessed than I. Now . . ." She rolled her eyes, then looked accusingly at Ingunn.

"Do not blame me. He hasn't been seeking my bed, either. He says he is tired." She whispered in Gwyneth's ear, "I think he is growing too old."

They were interrupted by Hildegard, her round face animated with excitement. "A ship has come. Let's go down to the sea to greet them. We rarely have visitors."

Wiping her hands on her apron, Gwyneth followed the three women through the door of the communal hall and down the narrow path. The quiet was disturbed by the sound of horns and the answering blasts. Looking towards the ocean, she could see the blue-and-gray, diamond-patterned sails of a Viking ship billowing in the wind.

She watched as the longship, its oars spread out, moved up the shoreline looking like a multi-legged dragon. "Whose ship is that, Ingunn?"

"I don't know. I've never seen it before," she answered, crinkling her freckled nose as she squinted to get a better look.

They watched as the ship was run ashore on the beach, the crew carefully securing the ship then wading through the water to unload several casks and chests. Gwyneth could see the familiar form of Selig striding towards one of the men, a large man. Soon he was slapping him on the back, his loud voice floating in the breeze.

"I told you I would capture him for you one day, but you didn't believe me. Now he's yours. A token of our friendship."

Selig's answer was muffled, but he did return the other man's gesture of friendship, patting him on the back enthusiastically.

"Who is that man?" Gwyneth asked.

"I think . . . yes . . . it is. Thordis, a Viking of great renown and a merchant."

The women twittered amongst themselves that the ship had brought wealth from the north—furs, ivory from walrus tusks, whale oil, and slaves, all of which would be bartered.

"Slaves?" She wandered closer to where Selig and the man stood. The ship was being unloaded—barrels and chests were lugged ashore by the crewmen. Others held their battle-axes and swords in hand, looking fearsome in the glare of the sun. It was a gruesome reminder of a very bitter day in Gwyneth's memory.

Selig stood watching as the cargo was put ashore. Gwyneth eavesdropped. The ship had been slightly damaged in a storm and needed repairs. Selig offered his hospitality.

The man named Thordis motioned to several of his men. "Bring the prisoner out." A tall, dirty figure was led from the ship. "You can see for yourself if this is the man who wronged you."

The prisoner was ragged and filthy, his hair and beard matted and long. His wrists were tied together and from his neck collar a chain protruded so he could be led. He moved about slowly, his head held downward as if weeks of abuse had broken his spirit.

"How cruel!" Gwyneth murmured, feeling pity well up inside her.

Selig strode forward, taking the prisoner's face in his hands and examining him as if he were a prized cow.

"By Thor's hammer, it is he," he remarked. He stepped back as the creature recovered his anger and lashed out at Selig.

"You will have to show him who is master, eh, Selig?" Thordis laughed.

"I'll teach him what it is like to be a slave."

"I would rather die than live as a slave among

heathens, you Viking dog! Kill me," the ragged, dark-haired captive snarled, tugging at his bonds. Something about the voice was familiar to Gwyneth. She ran forward to get a better look at the man. In that moment his eyes met hers and focused in recognition.

"Gwyneth? No . . . It can't be. Here . . ."

Her heart palpitated; she felt as if she couldn't breathe. "Jaenbert!" The prisoner was her kinsman, her cousin on her father's side. That he was also the same man who had been responsible for Selig's being sold into slavery was also unfortunately true.

"Gwyneth . . . help me . . . !"

"Don't expect a woman to come to your aid." Thordis gave Jaenbert a shove, sending him sprawling as Gwyneth looked on, horrified.

She threw herself at Selig, holding his arm tightly with her small hands. "Let him go, Selig. Don't condone this!"

Selig scowled at her. "I must!" He did not want to appear to be weak in front of Thordis. Gwyneth didn't understand the Viking way. The Viking had done him a favor by capturing his enemy. It was the supreme act of friendship.

"Please!" Her grasp on him tightened as her eyes met his. She read defiance there and fierce pride. "He is of my blood."

"Only distantly." His tone softened. "You have no idea what tortures I suffered at his hands."

"I do!" Jaenbert had been a cruel master. He had nearly starved Selig; he had beaten and taunted him unmercifully. "I remember the first day you were brought to my father. I wept for you and offered you what comfort I could."

"He deserves punishment."

"But it is not for you to punish him. God will do that!" She could understand how Selig could hate him so and want to seek revenge, yet Jaenbert was her father's sister's son. "If you cause him harm, if you condone his being mistreated, then you are no better than he."

Her words stung. He clenched his teeth, angry at her for causing a scene. "Go back to the hall, woman, and do not interfere in a man's business." He coldly turned his back upon her.

Ingunn tugged at her. "Calm yourself. It is not seemly for a woman to argue publicly with her man."

"But he is wrong!"

"It is the Viking way and in case you have forgotten, Selig is a Viking!"

"Yes, he is." Gwyneth realized at that moment that she had put that out of her mind, just as she had the differences between them. Now, brutally, she was forced to remember.

The hall was filled with the aroma of cooking food, tantalizing to all but Gwyneth. She watched as the soapstone oil lamps were suspended from the ceiling with iron chains. The air rang with laughter and chatter as the throng of men from the ship elbowed each other for a place on the bench close to the food. She could hear their boasts of their exploits and their travels across the seas.

She looked for Selig, but he was not in the hall and she wondered if he were still angry with her. Now that she had time to think clearly about the matter, she realized that she should have taken him aside, away from the presence of his friend, to speak with him.

As if her thoughts conjured him up, she saw him walking in the door with Thordis beside him. The other Viking spotted Gwyneth and glared his dislike at her. It was as if he deemed her guilty of her cousin's transgressions. She waited until he took a seat before she sought out Selig.

Hearing her footsteps behind him, Selig turned and gestured for her to follow him to a far corner, away from prying eyes and inquisitive ears. "If you have come to plead for him, save your breath," he said sternly.

"I can not stand meekly by while you keep one of my kinsmen in bondage," she whispered.

"If it were any other of your kinsmen I would free him without hesitation. But not him!"

"I hate slavery."

"And yet your people have slaves, valued at eight oxen, as I remember. So how can you be so self-righteous as to condemn me?" His voice was cold with none of the warmth she remembered.

"I condemn anyone who holds another in bondage," she replied, her tone just as icy as his.

"Thordis has bestowed upon me a great honor by capturing one of my enemies. I would insult him by refusing such a gift." He took hold of her shoulders, his eyes softening. "By the love you bear me, Gwyneth, try to understand our ways."

"By the love that you bear me, Selig, please free him. You have suffered the bonds of slavery yourself so you know that it is not fit for one man to own another. Free him!"

"I did not enslave him," he said, trying to avoid the issue. He didn't want to quarrel with her.

"He was given to you." Her lips trembled as she mouthed the word, "please." She didn't want to beg but she also didn't want her cousin to be enslaved here, a constant reminder of everything she wanted to forget.

For a moment Selig was torn. He didn't like slavery any more than she did. More importantly, he loved her. He had suffered slavery and she had freed him.

"Let me think the matter over," he said.

"Think about freeing a slave just to please a woman?" Thordis came up behind them. "Soon you will be staying in the hall to do woman's work." He laughed scornfully.

"I will do nothing of the kind," Selig answered. As if feeling the need to prove his manliness, he lifted his drinking horn high, swallowing more than usual. He laughed loudly at the ribald stories that Thordis told and told stories himself that made Gwyneth blush. Worse yet, he didn't look in her direction even once. It was as if he wanted to ignore her to prove that he was not in her power.

"What will you do with my present?" Thordis inquired, his eyes darting to where Gwyneth sat with the other women. "I say we should feed him to wolves, except as skinny as he is, even they would scorn the bastard!"

Selig flinched at his friend's words. He could feel Gwyneth's anger all the way across the room and found himself wishing that Thordis had never come to the settlement. His coming was responsible for the wall that had suddenly sprung up between Gwyneth and himself just when they were at the pinnacle of their happiness.

"No, I won't feed him to the wolves," he said loud enough for her to hear, hoping to reassure her.

"Feed him to Baugi then," Thordis goaded.

"Baugi is too tame. All he would do is lick him to death . . ." He wanted to put the matter of Gwyneth's kinsman to rest. "Tell me, have you heard about the lands far beyond the sea? I have heard that there are more lands than we know."

"Boasting. That's all it is. Boasting. If a ship sails too far they will fall off the earth. You know that, Selig."

Selig didn't believe that for a minute. He was one

of those who thought that the earth was curved. Perhaps it was even like an egg. Only the gods knew for certain.

Rising from the table, he made his way to the keg of mead where he dipped his drinking horn again and again in the brew, letting it numb his senses. He loved Gwyneth but he wouldn't let any woman make a eunuch of him before his men. Not even her. With that thought in mind, he drank until he was inebriated. He did not even notice when the women retired early with the small children to leave the men alone with their drinking and tale-telling.

Selig's vision blurred and his head buzzed as he continued to drink. He had never been one of the Vikings who let his drinking get out of hand. Why was he doing so tonight? Was it because he saw himself through Gwyneth's eyes—a cruel, bitter, vengeful monster who in truth was no better than the man who had brought such misery to him?

"Well, I guess you put your woman in her place," Thordis crowed, pounding him on the back.

"Yes, I guess I did," he whispered, wishing that words said tonight could be unsaid.

From her perch near the doorway to the hall, Gwyneth watched him. Her heart ached because of the bitterness between them. Even so, she couldn't have done or said anything else. Under different circumstances he might have done the same were it his kinsman.

"He might have set Jaenbert free if not for the other Viking." Well, if he wouldn't, then she would.

SIXTEEN

The hall was strewn with the inert bodies of Viking men who had imbibed too much mead the night before. The sound of snoring filled the air. Rousing from his drunken slumber, Selig put his hand up to his temple. He had a headache. His temples pounded, as if all the Valkyries of Valhalla were riding through his head. Mumbling his discomfort, he rose from the table, stumbling over the inert form of Thordis, who was still out cold.

"It will be a long time before I drink so much mead again," he said to himself, walking to the door to stick his head out for a breath of the fresh morning air. It acted like a potion to revive him. His thoughts immediately turned to Gwyneth.

"Odin curse that Englishman! First he enslaves me and now he is the cause of tearing Gwyneth from my arms." He tried to convince himself that it was the Englishman's fault, yet he knew he had to take most of the blame. It had been his pride, his stubbornness, that had goaded a quarrel. If not for that pride, he would have backed down and granted Gwyneth's request. He had no need for slaves. In fact, he loathed the practice of subjugating others for he knew how humiliating it was to be a slave.

Fighting against his wooziness, he made his way to the house he shared with Gwyneth with the purpose of making amends. He didn't like to have bad blood between them.

As he stepped through the door he saw her curled up in a ball, her arms around her pillow. Her long, silken hair flowed over the pillow like the morning tide upon the rocks. Just looking at her took his breath and his anger away. He couldn't blame her for her feelings. She was gentle and kind and the sight of anyone in trouble always seemed to plague her. It was just that in this instance her sympathy was misplaced. Her cousin deserved to be punished for all the evil he had done.

"You must remember what it was like for me," he murmured. More importantly, she had to understand that no man wanted to look weak in the eyes of another man. Though he admired her compassion and spirit, he had to remain strong on this matter. If only there was a way to compromise without looking ineffectual.

For a long time he pondered the matter as he looked at Gwyneth's peacefully sleeping form. At last he came up with a solution. There was only one way for a slave to gain his release—to prove his valor and strength in battle. Perhaps he could instigate such a combat between Gwyneth's kinsman and one of Thordis's men. That way he would not be showing weakness and Gwyneth's kinsman would at least have a chance to earn his freedom.

The very idea caused him to be pleased with himself. It was the kind of solution a lawgiver would decree at the gathering of the Thing, were they to have one.

"You see, I do care about your feelings," he said, gazing down at Gwyneth. "So much so that I can put aside my own anger just to see you smile." His eyes swept over her soft breasts and he reached out to take her in his arms.

She snuggled against him, slowly opening her eyes. "Selig?"

"No more harsh words between us, Gwyn," he said softly. "I have thought of a way to melt this wall we have suddenly built." He explained his idea to her, holding her close.

"You would do that? Give him a chance to win his freedom?"

"Yes." He reached down to slide her chemise from her shoulders. "Did you miss me?" He kissed her exposed breasts, first one and then the other.

A ripple of delight surged through her, yet she fought for control. "Maybe I did," she said with a smile.

He gloried in the touch of her, the smell of her, the sight of her. Why was it that whenever he was near her he forgot everything else? Slowly he slid her chemise from her body.

"Selig!" Without even knocking, Thordis barged into the house.

With a gasp, Gwyneth hastened to cover herself, angry at the daring of the Viking. Despite the fact that he was Selig's friend, she loathed him.

"What is it, Thordis?" Selig stepped in front of Gwyneth to shield her nakedness from his eyes as she rearranged her garments.

"The Englishman . . ."

"Yes . . . ?" Selig feared that the man was dead.

"He's gone!" He looked at Gwyneth as if she were the culprit.

"Gone?" It was the last bit of news he had ever expected.

"Yes, gone. Unless you freed him, he has escaped."

Selig shrugged. "He must have been stronger than we imagined."

Thordis furled his brows. "So strong that he could unbolt the door from the outside? That would take magic, my friend." His eyes turned toward Gwyneth, accusing her without saying the words.

"The door was unbolted?" Selig asked in disbelief. He remembered locking it himself.

"Yes. It seems your *woman* has had her way." There could be no misunderstanding what he meant. He was openly accusing her. "Who else would do such a thing?"

"She would not . . ." Selig began, fighting against his suspicions. He didn't want to believe that she would go against him.

"Then tell me who did!" Thordis strutted around triumphantly. "She is the only one who would have reason to free an Englishman."

Selig could not think of an argument that could convince Thordis otherwise. He turned to Gwyneth. "Did you free him?"

"No!" She had been determined to set Jaenbert free last night but had decided that persuading Selig to set him free was the better way. "I wanted to, but I didn't."

"Then who did?" His words were a challenge to prove her innocence by thinking of an alternative culprit.

"I don't know." Tears brimmed her eyes. "It was not I."

Thordis stepped in between Selig and Gwyneth. "Can you say that you are sorry that he escaped?"

"I am not sorry!" she answered truthfully. "But it was not by my hand that he was freed. I would not so betray Selig." She waited for Selig to agree, to come to her defense, but he did not and his silence hurt her deeply.

The evidence was against her. Who would believe that she had not freed Jaenbert? If the truth were told, she had come very close to freeing him. She had even walked by the storehouse where he was imprisoned, determined to unlock the door. Then, as she reached out, something in her heart had stilled her hand and she had turned and walked away.

"I don't believe you! And neither will Selig when I have gathered my witnesses against you."

"Witnesses who will say anything that you want them to say?" For some reason, Thordis had declared himself her enemy. Well, he would soon see that she could be just as determined as he.

The great hall was in shambles. Chairs and benches were overturned, tankards and flagons were strewn over the floor haphazardly, spilled mead soaked the floor. Thordis and his men had left the large room in a clutter in their drunken frenzy.

Determined to keep busy, she bent down and started to clean up the mess. Ingunn and Kadlin helped her.

"He doesn't believe me," she mourned.

"That's because Thordis can be very persuasive and because Selig owes him his life," Kadlin explained.

"And because men are men, after all. Prideful to the end," Ingunn added. "What you must do is to think the matter out. Who would seek to free your kinsman?"

"I don't know . . ." It was puzzling. "Unless Jaenbert bribed one of the men with promises of gold if they would help him."

"What if the reason were a more sinister one? What if someone wanted to kill your kinsman and thus set him free to make his murder possible."

"What of Thordis? Maybe he regretted his generosity in giving the man to Selig. Perhaps he reclaimed the slave and then placed the blame upon Gwyneth to keep from angering Selig."

SEVENTEEN

It was dark in the storehouse. Gwyneth paced back and forth, tripping every so often over some object and losing her balance. Fumbling around in the dark, she felt the cold metal of an iron sword—as cold as Selig's heart, she reflected angrily. She tried to adjust her eyes to the darkness, searching for any familiar object, fearful of this blackness they had thrust her into.

"Why wouldn't he believe me? How could he take the word of that vile Thordis over mine?" If she had actually freed Jaenbert she would have told Selig the truth and faced her punishment bravely. She wouldn't have set him free and then lied about the act. Selig should know that. He should have trusted her.

She had gone beyond hurt, beyond anger, and now felt only the darkest despair. It was difficult to believe what had happened—or Selig's rejection of her. How could she have ever believed that he loved her? If he did, he would have trusted her.

She reached out to feel the shapes and textures of her surroundings. It was strange how her sense of touch took over for the missing sense of sight. She felt the sharp edge of a battle-ax and drew back her hand in revulsion, wondering how many men it might have killed.

Crawling on hands and knees, she soon found

what she sought—a pile of furs and soft-stitched tapestries. At least she would have a bed. Trembling, she pulled one of the tapestries over her body and wondered if it was Selig's intent to leave her in this prison until she grew old. If he expected a confession from her for something she had not done, that was how long she would be in this prison.

No matter how miserable she was, Gwyneth would not cry out to Selig or plead with him to let her go. If he loved her he would come and take her away from this darkness and humiliation.

"If he loved me." She clutched at the tapestry. "Perhaps I should have freed Jaenbert. At least then I would be suffering punishment for something I did," she whispered angrily.

She was infuriated with Selig and worried at the same time. Who freed Jaenbert and why? Whoever it was could be dangerous.

Selig walked back and forth in his house, staring at the bed, remembering the nights he had spent with Gwyneth. He ached to hold her now, to comfort her. It took all of his self-control not to run to where she was imprisoned and gather her in his arms. He wanted to more than anything and yet each time he moved in that direction he was stopped by his stubborn pride. His honor was at stake, his reputation, all that a man had upon his death.

He was torn between his duty and his emotions, so tormented that he let out a loud, futile cry to vent his frustrations. A yell so loud that he was certain they could hear it all the way to Asgard, the home of the gods.

Over and over again he asked himself which he treasured more, his friendship with Thordis or his love for Gwyneth. Was it more important for him to save face with this man or to learn the truth?

A voice deep within him shouted that he had lost a treasure more precious than all the riches in the storeroom. Even so, he had felt he had to ignore the pleading of his heart. It was the Viking way to value strength and leadership. How, then, could he openly show that his love for Gwyneth was so strong that he would go against the laws and code of his Viking brothers and open himself up to rebellion and misconduct? No matter which way he turned, no matter which path he chose, he was doomed.

Selig paced until his feet tired. At last he left the house and roamed aimlessly around the settlement, with Baugi trailing along behind. He found himself wanting to take Gwyneth away from the settlement, to sail the ocean just the two of them, to leave his friends behind so he could insure that he would not have to keep her imprisoned.

Walking by the hall, he could hear laughter. Thordis and his men were enjoying the hospitality of their hosts as was the Viking way. Selig found himself feeling angered. He wished Thordis had never come here. If he had not come and brought the Englishman, then Gwyneth would be safe and all would be well.

Back at the house, he threw a log on the fire and stared at the flickering flames. Why had Gwyneth betrayed him? How could she have so blatantly freed her kinsman when she knew that he would be angered? Had she foolishly thought that because of his feelings for her he would let her escape punishment? Or was she telling the truth?

How can I blame her for feeling sympathy for one of her own? What would I have done in her place?

"But she lied to me!" That perhaps was what he could not forgive. Selig had always valued the truth.

Running his hands through his hair, he contemplated her every word, every gesture, and the look in her eyes when she had denied the accusations against her. What if it were true?

"There you are, Selig. You should be drinking with me and the others!" Thordis stood in the doorway, beckoning Selig to join him. "This is just like old times!"

"I'm not thirsty!"

"Pining over your woman?" Thordis shook his head. "Women are like waves in the ocean. There will always be another and another and another."

"There will never be another woman like Gwyneth. Never!"

Thordis shrugged. "You are right. She is a beauty, even if she is deceitful and disobedient." He stepped inside. "If it were me, I would sell her and make her take the place of the slave that she set free."

"Well, I am not you!" Selig shouted. No matter how angry he was at what Gwyneth had done, he would never do such a thing. Life without her was already too lonely even to contemplate what Thordis was saying.

"Soooo, she has gotten under your skin. I never thought any woman would do that, Selig."

"I'm trying to be fair. There is no proof that Gwyneth did anything wrong and yet you are assuming that she is guilty. If she were a man she would at least be allowed a trial by combat to prove her words to be true."

The Vikings prided themselves on their system of law and yet Selig could see that Gwyneth had been wronged.

"If she were a man you wouldn't care so much about her guilt or innocence," Thordis countered. "But what a woman has between her legs is more persuasive even than facts, it seems, at least to you."

Rather than humiliating Selig, Thordis's barbs goaded him to anger, not at Gwyneth but at the perpetrator of the trouble. "Gwyneth is not like that. She deserves respect."

Without even realizing what he was doing, Selig pulled back his fist and punched Thordis in the jaw. Then he grabbed him by the hair and forced him to his knees.

"Unlike the Christians, we hold women to be our equals in matters of the law. Were Gwyneth a man she would be able to fight for her honor. Since she is not a man I will fight in her place and then if I win you will go to her on bended knee and apologize for the way she has been treated."

Thordis pulled away and stood up. "You must be mad!"

"No, to the contrary, I am thinking clearly for the first time since you came."

"You will fight me?" Thordis raised his fist ominously.

Selig nodded.

"You will lose. What then?"

"I won't lose!"

"But if you do, Gwyneth will be deemed guilty before all and will have to pay the price."

Selig knew what he was risking. He also had the feeling that he would not lose. He didn't dare!

Clutching the keys to the storehouse, Selig made his way to where Gwyneth was imprisoned. Opening the door and lighting a torch, he searched the room for her, panicking when he didn't see her. For a moment he feared that she had escaped and that perhaps Jaenbert had come back to take her away with him. Then he saw her in the far corner, curled up on a pile of furs. She looked so fragile, so beguiling and so innocent, that any doubts he might have had were swept away.

"Gwyneth . . ."

She turned slowly and for one fleeting moment their eyes met and held in the torchlight. Her breath stopped as she recognized the look in his eyes. He believed her. That was why he had come. Finally he had listened to his heart and not the hissing voice of Thordis.

"I've come to set you free and to ask for your forgiveness. And to tell you that even one night without you was an eternity of loneliness."

"Loving is trusting," she whispered. "Everything I have said to you is the truth. I thought of freeing Jaenbert; I wanted to; I even walked past the storehouse not once but several times. I was tempted, but I did not let him out. Instead I was going to . . ."

"Hush!" He took her into his arms, satisfying himself by holding her for a long time. The touching of their bodies brought forth a spark between them that might have erupted into lovemaking had it been another time, another place. At last he said, "Come . . ." He took her by the hand.

Stepping outside, Gwyneth looked at the bright rainbow of colors in the sky. It was as if God's very hand had painted the sky with brilliant hues.

"It's a sign. All will be well from now on, I know it."

Together they walked to the communal hall where a crowd was gathering.

"What's this?" She turned to look up at Selig. "What's going on?"

He hurriedly explained the law of combat. "Since you can not fight Thordis, I am going to fight for you."

"No!" It seemed the most barbaric thing she had ever heard of in her life. "You could be killed!"

"You said that love was trust. I love you, Gwyneth, and I trust in your innocence. So much so that I am willing to risk my life."

EIGHTEEN

The combat was to be on a level stretch of hard ground covered with a dusting of wild grass and surrounded by rocks upon which the spectators sat. Gwyneth's heart was in her throat as she watched the two men walk onto the field. Though Selig was a strong man, Thordis seemed to have a violence about him that worried her.

She heard wagering going on, men in the crowd deciding a winner and placing bets on the outcome. She was appalled that these men she had lived among placed wagers on a test of strength and truth. Though she longed to plead with Roland to stop the battle, she knew she didn't dare. This was the only way to prove that she was not guilty.

"Please, God . . . be with Selig . . . and I will never ask anything of you again . . ."

"This is to be a trial by combat. Let it be proven before all this assembly whether or not the accused is innocent or guilty. By the might of Thor, we begin this combat," Roland shouted out.

Voices rose in a cheer as Selig and Thordis took their places, removed their tunics, and threw them to the ground. Just as the English fighters did in battle, they would fight nearly naked and though there was much at stake, she felt a stirring in her blood, a languid heat that brought forth a longing.

She wanted this to be over so that she and Selig could go back to their own home.

There was an eerie feeling as the two adversaries advanced, swords leveled. The swords glowed in the sun, their engraved hilts casting bright lights from afar. Selig inspected his carefully, satisfied that it was exactly like the one that Thordis would fight with.

Roland, who was acting as lawgiver, set forth the terms of the combat then brought his hand downward to begin the fighting. In grotesque dance, they bent and swayed. The air rang with the sound of blade on blade. It was a brutal fight. Grueling. Dangerous. Gwyneth was dismayed to see that Thordis was making a good showing for himself. Too good. Just as she had suspected, he was the kind of man who would win a fight at any price. Certainly he was giving as good as he was getting.

"Selig . . ." She grimaced as he narrowly ducked out of the way of his opponent's sword. The battle was growing fiercer and fiercer.

The sun beat down full force as the two men lashed out at each other again and again. Sweat ran into Selig's eyes, blinding him for an instant. Gwyneth could nearly feel the pain as the tip of Thordis's blade tore the flesh of Selig's arm. Covering her mouth with her hand, she stifled a cry.

Selig's arm blazed with pain. Despite his torment, however, he used his wits. He pressed in, driving his brawny opponent back as he tried to maneuver him onto the rough ground and over the rocks. Selig plied him on the right side, then on the left, moving with the grace of a mountain cat.

"Look at him. He moves like some ancient god," Ingunn cried out in awe. "If I wasn't a married woman and if he wasn't spoken for, I could fall in love."

Selig pulled himself from the ground, keeping his eyes on his adversary's sword, feeling his head grow light as the blade whistled before him. He could feel his breath hammering inside his chest and knew that he was winded. His arm felt so heavy that it took great effort to lift it.

"You won't escape me so easily this time." Locked together in combat, the two men rolled upon the ground as the Vikings rumbled their excitement.

Freeing himself from the large man's grip, Selig stood up. This time it was he who initiated the assault, diving for Thordis's legs. With a sudden burst of strength, he tore the sword from his adversary's hand and hurled it away. Was the crashing in his ears from the onlookers or from his heart? He fought to catch his breath, certain that his lungs were so cramped there would be no room for any air.

Thordis scrambled to retrieve his weapon. The sound of sword on sword rent the air again as the two men renewed their furious battle, a test of strength, courage, and fortitude. Selig's aching eyes seemed to imagine three men at one time hurtling toward him, lunging, striking. Shaking his head, he sought to clear his vision as Thordis plunged forward with the tip of his blade. Pain pierced Selig's shoulder. The warmth of his own blood seeped from the fresh wound, mingling with the first wound to run in a rivulet down his arm.

Thordis was trying to maneuver him along the slope of the ground to gain advantage but Selig would have none of that. Over and over again, he remembered tales of prowess and how the heroes of old had won their battles. He mimicked their daring.

"Look! Thordis is getting angry," Ingunn said, poking Gwyneth in the ribs. "And when he does he sometimes loses his head."

Gwyneth looked towards Selig's opponent. Thordis was brawny and strong, it was true, but what he had in strength he lacked in brains. It was clear that Selig was easily outthinking him, goading him into foolish moves.

"Come on. Come on," Selig taunted, baiting his combatant. He had to win! He *would* win. For Gwyneth's sake. For the sake of his honor. For the sake of truth.

Again and again Thordis lunged, his anger at being so easily thwarted making him careless. His senses honed by danger, his sword arm swinging forward, Selig blocked each thrust until, with a sudden burst of strength, he knocked his enemy's sword from his hand again.

Gwyneth blinked her eyes and in just that short span of time Selig had Thordis on the ground, the blade of the sword pressed against his neck. The Vikings roared their excitement.

"Say it!" Selig cried out. "Tell them. Tell them all!"

Thordis nearly choked on his words. "As has been promised, the woman is declared innocent of any wrongdoing."

His announcement was met with shouts and cheers for there wasn't anyone among them who did not place value on a winner. Nor would anyone dare doubt her innocence from now on. It was a victory. Hers and Selig's. And yet, her joy was marred by the anger clearly written on Thordis's face as he brushed by her.

"You will live to regret this," he shouted out to Selig.

How easily their friendship turned sour, Gwyneth thought, regretting any part she might have had in what happened. She felt a sense of foreboding as Thordis gathered up his men and they made their way to the ship.

* * *

Gwyneth was relieved to find out that Selig's wounds were superficial. Washing off the blood, she wrapped his arm and shoulder tightly with linen, then bent to give him a kiss. For the moment, at least, all was forgiven.

"Have I told you lately how much I love you?" he asked softly.

"Not lately," she answered.

"Then I'm telling you now. I thank the gods that you are mine." His hands tangled in her hair as he kissed her. The kiss was long, satisfying to them both, an unspoken affirmation of their love. "Nothing this side of Niflheim, world of the dead, will ever part us again."

"I hope not!" she whispered. She wanted to believe that they were destined to be happy forever but at the back of her mind she questioned that possibility. They loved each other, it was true, but that deep affection faced a multitude of obstacles. For the moment, however, she put any misgivings out of her mind.

NINETEEN

The sound of wood splintering followed by a loud crash shattered the silence of the early dawn. Rudely awakened from her peaceful slumber, Gwyneth sat up in bed, sensing danger despite her drowsiness. She barely had time to awaken Selig before a nightmare descended upon them.

She screamed as she saw the silhouette of an upraised sword. A Viking stood in the doorway. Memories of the attack on her kinsmen flashed through her mind.

"Selig!" Her warning gave him time to arm himself just a moment before the Viking lunged at him.

"Gwyneth, run! Get away!" he shouted, lashing out with his sword as two other Vikings joined their companion.

"No." She wouldn't leave him alone to face three men, particularly when he hadn't fully recovered from his wounds yet.

Selig stood with his legs astride, sword in hand, dodging an ax which missed him by the width of a finger. His sword blow hit its mark and one of the Vikings fell to earth like a massive tree. Now it was two against one as the conical-helmeted Vikings pushed forward.

Gwyneth recognized one of the men by his profile and realized it was the Viking who had tried to rape her. Selig had banished him and now it seemed he had returned for revenge. "Jokul!"

"I should have killed you while I had the chance," Selig swore as he, too, identified his enemy. "Who have you brought with you?"

"Friends," Jokul declared. He swung his sword and struck a blow that Selig only narrowly dodged. His sword embedded itself in a small wooden bench, nearly cleaving the wood in two. The other Viking stepped forward to take his place, swinging his battle-ax. Selig thrust his wooden trunk forward, nearly knocking the man off balance.

Though she loathed violence, Gwyneth sought any weapon she could use to aid Selig. She found a long-handled baking plate right outside the door. It was made of iron and wood and when she swung it like a club, it struck Jokul a blow that sent him sprawling. Raising it, again she brought the rounded surface down upon his head to knock him unconscious.

"Well done, Gwyn!" Selig said in praise; then, wincing at the pain in his shoulder, he continued his own fight. "At least now the odds are more fair."

Selig and his adversary crossed the room, back and forth, first one striking out, then the other. The contest was evenly matched. All Gwyneth could do was stand aside and watch.

Suddenly Selig's foe, an older man, tired and seemed to lose power. Selig's sword struck out and sliced through the Viking's shoulder, rendering his sword arm useless. Gwyneth had no doubt that the man would bleed to death within a short while; there was nothing she could do to change his fate. She wondered if she even wanted to try. He would have murdered Selig had the fight gone the other way.

"God forgive me, I'm becoming more Viking than I realized," she said aloud.

Selig put his arms around her. "Aye, you have acted like a Viking woman should. I could not have asked for more."

The man who had just been wounded made a rasping sound that she knew to be the sound of death. Selig knelt down beside him while Gwyneth tied Jokul securely with ropes. He opened his ice-blue eyes and squinted as he looked into her eyes. She read hatred there, a desire to cause her injury.

"Bitch!" he swore. "You have not seen the end of this."

"But you have!" Selig answered.

Gwyneth turned towards Selig and saw that he was staring transfixed at the face of the dead man whose helmet he had just removed. "Who is he?"

"A Dane!"

"Are you certain?"

"Look at his hair. It's as dark as the night." He nudged Jokul in the ribs with his bare foot. "So, you go against your own and join with the Danes! I should kill you but I won't. Not until you tell me what I want to know."

Jokul glared up at him. "I won't tell you anything!"

"I think you will. You know as well as I the ways we have of making a man loosen his tongue."

"You will torture me!"

Selig's grin chilled Gwyneth's heart. "You wouldn't . . . !" she rasped. No matter what Jokul had done, she didn't think she could witness suffering.

Taking her by the arm, Selig led her outside. Several bodies lay on the ground, enemies as well as those from the settlement, but it was clear that Selig's people had been victorious. Several houses had been burned to the ground and from afar they could see the blaze of the fields that had been set on fire. Selig didn't lose any time in gathering a party of men to fight the flames. Gwyneth sought out the women to aid the wounded.

There was no time for talk as women and men alike fought hard to save the settlement. The men returned with faces blackened with smoke but with the knowledge that most of the crops had been saved. The women knew that they had done their best to mend injuries and soothe the dying.

Only when he knew that the settlement was safe did Selig turn his attention to Jokul again. "Who sent you or did you think up this treachery? Where is the ship that brought the Danes or did they come across the land to join you?"

"You know that I won't tell you!"

"And if I threaten to boil you in oil if you do not tell me, what then?" Selig countered.

"Selig . . ." Gwyneth shuddered at the thought. Surely he wouldn't actually do such a thing!

He silenced her with one word. "Hush." He turned back to Jokul. "Tell me what I want to know or I swear by Thor's hammer that I will do it!"

Jokul snarled his defiance. "I am not afraid of death at your hands. Do what you want."

Selig grabbed Jokul by the front of his blood-stained tunic, lifting him off the ground. "I hate Vikings who betray their own. You will beg me a hundred times over to let you die quickly but I will make certain that yours is a slow death."

Something in his voice, his expression, took away Jokul's bravado. He did not mind dying and going to Valhalla, but to die the way that Selig intended him to die was another thing. He thought a moment. "If I tell you, what will be my fate then?"

"I'll see that you are sent to Norway, to serve your fellow Vikings there."

"I will not live one day as a slave."

Selig looked at Gwyneth and she looked at him. "Not as a slave, but as a peasant bondi. The muscles of your sword arm will be severed so that you may never again take up arms against your brothers. It is better than you deserve." He stood with hands on hips, looking down at the traitor.

Jokul was silent for a long time, pondering the matter. He chose death over life and Selig again stated his terms. "Tell me and I will have you killed quickly."

"You can't murder him . . . !" Gwyneth was horrified.

Selig looked daggers at her. "Don't interfere! Because of this man there has been death here." He was bluffing, hoping he wouldn't have to kill him in her presence but he would if that were his only choice. For the sake of the settlement he could not allow Jokul to cause any more trouble.

"You won't kill me in front of her. She has made you weak."

"No, because of her I am even more determined to see to the safety of the settlement." Walking to the outdoor fire, Selig threw several logs into the flames, then set a large cauldron on the fire. He filled the cauldron with water and waited for it to start boiling. "Roland, help me put him into the cauldron."

Gwyneth gasped, but she didn't say a word. Even the Holy Book spoke of an eye for an eye but she could only pray that Selig was deceiving Jokul and would never carry out his threat. Still, as Roland and Selig picked Jokul up by his legs and arms, it appeared that he intended to proceed.

"No! Wait!" Selig and Roland put him down, none too gently. "The raid was led by Harold Blacktooth. They came by ship."

"And where is that ship now?"

"Sailing north, past the eastern coast of Scotland, headed for the Hebrides."

Gwyneth knew without even asking what Selig was going to do now. He was going to follow.

The *Sea Dragon* sailed immediately, her sails billowing with the summer winds. From his place at the prow, Selig watched the dark-haired figure of Gwyneth grow smaller and smaller. The farther away he went, the more determined he was to catch up to the Danes and do battle for the only way to end the menace of the dark Vikings was to defeat them once and for all.

Selig scanned the horizon for any sign of the ship but saw only an endless expanse of blue. Deciding to sail further inland, they traveled up the coast of England, then Scotland, until it was a black line to starboard. There would be no moon, but the sky was clear; thus they decided to sail all night, using the stars as their guide.

"How long are we going to sail?" Roland asked.

"Until we find them!"

"And if we don't?"

"We will!"

Roland hung lamps of tortoiseshell filled with whale oil and lit the floating wicks. The light reflected on the dragon's head, making it seem real.

The sea was loud, rushing beneath the ship. Selig could hear the water slapping against the prow. Now and again he could feel the cool kiss of spray upon his face. The night air was filled with the voices of the men who sang a song about Aegir, god of the mighty ocean, and his wife, Ran, who was said to wait with her net to catch drowned sailors. *"In the greenish gloom that spells your doom, no fires can burn. The hall is lit by the treasure pit and the gleam of its golden urn. The clang of a bell in Aegir's hall sends chills up the spine of the brave. Then Ran swims up and fills her cup with the coins as they float on the waves. For the gurgling fools must pay with the jewels if they lust for a welcome from her."*

"Wait . . . hold . . ." Selig gestured for the men to be silent. Was it his imagination or did he hear the faint sound of another ship splashing through the waves.

TWENTY

The silhouette of a ship hovered on the dark waters, illuminated only by the tortoiseshell lamps hanging on the *Sea Dragon*'s prow. The oars of the other ship protruded from the sides like legs on a spider. Selig knew at a glance that it was a Viking ship.

"The Danes!" He clenched his jaw as he reflected on the damage and death they had brought to the settlement. Tonight they would pay.

"What are we going to do?" Roland had left the tiller. His gaze was riveted on the shadow of the ship.

It seemed to Selig that the dragon head on the ship strained to take the wind like a living being. It was as if it were urging him on to do what must be done. The ship or Odin!

"We will attack!"

"But it's dark." Roland had his reservations.

"If we wait until it is light, the Danes may elude us and we will have come all this way for naught!"

It was a decision made of anger, yet the judgment had been made. Preparations were quickly underway for those at the oars to increase the strength and speed of the ship in order to ram the other vessel. The god Aegir and his wife Ran would have plenty of visitors. Selig hoped that Ran's nets were ready to catch the fallen Danes.

"We will ram them and do as much damage to the ship as we can—then we will board them."

"Board them? How?" Roland's furrowed brow showed that he was against the idea.

"We'll find a way." Selig's hazel eyes were black with intent. His face was shadowed. "We'll use ropes or crawl over the oars if we must. Then we'll bring them the same terror they brought to us!"

Selig knew that his crew would never know how violently his insides were churning. He masked any misgivings with bravado for he knew they had to win. The alternative was too devastating to contemplate.

Selig watched as some of his men maneuvered the sails, allowing the ship to take advantage of the wind. That, added to the oar power, would enable them to overtake the other ship with a violence that would stun the Danes, at least for a time.

"Steady."

Speeding upon the sea like a winged dragon, the *Sea Dragon* overtook the Danish ship, veering sharply, angling in the direction of their stern. Then it rammed it at full speed. The impact caused men and debris to be hurled into the air. The Danish ship was badly wounded. It would be forced to fight defensively.

"Board her!"

Goaded on by an anger that matched Selig's own, the crew swarmed onto the other ship, their swords ready to shed blood. Soon the clang of sword against sword would vibrate in the air.

Selig was the first to board. In the dim moonlight, his eyes scanned his surroundings. He was intent on finding the leader and that was exactly what he did—a tall man with golden hair. Selig waited for him to throw himself into the battle but strangely the man held up his hand.

"We are outnumbered. Take what goods that you must and leave us be."

Selig could barely control his anger. "Leave you be? After the death and destruction you brought?"

The blond man took a step forward. "We did not bring anything to you. Whatever has caused you to attack a peaceful merchant ship is a mistake!"

Mistake! The word echoed in Selig's mind. He lit a lamp and looked around him. His men were poised for violence but he gestured for them to hold steady until he had scrutinized the enemy ship. What he found made his face flush with confusion and dismay. Not only did the goods on board prove the other Viking to be telling the truth but it was obvious that the ship was not manned by dark-haired Danes at all but by blond Norwegians. Not one of the men on board was recognizable as having taken part in the assault on the settlement.

"I . . . I don't know what to say," Selig stammered. It was the most embarrassing moment of his life.

"You could start by explaining why you attacked." Now that it appeared that there wasn't going to be a battle, the leader of the damaged ship showed his anger. "You have crippled my ship, impeded my journey, and caused injury to my crew. I think that entitles me to know why."

"My settlement was attacked by Danes. One of the attackers who was left behind told me that the ship manned by our attackers was on its way up the coast to the Hebrides. In our pursuit of the guilty I blundered and ordered an attack on what I thought to be my enemies."

Selig assessed the damage his ship had done to the other. There was a large hole that made it dangerous for the ship to sail any great distance. Several of the crewmen had been shaken up, bruised, and battered but there were no serious injuries. It would not be difficult to make amends.

"I propose that I tie your vessel to mine, tow you back to our settlement, and make repairs to your ship."

The other Viking shook his head. "No. I think it better to go our separate ways." He wore an expression of distrust.

Selig was insistent. "One of the best ship builders known in the Northland is in my settlement. I promise you that he will repair the hole so well that you won't be able to see a remaining scratch." He paused. Being humbled was a new experience. "I am offering you my hospitality and my apology."

The Viking thought the matter out carefully, at last agreeing. "We won't stay long enough to impose on your generosity. As soon as we are able, we will set sail." He introduced himself. "My name is Torin Rolandsson. My wife and crew and I were on our way from Alba to Hafrsfjord in the Northland."

He motioned to a tall, silhouetted figure whom Selig had not noticed before. Coming closer, she pushed back the hood from her cloak to reveal an attractive face and long, flaming-red hair. Except for Gwyneth, she was the most beautiful woman Selig had ever seen.

"This is my wife, Erica."

The lovely woman held her head high and looked him eye to eye. "Are ye always so rash in your actions?" she asked him. If her husband was quick to forgive, she was not.

"As I explained to your husband, my settlement down the coast was attacked by Danes. Several were killed—they set fires and would have done more except that my friends and I rallied. I captured one of those responsible. He told me, upon threat of death, that the Danish ship was headed up the coast. Your ship was there, it was dark, and I thought . . ."

"That we were the guilty ones."

"Yes." He was bold enough to take her hand. "But forgive me. I have not told you my name. It is Selig."

"Selig . . ." she repeated.

Motioning for Roland, Selig gave orders for the two ships to be tied together by ropes, then he turned back to Torin Rolandsson and his wife. There was something about the two of them that piqued his interest.

"So, you are merchants."

This time the red-haired Erica smiled. "Not exactly. My husband came to Ulva and Mull with something else in mind and got more than he bargained for." She and Torin exchanged loving glances. "He came searching for one of the sons of Ragnar Longsword."

Selig paled. "Sons of Ragnar Longsword!"

She didn't notice the way Selig was suddenly staring as she laughed softly. "Aye. My father thought that he had sired a son in Alba but he was wrong. As ye can see, I am not his son but his daughter."

"That is plain to see," he whispered. His thoughts were muddled, his emotions in chaos. All this time he had foolishly assumed that he was the only offspring of the infamous Viking leader. Suddenly he had, through his own actions, come face-to-face with his half-sister. It was hard to believe.

"My Uncle Coinneach was loathe to give up a quarrel that began the day I was born but my dear Torin came to the rescue." Moving close to Torin, she entwined her hands with his. "Let me make a long story short by saying that it was his idea to establish trade between my uncle and my father for the betterment of both our peoples."

"And you were sailing back when my ship came upon your ship." It was so strange, so eerie, that

Selig could only suppose that it had been fated that he cross paths with this ship.

"Aye. But perhaps some good can come of all ills. Perhaps there can be trade between my uncle's kinsman and your settlement."

Torin laughed. "Spoken like a true merchant." He kissed her lightly on the lips. "Will you never cease to surprise me?"

Their happiness was infectious, but for the moment Selig was immune as old resentments against his father resurfaced. The woman named Erica had said that Torin was looking for the sons of Ragnar and he could not help but wonder how many there were. How many women had his father taken to his bed and then deserted?

For a moment he wondered what Torin and Erica would think if he told them of his own blood ties to Ragnar Longsword; then just as suddenly, he decided not to say a word. In his way, his father was looking for him and it seemed a sort of revenge to keep silent on the matter of his parentage. Let Ragnar search for him forever for all he cared.

It was a long, tedious journey back to the settlement but the welcome that he received soon put Selig in a better frame of mind. Throwing her arms around him, Gwyneth laughed and cried at the same time.

"I was afraid . . . I thought . . . that I might never see you again!" Tears of happiness flooded her eyes. It was only much later that she noticed the strangers on board his ship. "Who . . . ?"

Selig quickly explained all that had happened, flushing as he told her about the mistake he had made. He then preceded to introduce Gwyneth to Torin and his wife, Erica.

The two women eyed each other up and down

and decided immediately that they were to be friends. Gwyneth held out her hand, clasping Erica's warmly to demonstrate her welcome.

"You are so tall, you make me feel like a child. I've never seen hair the shade of yours before. It reminds me of fire."

"I've been told that I hae a temperament to match," Erica said with a slight smile, "but that is only when I am angered."

"Then I'll try not to make you lose your temper," Gwyneth countered. Leading Erica inland towards the settlement, she asked her all about the fearsome Scots she had heard so much about.

"Is it true that they fight with such a huge sword that it takes two to lift it?"

"We have a sword like that but my kinsmen prefer their own swords so they can fight alone."

Finding a quiet spot near the communal hall, Gwyneth and Erica engaged in small talk, each finding out about the other. Erica revealed the story of how her husband, Torin, had come to Alba on a quest to find a young man only to find out that the young man was in actuality a young woman.

"It's strange but when I went back to Alba I felt out of place. Because I love him, anywhere my husband is feels like my home," Erica said with a sigh.

"That's how I feel," Gwyneth responded, "yet there are times when I long to see my family for a few moments so I can explain my feelings and give my father warning about those who have deceived him."

Gwyneth told Erica about the attack on the church during her wedding ceremony and of how surprised she had been to find out that Selig and the young Viking she had loved and had freed from slavery were one and the same.

Reaching down the front of her gown, she touched the dragon's tear and proudly held it up for Erica to see. "He gave me this the night I cut his bonds. Later, when he raided the church, he saw it and knew that we had been reunited."

"The pendant . . ." Erica's eyes were riveted on the silver dragon with its sapphire tear.

Gwyneth noticed the way she was staring. "What is it?"

"Torin has been searching for . . ." She reached out and touched the pendant, turning it in several directions as she examined it. "Has Selig ever told you about his father?"

"No." Gwyneth watched as Erica reached beneath her arasiad and gown and brought forth a pendant strikingly similar to her own. It was of the same intricate craftsmanship. The difference was that one was a raven with a garnet eye, the other a dragon set with a sapphire.

TWENTY-ONE

The beached merchant ship was secured by a netting of ropes that looked like a giant spider's web. A crew of Selig's men immediately began to work on the hull, recaulking and refitting sprung and broken planks.

To repair the ship they were using tree nails, or wooden pegs, and overlaps made watertight with moss mixed with tar. In some places iron nails and animal hair were used; thus once again Baugi came to the rescue.

"We need to gather some pitchy logs to tighten the seams. That will work wonders and make the ship airtight," said Godric, the shipbuilder.

Selig was in a boastful mood as he pulled at the old nails in the merchant ship, trying to straighten them out so they could be hammered in again and used to hold new wood. He grinned at the man named Torin.

"Your ship will be better than it was before. You might even thank me for bumping into you in the night."

"We'll see," Torin replied, picking up a chisel to work at the splintered oar holes.

Because of the shipbuilder's technique of splitting green logs in a radial pattern, all hull planking had the same cross section which guaranteed uniformity of strength and resilience throughout the ship. Selig knew that his ships were crafted superbly and that his shipbuilder had achieved strength through resilience and lightness. Now these same skills would make the merchant ship stronger than before.

Side by side, Selig and Torin labored. They pared the planking to a thickness of two centimeters, a finger's breadth, and trimmed every sliver of excess wood from the rib frames. As they worked, a bond formed between the two men, born of their love of the sea.

"How long have you been a merchant?" Selig was curious about Torin. He seemed much too muscular and skilled with a sword to have confined himself to trading goods.

"This is my first time sailing a merchant vessel. I am trying to bring peace between the Norsemen and the Scots in my wife's lands of Ulva and Mull." Torin explained that he had accompanied Ragnar Longsword on innumerable raids prior to this voyage. "You have heard of Ragnar Longsword?"

Selig stiffened. "I have. He has a reputation that has spread farther than his raids."

Ragnar Longsword was a big-boned giant of a man in the autumn of his years whose skill at fighting was not to be equaled in all of the Northlands. He was feared all the way from the Hebrides to Kiev. The very glimpse of his Viking ships with their square sails and dragon-headed prows on the horizon struck fear in the hearts of anyone who sighted them.

For twenty-seven years Ragnar and his band had burst upon the coasts like bolts out of the blue, targeting villages, castles, and monasteries alike in their quest for plunder. The raids had brought Ragnar and his men wealth, land, reputations for being both ruthless and bold, and an armed following to support Ragnar's ambitions at home.

"In his youth Ragnar terrorized his enemies but

now as he has grown older he has become a fair man whose goal is peace," Torin added.

"Peace?" Selig laughed derisively.

"Yes, peace." Torin insisted that Ragnar was intelligent as well as strong. "He has proven himself an able administrator in the lands he has subjugated. He realizes that a man has to be a creator as well as a destroyer and must reach out to other cultures, to learn from them and absorb their influences and ideas."

Torin told Selig that his own father had been one of Ragnar's fiercest foes, a man Ragnar had outlawed as a murderer, a coward, and a traitor.

"Then you must hate him!"

"No. I respect him and I have come to understand that it is men like him who change the world." Torin paused to wipe perspiration from his forehead. "Ragnar has been like a father to me."

"A father!" Selig clenched his jaw in anger as he thought about his boyhood days and how he had ached for a father. Ragnar had deserted him and left his mother to face scorn and ridicule all alone.

"At first we were at odds but I worked hard at all the duties I was given. I found time to watch the men at their mock battles and mimic them. Ragnar noticed my interest and taught me how to use a sword. More importantly, he taught me the thought behind each movement. In the end I won him over."

"How fortunate for you!" Selig snapped. Though he knew that he had no reason to be angry with Torin, he could not help being surly at the reminder of the wrong Ragnar had done to him. And to his mother!

Selig was assailed by so many memories. He thought about his mother, Cynnefed, and the pleasant hours he had spent with her when he was just a boy. She had been like a light in a dark, cruel world, telling him stories of her love for a Viking chieftain, who was his father and teaching him the Viking language in hopes that one day they would all be reunited.

Like a mosaic, the pieces of his life formed in his mind's eye. As a boy, Selig had been reviled because he was fathered by a Viking, despite the fact that his mother was betrothed to an Englishman. The very name "Ragnar" had been like a thorn in his flesh.

"Ragnar!" He swore softly to himself. The infamous Viking had thundered his way into Cynnefed's life with all the violence of a thundercloud. Despite her protests, he had swept her up in his arms and carried her off to his encampment, then forced her to marry him in a Viking ceremony. His mother should have hated the man who took her virtue and yet, strangely, their stormy encounter had turned to love.

As if it were only yesterday, he remembered Cynnefed vividly. She was a woman who always smiled, her thoughts soaring beyond the hostile reality of her surroundings. She had conjured up a world of contentment where troubles could not bother her. He had sensed that she counted the days until the man she loved would return to reclaim her. Selig had found himself sharing her dream, wanting desperately to have a father. But Ragnar never returned from roving the seas, and a bitterness had welled up inside the boy like the poison of an ill-tended wound.

Selig had been told many times that he favored his mother in looks. The thick blond hair, hazel eyes, and full, sensual mouth all marked him as his mother's son. In truth, he had inherited her gentle temperament as well until the cruelty of others forced him to be strong and domineering.

Many an early morning and late afternoon had been spent sparring with the other youths. He had received more than a few lumps, scratches, bruises, and black eyes defending his mother's name from those who taunted him, saying that his mother was a Viking's harlot. He had been called a bastard more times than he could count, learning at an early age that strength was his only defense.

He remembered how his mother's English husband had told him that a child conceived in sin stood in mortal jeopardy of his soul. He had made the boy work unmercifully hard, cuffing him if he dared to complain. Selig had toiled from early morning until long into the night.

At last the abuse to his spirit and pride had become unbearable. Though Selig had loved his mother fiercely, he ran away and it was then that he had been captured and sold as a slave.

Now he was a man of consequence, a Viking with his own settlement and ships. He had never asked his father for help. Not even when he faced slavery. Nor would he ever ask anything of him now. Let Ragnar face old age alone or with the other "sons" he sired.

Selig picked listlessly at the food on his plate as he sat across from Gwyneth at the morning meal.

"How is work going on the ship?" she asked, trying to initiate a conversation.

"One more day and Torin will be able to sail." He saw the look of disappointment that flickered in her eyes. "You like them, don't you?"

"Yes, I do. Erica and I have a lot in common."

He looked up, his eyebrows drawn together. "What?"

"We are both women." She was pleased when she saw a faint smile. "We are both Christian. We both love strong, handsome Vikings. And each of us has been gifted with a pendant." Taking out the dragon's tear, she gazed at it lovingly. "Erica has one similar to this except it is a raven with a red stone."

"Is that so?"

Gwyneth looked at him out of the corner of her eye. "She told me that Torin is looking for two pendants similar to hers. She thinks perhaps my pendant is one of them."

Selig dropped his spoon with a vehemence that stunned her. "I don't want you talking about the dragon's tear to anyone. Especially to her. Do you understand me?"

"I . . . I think so . . ." She covered her face with her hands as all sorts of thoughts came to her mind. At last she said, "So, then it is true. Torin is looking for the owner of the pendants and he has found one. You."

He shook his head violently. "No!" The lie tasted sour on his lips.

"Yes. You are the Viking Ragnar's son. Don't try to deny it, Selig, because your face tells me otherwise."

He stood up, pushed the bench aside, and paced the earthen floor with such a forceful stride that she feared he would soon wear a path in the dirt. At last he admitted what she had already guessed.

"Ragnar Longsword is my father, yes. Though I am loathe to admit it. If I could drain every drop of blood that binds me to him I would."

Gwyneth could feel the pain that he felt at that moment for it seeped from every pore. "You have never spoken of your boyhood or of your parentage."

"Because the wounds are much too deep."

She quickly came to stand beside him, reaching out to touch his hand. "Tell me what happened. Perhaps if you talk about it you can exorcise the demons that have haunted you for such a long while."

He was silent for a long, drawn-out moment, then he said, "Perhaps . . ."

What followed was a story that tore at Gwyneth's heart. Selig told her about his mother and how she had been abducted by Ragnar Longsword and carried off to his camp as part of the "spoils." At first Cynnefed had violently resisted but as her anger had turned to affection she had at last capitulated. After the Viking had married her in a ceremony in the woods she had given him her body and her heart.

"She wanted to go with him when he returned to the Northland, but he told her to wait for him and that he would come for her in the spring." He clenched and unclenched his fist. "He never returned."

There was a long pause before Gwyneth asked, "What happened?"

"My mother's family found out about my impending birth and tricked her former betrothed, a Mercian man of high renown, into marrying her quickly. A few months later I was born." He coughed. "Being a man who could count on his fingers, he knew at once that I was not of his seed. I suppose that is why he always hated me."

"How could anyone hate a child?"

"He did and made me suffer twofold for my mother's so-called sin."

Nor had his mother had an easy time of it. Though she spoke not a melancholy word and always soothed his spirits, he knew she hated her husband and his family, particularly the brother-in-law who made it obvious that he intended to claim her once his brother was out of the way.

"To make a long story short, I suffered at my mother's husband's hands until I could stand no more. I ran away and you know the rest . . ."

"I do and I am so sorry . . ."

"You helped me escape that night and gave me

a second chance at life." He brushed his hand against her face, then continued his story. "I established myself as a Viking of renown. I vowed that if my father would not return from the Northland to rescue my mother then I would!"

Selig had returned to Mercia, his arms piled high with gifts, only to find that his mother had been killed. The treasures he had brought home would never belong to her. He had taken too long to return and now it was too late. The bitter truth had hit him like a fist. It was the only time in his entire life that Selig had cried.

"I blamed my father and I blamed myself!"

Gwyneth tried to soothe his conscience. "It wasn't your fault! Place the blame on he who actually killed her. It wasn't you and it wasn't your father."

"I place a share of the blame on Ragnar's shoulders. At the very least he should have offered my mother protection," he said more to himself than to her. "He must have known of the warfare raging among the Anglo-Saxons and that she would be in danger. Instead, it appears as if he forgot her . . . and me!"

"No, you are wrong!" Gwyneth had listened to Erica's story of how she, too, had been abandoned by Ragnar before she was born. "Erica told me that Ragnar never forgot about her mother, or about her. He told her that he wanted to make amends. That's why he sent Torin out to find the three pendants and his grown offspring."

"He wants to make amends," Selig said and snapped his finger. "Just like that!" His expression turned stormy. "Well, he can't! There is nothing he can do to make up for all the pain he has caused or the promises he's broken."

Gwyneth started to say more but Selig held up his hand. "No more talk! Let Ragnar go to the ends of the world if he wants but he will never find me!"

TWENTY-TWO

Rain fell from the skies like ribbons of water, drenching the earth below. Though it was a summer storm it was nonetheless fierce and interfered with visibility and work on Torin's ship. Somehow it seemed to be an omen, though of what, Gwyneth wasn't exactly certain. All she knew was that it delayed the departure of a woman she had quickly come to know as a friend.

"We Christians believe in forgiveness and honoring our father and mother. Oh, Erica, how am I going to make Selig see that by shutting out his father and holding on to his anger he is harming himself?"

"Selig must see that for himself!"

Gwyneth's voice was shrill. "But how is that possible when he has put up a wall around himself and refuses even to talk with me about his father?"

Rain beat against the roof and splashed through the cracks in the walls of the small house. As they talked, Erica and Gwyneth were placing tankards, bowls, and cups under the leaks to keep the earthen floor from getting wet and thus making it uncomfortable.

Erica sighed. "Ye should know by now that men can be stubborn, hinny."

"Stubborn and unreasonable." Gwyneth finished with the last "raincatcher," then sat down on the chest and crossed her arms. "How can I convince

Selig to do as you have done and at least seek out his father and give him a chance to explain?"

"Perhaps I can help." Walking over to the vertical loom in the corner, Erica ran her fingers over the threads, stirring up a cloud of dust. "I see ye are not fond of weaving."

"I never learned how."

Erica's eyebrows arched up in surprise. "Never learned?"

"My father had churls to do the household chores," Gwyneth confided with downcast eyes, "but I would like to learn. Can you teach me?"

Erica laughed softly. "Come. It's simple. Though it is not one of my favorite things to do, I'll show ye."

She sat down on a chair in front of the loom and explained that there were threads that ran up and down on the loom called *warp* and those used cross-wise called *weft*. The warp threads were kept taut by means of stone weights tied at the bottom.

"The weft threads are interlaced under and over the warp threads by means of a *shuttle*," she pointed to the small wooden stick, "like this. Basic weaves can be varied by alternating the interlacing of the weft over the warp to include two or even three threads."

It seemed foolishly simple. "Let me try!" Gwyneth took Erica's place in front of the loom, interlacing the threads. "Were you angry at Ragnar for not returning to Alba, Erica?"

"No, perhaps because my mother had told me an imaginary story of how wonderful it had been when my father was with us. I was hoping that he would return one day, gather me into his arms, and take me away with him to the Northland, but it didna happen that way. Instead, he sent Torin to find his youngest son, Eric." She laughed heartily. "Ye can imagine that my dear Torin was in for a surprise."

Her laughter was infectious, spreading to Gwyneth, who laughed even though she had heard the story before. "You proved that you were more than a match for his male arrogance and supposed superiority. You saved his life."

"Aye, that I did."

"And then traveled back to the Northland with him?"

Erica shook her head. "Nay. Despite my love for him I would hae stayed in Alba had it not been for the men on Torin's ship. They kidnapped my beloved little brother, Geordie, and in order to save him I followed. All the way to the Northland and my father's hall."

Gwyneth listened in fascination to the details of Erica's story of how Geordie had cleverly left scraps of cloth as a trail for her and Torin to follow. She was awed as Erica told of how she had fought side by side with Torin to free her brother.

"You wielded a sword?"

"Aye! It was me who taught Geordie to fight. I suppose it was a wee beastie in me, trying to prove that even though I was female born I could make my father proud."

"I wish you could teach me . . ." Closing her eyes, Gwyneth imagined herself fighting beside Selig, only not with a long-handled baking plate but with a sword.

"Och! Careful, hinny, ye are tangling the threads."

Gwyneth dew in a deep breath and let it out slowly in a sigh. So much for dreaming. "I'm sorry— I wasn't paying attention to what I was doing."

"Here . . ." Erica showed her how to pluck at the wool, hastily rectifying the situation by untwisting the thread, then passing it more cautiously back and forth.

Gwyneth focused her attention on the loom,

watching as Erica rolled up an end of the finished cloth to make way for a new length of weaving, then unwound the spindle and measured off more thread to be used as the weft.

"Back on Mull and Ulva my cousin and the other women always said that I was all thumbs," Erica whispered. "I think it was because my mind was always elsewhere."

"It's no wonder." Gwyneth grasped the shuttle more tightly. In and out, in and out, she worked with the spindle. "So you would have stayed in Alba had it not been for Geordie."

"Aye."

"Perhaps Selig needs something like that to happen to make him forget his anger," she said more to herself than to Erica. But what? There was no Geordie to be kidnapped, no little brother to be saved.

Gwyneth tangled the threads again, only this time she straightened them out. "Surely weaving is tedious work." Even so, Gwyneth was determined to prove that she could master it. She would weave this thread into cloth if it killed her and then make a new tunic for Selig. She was equally determined about something else. Somehow, some way, she had to convince Selig to travel to the Northland to meet with his father.

The hall was warmly lit, the roaring fire inviting, but nonetheless Selig felt cold. "I hate rain," he said to Torin. "It is the one thing that a man can not control!"

"Rain and women," Torin answered. "Stormy and unpredictable, yet necessary to a man's well-being." He motioned for Selig to sit across from him at the small table. "Are you familiar with *hneftafl*, my friend?" He pointed to the wooden game board dotted with holes.

"No! I have been too busy for games."

Torin shrugged. "Well, with all this rain you won't be busy today, at least until it stops. Come. It is a game of skill. It will relax you and maybe turn that scowl into a semblance of a smile, my friend."

Despite his grumbling, Selig took a seat. "What is the purpose of the game?"

"To protect the jarl," he picked up an amber gaming piece shaped like a man's head, "this one." Hurriedly he explained the rules and that the amber pieces were to be moved across the board in the manner of a small army of Vikings. Each player had to defend his men from attacking forces.

"That shouldn't be too difficult. Prepare to be defeated," Selig challenged.

The two men began the game, each playing with the same intensity. Selig was interrupted only when Baugi nuzzled his hand, wishing to be petted.

"Where did you get the dog? I would like to have one."

Selig grinned. "There is only one Baugi, but I know where there are other black bear dogs."

"Have you ever thought of getting others and training them? Gwyneth told me about how the dog saved your friend Roland from the sea. It would seem to me that such dogs would be a treasure."

"It's a thought. Baugi has saved a great many men from being swallowed by the ocean." He patted the dog's head affectionately, then turned his attention back to the game, cursing when he lost. "Let's try another game."

This time Selig played with Torin's game pieces as if they and not Torin were responsible for the win.

"Erica tells me that you gifted Gwyneth with a pendant shaped like a dragon . . ."

Selig stiffened, pausing as he started to make a move with his game piece on the board. "And if I did?"

"I'm looking for a man, one of the sons of the jarl that I serve. Each son's mother was given a pendant to hang around her son's neck when he was born to protect him."

Selig put his game piece in a hole to the left of Torin's game piece. "There must be many such pendants," he answered, trying to make light of it. "They come in all shapes and sizes from ships to Thor's hammer."

"This pendant was a silver dragon set with a sapphire cut from Ragnar's jeweled sword. The sapphire is below the dragon's eye and makes it look as though the dragon is crying."

Selig's mouth contorted into an angry frown. He felt that Torin was violating his privacy and prying into matters that did not concern him. It took all of his self-control to remain silent.

"I want very much to find Ragnar's son," Torin said softly.

"And what if he does not want to be found?"

For a long moment there was silence as Torin mulled over his answer. At last he said, "Ragnar is growing older. He wants to find a successor to carry on all that he has accomplished."

"What Ragnar wants does not concern me!" Selig dropped one of his game pieces, staring as it skimmed across the game board and hit the ground.

Torin pushed the matter. "I think it does concern you. I think that the pendant Gwyneth wears around her neck is the same one that Ragnar gave to his beloved Cynnefed. I think that you are the man I have been sent to find."

Selig bolted to his feet with a suddenness that overturned the board. Game pieces rolled everywhere. As Torin bent down to pick up the amber

figures, Selig stalked out the door into the pouring
rain.

Gwyneth lay alone on the bed, staring at the walls,
longing for Selig. She was worried about him. Since
he had stormed out into the rain, angry with Torin
for talking about the pendant and its implications,
he had not been seen or heard from.

*His anger at his father is poisoning him and he just
doesn't see it,* she thought. If only he could make his
peace with his father! But how was that going to
come about when the very mention of the name
"Ragnar" put him in an irate mood?

Ragnar wants to make amends, she thought, remembering Erica's words. He wants to make one of
his sons the next jarl. It would be the fulfillment of
all his dreams for Selig to have such wealth and
power. The odds were in Selig's favor since he was
the eldest of Ragnar's offspring, but only if he forgot
the bitterness of the past and sailed to the Northland to confer with his father.

Suddenly it seemed as if there were obstacles to
Selig's happiness. Obstacles of his own making. "He
is being stubborn!"

Again she thought of Erica and how it had
brought her peace of mind to come face-to-face with
her father. It had been a healing process, setting
aside the ghosts of the past as they had learned
about each other. Father and daughter had bonded
as the truth had been revealed. Erica had said that
she learned Ragnar's many regrets from his own
lips. If only she could make Selig see that he had
to give himself a chance to find out the truth and
come to know his father just as Erica had. But how?

Hearing the sound of footsteps, she stiffened.
Selig had returned and she couldn't help but wonder what kind of a mood he was in. Would he be

angry with her for mentioning the pendant to Erica?

"Gwyneth . . ." His voice was soft.

It was dark in the room. With trembling fingers he found the soapstone dish and filled it with oil; then, working with the flintstone he lit the lamp. The room was filled with a glow.

"I've been worried," she whispered.

He seemed to be in a brooding sort of mood. By the smell of his breath she could tell that he had been drinking. "I needed to do some thinking alone . . ."

She wanted to run to him but something in his eyes held her back. "What is it?"

"Torin knows who I am."

"Perhaps it is just as well. You can't hide forever." She regretted her words the moment they were spoken.

Selig's expression was bitter. "I'm not hiding. It's just that I want to manage my own affairs."

She had never heard such bitterness in his voice and it worried her. "Torin and Erica mean well."

"I know. I am not angry with them, only with Ragnar!"

"He's your father! Can't you at least give him a chance to explain? Maybe there is much more to the story than you know."

He was silent as if he were at least contemplating her words. Because he wasn't arguing, she was encouraged to continue.

"Ragnar is growing older. Erica says he has been ill. How truly sad it would be were he to die without your having heard from his own lips why he did what he did!" She raised her arms and entwined them around his neck.

"Why he deserted my mother and me?"

"You seem to be so certain that he didn't care about her or about you but if that were true, why did he give her the pendant for you to wear for protection? And why does he bother to search for you now?"

"I don't know, Gwyn," he whispered against her hair. "I've spent so many years hating him. I can't forget what happened and I don't know if I can ever forgive."

Gwyneth pulled away and looked deep into his eyes as she remembered the violence and destruction he had brought to her family. "I forgave you . . ."

TWENTY-THREE

Selig brushed the damp hair out of his eyes and looked across the waters at the bright sun on the horizon. The days were becoming longer and longer now that summer was here. It was a perfect time to sail and he found himself envying Torin. Tomorrow at dawn the merchant ship would sail.

The sound of hammering echoed through the forest as Roland and Selig's men worked at the edge of the woods to cut and carve the necessary wood to repair the settlement. The hammers reverberated in Selig's head, reminding him that he had imbibed too much mead the night before in his effort to forget his anger at Torin's goading. Now he was the one to pay.

"Ah, my friend, it appears that with your help we will soon be setting out to sea," Torin said, coming up behind him.

Selig waited for Torin to chide him about their quarrel the day before but he had seemingly put it out of his mind. Well then, so would he.

"There are a few more repairs that need to be done." He motioned for Torin to follow him towards the ship. With chisel and hammer, they carved grooves in the sides of the ship, then set their sights on replacing two oars that had been damaged and nearly broken in two by the impact of Selig's ship hitting the merchant vessel.

to go on the journey. He stammered as he said, "A-agreed!"

"Good, then it is settled." Having made his decision, Selig gathered together the people of the settlement. There was still a lot of rebuilding that needed to be done; thus he realized that there would be many men who would choose to stay. But there would also be those who would welcome a chance to visit the Northland.

Roland was the first to step forward. "I'll go!"

He was joined by Thorne, Aki, Frodi, Harek, and several others, though Selig accepted only enough men to man the Viking ship's oars. The rest would stay behind.

"So you are going!" Gwyneth entwined the fingers of her hand with his.

"We are going!" he answered, burying his face in the softness of her fragrant hair. "Together we shall cross the waters to Norway so I can introduce you to this father I have never seen. And when we get there I want you to marry me before all!"

"Marry . . . ?"

He covered her lips with his fingers. "I don't want to hear no."

"Then as a brave woman from my Holy Book once said, 'Whither thou goest, I will go . . .' "

Preparations for the journey were made, including provisions. Dried food, pickled herring and other fish, and fresh fruits, grains, and water in skins were put aboard the ship.

Watching the flurry of activity from the doorway of her small house, Gwyneth felt proud of herself for she knew that what she had said had been at least partly responsible for Selig's decision. She could only hope that Ragnar was everything that Erica proclaimed him to be and that he and Selig could find a way to bury the past and establish a relationship.

Introducing Ballad,
A LINE OF HISTORICAL ROMANCES

*A*s a lover of historical romance, you'll adore Ballad Romances. Written by today's most popular romance authors, every book in the Ballad line is not only an individual story, but part of a two to six book series as well. You can look forward to 4 new titles each month – each taking place at a different time and place in history.

But don't take our word for how wonderful these stories are! Accept our introductory shipment of 4 Ballad Romance novels – a $23.96 value – ABSOLUTELY FREE – and see for yourself!

*O*nce you've experienced your first 4 Ballad Romances, we're sure you'll want to continue receiving these wonderful historical romance novels each month – without ever having to leave your home – using our convenient and inexpensive home subscription service. Here's what you get for joining:

- *4 BRAND NEW Ballad Romances delivered to your door each month*

- *30% off the cover price with your home subscription.*

- *A FREE monthly newsletter filled with author interviews, book previews, special offers, and more!*

- *No risk or obligation...you're free to cancel whenever you wish... no questions asked.*

Passion-
Adventure-
Excitement-
Romance-
Ballad!

*T*o start your membership, simply complete and return the card provided. You'll receive your Introductory Shipment of 4 FREE Ballad Romances. Then, each month, as long as your account is in good standing, you will receive the 4 newest Ballad Romances. Each shipment will be yours to examine for 10 days. If you decide to keep the books, you'll pay the preferred home subscriber's price – a savings of 30% off the cover price! (plus shipping & handling) If you want us to stop sending books, just say the word...it's that simple.

Get 4
Ballad
Historical
Romance
Novels
FREE!

A $23.96 value – **FREE** No obligation to buy anything – ever.
4 FREE BOOKS are waiting for you! Just mail in the certificate below!

BOOK CERTIFICATE

Yes! Please send me 4 Ballad Romances ABSOLUTELY FREE! After my introductory shipment, I will receive 4 new Ballad Romances each month to preview FREE for 10 days (as long as my account is in good standing). If I decide to keep the books, I will pay the money-saving preferred publisher's price plus shipping and handling. That's 30% off the cover price. I may return the shipment within 10 days and owe nothing, and I may cancel my subscription at any time. The 4 FREE books will be mine to keep in any case.

Name _____

Address _____ Apt. _____

City _____ State _____ Zip _____

Telephone (___) _____

Signature _____

(If under 18, parent or guardian must sign)

All orders subject to approval by Zebra Home Subscription Service.
Terms and prices subject to change. Offer valid only in the U.S.

DN062A

Passion....

Adventure....

Excitement....

Romance....

Get 4
Ballad
Historical
Romance
Novels
FREE!

lllııılıılllıııılllılılılıllılılılıılıılıılllılıllıllıılllıııl

BALLAD ROMANCES
Zebra Home Subscription Service, Inc.
P.O. Box 5214
Clifton NJ 07015-5214

Looking behind her at the room, she bade fare-well to the memories she had gathered there and looked forward to her voyage which would take her to the realm of the midnight sun.

PART TWO

Land of the Midnight Sun

Norway

TWENTY-FOUR

The carved dragon figurehead nosed its way through the ocean, shaking itself free of sea spray like the head of a real beast. Shields were lapped over the nets like dragon scales and presented as formidable a defense as armor.

A single bank of rowers on each side pulled the oars with steady, even strokes in unbroken cadence. Their chests swelled, their mouths grimaced, and their arms bulged as they rowed in seemingly perfect unison. They sang a rowdy song extolling their pride in being Vikings. Not until the wind came up and the ship's sails billowed did the men set aside their oars.

Gwyneth watched as the view of the coast changed from clusters of thatched cottages to large areas of uninhabited forest, then from rough and rocky cliffs to small, placid bays, then back to rocky terrain. Soon the shores of the settlement would be little more than shadows in the distance.

Selig stood on deck, balancing himself against the rocking and swaying of the deck beneath him. Oh, how he had missed this, he thought as he ran his fingers through his wind-ruffled blond hair. The sea was in his blood.

"Freedom. Ultimate freedom . . ."

He laughed as a wave sent salt spray into his face.

He even relished the taste of the ocean, he thought, licking the water from his lips.

Sitting on a hard bench, gazing out at the ocean, Gwyneth felt the same surge of excitement. This time the voyage held no fear for her, only a sense of anticipation to see the land that Erica had told her about. The Northland!

Selig is doing the right thing, she said to herself, content to know that she had urged him to meet with his father.

If she had any regrets at all, it was for the lack of privacy that she and Selig had. Although he had erected a tent on deck to hide them from prying eyes she felt uncomfortable and longed for the time when they would once again be unafraid to verbalize the intense fulfillment they felt while making love.

"You feel the surge of excitement upon the ocean also," Selig said aloud, coming to stand beside her. "I can see it in your eyes."

"It's as if the world has ceased to exist and the only thing real is this ship floating upon an endless sea beneath an endless sky . . ."

He liked her analogy. "Sometimes I feel as if I could sail on forever . . ."

Selig was thankful that so far there hadn't been any storms to compare with the one he encountered when Roland fell overboard. But if there were, Baugi was ready.

"You aren't afraid this time, are you?"

"I've learned to conquer the fear of things I cannot control." She smiled at him. "Besides, I'm with you."

She had learned that Selig was a powerful man. He had the ability to fulfill that need in her for someone strong. More than anything else, that was what had drawn her to him—perhaps, Gwyneth reasoned, because she desperately longed for love and security and needed to be sustained by his strength.

He noticed that her gaze was riveted on the muscles of his arms. "Do you know why we rule the sea?" When she didn't answer, he said, "Strength and something more important. Our respect for the ships that we build. To me this ship is a living thing."

"Like your gods and goddesses?" She was troubled to be reminded of his pagan beliefs.

"No. I think of this ship like a father does of a daughter. She is a part of me. I designed and created her. I watched as she was being built. I carved the dragon head with my own hands. I supervised every detail." He pointed to the sides of the ship. "See how she heaves and bends but never breaks?"

Gwyneth looked over the side, watching as the ship sailed the waves.

"The planks expand and contract as if she is breathing."

"You speak of the ship as if it were a female . . ."

"In some ways it is like a woman for the ship responds best to gentle handling . . ." He brushed her dark hair from her face as it blew in a swirl around her face, then he held onto her tightly. "What are you thinking?"

She was honest with him. "I'm wondering what this mysterious Northland is really like. I sense it will be different from the settlement." He had asked her to marry him but before she said yes she wanted to see what it would be like to live among a large number of Norsemen and be a Viking wife.

"You're frowning. Why?"

She sighed. "Erica told me that she and Torin were married by a priest and by a Viking ceremony as well. Would you? Could you?"

He shook his head. "Torin made that choice. As for me, I have seen too much violence from Christian hands ever to bend my knee to any of them.

Even a priest." The matter was settled, at least in his own mind.

For just a moment Gwyneth stiffened. Could she ever reconcile her religious beliefs with those of people who believed in several gods? Men who had plundered the churches of her own people?

"I won't think about it . . ." she whispered aloud.

"About what?"

"About anything except this moment with you . . ."

Feeling contented, Gwyneth lay her head against his chest. If only they could stand like this forever, gazing out at the sea, heedless of all worry, feeling only the joy of being together. If they could forget about the men who had wronged them, about being Viking and English, she would have asked for nothing more.

For a long time they just stood looking out at the ocean but then at last she ended the quiet asking, "What are you going to say to your father?"

His brows furled. "There are many questions I want to ask him. I want to vent my fury at him. I want to tell him how I have hated him all of these years."

She pulled away from him. "How can you be so sure that he doesn't have a good explanation for what happened?"

"There can be no explanation for loving, then leaving, a woman," he exclaimed. "I vow to Odin that I would never do such a thing to you! Especially if you gave me a child." He gathered her into his arms again. "I so long for a child!"

"A child!" Gwyneth trembled at the thought of bearing a child out of the bonds of wedlock. She would have to be careful and faithfully drink the potion that Ingunn had given her and pray that she would not be damned for all eternity for doing so.

* * *

It was growing dark. Gwyneth looked up at the murky vault of heaven. It seemed deep and remote though the stars were bright. Closing her eyes, she listened to the sea. It was loud as it rushed beneath the ship. She could feel the water on her face as the ocean spray kissed her forehead and cheeks.

What am I going to do? It seemed that no matter what choice she made she would be the loser, either of her happiness or of her soul. In the eyes of the Church she was living in sin; yet to marry a heathen, a Viking, would not be tolerated by her family, her priest, her church . . . but what about God? How did He feel about the tumultuous situation she found herself in? Was He really a loving and forgiving God or was He like those who wore his anointed robes?

I can't give Selig up! When she was with him she didn't think of him as a pagan but as her love.

Though she had put them out of her mind while in the settlement, Gwyneth thought about her family. Her parents, particularly her mother, had treated her like a child. She had been expected to obey and marry Alfred without question or complaint. And she had mindlessly complied. And all the while Alfred had been planning the most hideous treachery imaginable! Alfred—good, noble, professed-Christian Alfred who could not excuse his sins by being a pagan. Yet evil though he was, her parents would still hand her over to him rather than see her spend the rest of her days with a Viking.

"How sad . . ."

Selig left the tiller to come and stand beside her again. "Nothing can be sad on such a night as this." He looked up at the stars that flickered in the night sky. "Someday I'll show you how to read the stars . . ." He was proud that he could sail as well by night as by day.

"You never get lost?"

"Lost?" He laughed. "Never!" He studied the night sky, then adjusted the direction of the tiller.

Together they watched as Roland and a few of the others dropped nets overboard to catch fish for the evening meal. The ship would be put ashore so they could cook on fires, eat, then sail back out to sea. It would be a rare treat, for once the ship was farther out to sea they would have to eat dried and salted provisions.

The wind sang in the sails. Though she had not sung in a long time, Gwyneth was inspired to sing a Latin hymn the priest had taught her.

"You have a lovely voice. You should sing more often," Selig complimented. He started to hum along. "What are the words? What do they mean?"

She shook her head. "I . . . I don't know." The words spoken in church were always in Latin and she found herself wondering why. Was it because Latin was God's language?

The ship pulled in to shore. On the rocky beach the men built fires, then filled traveling cauldrons with saltwater and set them on the fire. The women cut up cabbage and onions. The fish was gutted and cooked on hot rocks while the men sat and talked about what to expect in Ragnar's hall. The women talked about weaving, spinning, and children, turning Gwyneth's thoughts once again to the subject of her and Selig.

"What am I to do?" She couldn't run away forever. One day she would have to face their differences. What then?

Roland began ladling up the vegetables and dividing portions of the fish. Some ate with spoons and some with their fingers, sopping the vegetable broth up with dark rye bread.

Gwyneth was famished and ate quickly. Then she filled a bowl with water and moved to a secluded spot on the rocky beach. There she sat down and sponged herself, dabbing on scented oil she had taken from Selig's wooden chest. She ran an ivory comb through her thick mass of dark hair, wondering if she would ever get the tangles out. Surely her hair was as tangled as her life had become.

"Here, let me help you!"

Gwyneth looked up, surprised to see that Selig had left the men and followed her. He took the comb from her hand, gently but firmly working it through the strands in back where she could not reach. It felt gloriously relaxing and sensual.

"The darkness of your hair reminds me of the sea at night."

"I'm afraid the wind tied it into knots . . ."

"I can get them out. All it takes is patience." Setting the comb aside, he ran his fingers through her hair, unsnarling tufts. "I remember how beautiful I thought your hair was when I first saw you. I wanted to reach out and touch it and see if it was as soft as it appeared."

Gwyneth remembered that first meeting as vividly as if it had been yesterday. "And was it?"

"Yes. When I finally got a chance to hold you in my arms I found not only your hair but you to be everything I have ever wanted . . ." Putting his arms around her, he molded his body to hers. "Now that you belong to me I don't ever want to let you go. I want you with me forever."

Though she knew that he meant his words to be an expression of endearment, they troubled her. "Forever is a long time."

He tightened his hold, crushing her so hard against him that for a moment she was afraid she would break in two. "Not long enough for me."

"One never knows the future, Selig." She wondered what he would do if she wanted to return to see her family. Though she loved him there was something about his possessiveness that was frightening.

"I will never give you up, Gwyneth. Never."

He loosened his embrace but continued to hold her for a long while; then, as if having made a decision, he took her by the hand and led her back to where the other Vikings were cleaning the cauldrons and gathering up the unused food to take back to the ship. Taking off one of his arm bracelets, he held it up for the others to see.

"Before all I pledge to make Gwyneth my wife!" Reaching for her hand, he slowly, ceremoniously slipped the bracelet onto her arm; then, he clasped her fingers and slowly raised both of their hands to a position high over their heads as the others cheered.

It had happened so suddenly that Gwyneth moved as if in a daze, watching as Roland poured mead into a cup and brought it to them. He nodded to her, waiting expectantly as he held it to her lips.

"Drink."

She hesitated, shaking inwardly as she obeyed. It was as if Selig were somehow forcing the issue, making her decision for her. Yet, if this was some kind of betrothal ceremony it didn't seem to be too heathen. She took a drink of the mead and gulped it down. Selig took the cup from Roland's hands and swallowed more of the mead than Gwyneth had.

"I should have done this long ago . . ." he exclaimed, choking as Roland suddenly pounded him on the back.

Though Gwyneth had seen the bracelets on Selig's arms and had even touched them while they were making love, she was more curious now that one adorned her own arm. She started to take it off, but Selig shook his head.

"No." He grabbed her wrist. "Now that I have

given it to you it is bad luck to take it off because of what it symbolizes. It is a promise."

"A promise." She satisfied her curiosity by just touching it, running her fingers over the carved design she imagined to be a dragon's head at one end.

Selig noted her interest. "It's a replica of the giant serpent of Midgard that holds up the world," he said proudly. "When he is wrapped around the arm he eats his tail, signifying eternity."

The metal was cold but it was as if it suddenly burned into her skin. "It's a snake!" A symbol of evil! The snake had tempted Eve to eat the apple and to seduce Adam into a sin so grave that it exiled them from Paradise. Without further contemplation or hesitation, she reached up and tore it from her arm.

TWENTY-FIVE

It was a cold voyage the rest of the way, made even more so by the iciness in Selig's voice and eyes whenever he came near Gwyneth, which was seldom. Though she had not meant to do so, she had humiliated and rejected him in front of the others and she feared it would be a long time before he could show his love for her again.

"I don't understand why you did it," Ingunn scolded gently. "Selig is a proud man and you wounded that pride along with his heart."

Gwyneth tried to make her friend understand why she had reacted so violently. "The snake is loathsome to us. The priest has told us how God created Adam and Eve and put them in His Paradise. The evil Satan manifested himself in the form of a snake and tricked Eve into eating the apple from the forbidden tree." She paused and took a breath before rambling on. "Eve in turn tempted Adam to bite into the fruit and because of this they were thrown out of Paradise. Since then the snake has had to crawl on its belly, men have had to work by the sweat of their brow, and women have been cursed to bring forth children."

Ingunn shook her head. "Loki is a shape-changer just like this Satan. He has tricked the goddess Freyja and several of the other gods many times."

She seemed puzzled. "But we as well as Odin have always forgiven him."

Ingunn explained that Loki was fair of face but had an evil disposition and was very changeable of mood. She spoke of how he excelled all men in the art of cunning and because he always cheated. Though he was continually involving the gods in great difficulties he always helped them out again by guile.

"You speak of Loki with amusement but there is nothing humorous about Satan. Because of him all women have been accused of being sinners and have been blamed for mankind's fall."

"Women have been blamed? Why?" Ingunn didn't understand.

"Because Eve tempted Adam to take a bite of the forbidden apple."

"Argh . . . !" Ingunn put her hands up to her ears. "I do not like that story at all. Perhaps you Christians can blame Eve for eating the fruit, but how can she be blamed because Adam did? He could have said no. It seems to me that he was as guilty as she but that poor Eve took all the blame."

Gwyneth had never thought of it quite that way before. For a moment she was taken aback, realizing how she had given little argument to things the priest had told her. Her eyes moved to where Selig stood talking with Roland and she felt a twinge of regret for her reaction to wearing the bracelet.

Ingunn sensed her feelings. "If I were you I would run to him, go down on bended knee, and ask his forgiveness."

"No. I can't! I won't."

Ingunn shrugged. "Then I feel sorry for you because it is going to be a long, lonely voyage."

In the days that passed, Gwyneth reflected that Ingunn didn't know how right she was. Not only Selig but the other Vikings shunned her as well.

Only Baugi and Ingunn gave her any kind of companionship.

As the ship moved northward the air at sea became colder and colder. Alone, Gwyneth huddled inside the small tent Selig had erected, pulling a woolen cloak up to her chin. She found herself longing for the warmth of a fire. Only when the ship touched land so that the Vikings could occasionally hunt, replenish the fresh water supply, and forage for wild fruit were they offered the opportunity to warm themselves.

It seemed that the ship sailed forever, but at last a sense of expectancy hovered in the air and Gwyneth sensed that they were on the last days of the journey to the place called Hafrsfjord."

Gwyneth ran her fingers through her wind-tousled hair, remembering the gentleness with which Selig had combed out the tangles. She missed his nearness and his warmth more than she had ever realized; she could only wonder how he would react to her when they at last reached land.

"I wonder if I will ever get all the snarls out of my hair," Ingunn complained, mimicking Gwyneth's actions.

"The first thing I'm going to do is wash my hair in rainwater and take a bath," Gwyneth confided. And then what? She shivered at the thought of finding herself among so many strangers without Selig's love to shield her, but then perhaps it was time that she relied upon her own strength. She had admired Erica right from the moment she had first met her. Perhaps she, too, could fend for herself if given the chance. It was a thought that calmed her fears as they sailed along.

Gwyneth found that the beauty of the "land of the midnight sun" was not a myth. From the moment she saw it rising in the distance she could see that it was a world of magnificent blue sea, dark green forests, and majestic mountains that proudly displayed their crowns of snow-capped peaks as they rose up to the sky.

"Those are called fjords," Ingunn said, pointing to narrow inlets of the sea that cut into the cliffs, allowing the huge ships to sail between their wondrous, towering rock walls.

"I've never seen anything like this before!" Gwyneth exclaimed as the ship steered frighteningly close to the elongated rock formation. She was so mesmerized by the beauty that she didn't realize Selig was standing beside her until he spoke.

"I thought you might want this." He held out a bundle wrapped in one of his cloaks.

She took it from his hands, hoping that it was some kind of peace offering. "What is it?"

"The silk dress that I gave you once. It is yours to wear when we reach my . . . Ragnar's hall." His tone was not hostile but neither was it warm. "I hope that you will not see fit to reject this present and embarrass me anew."

His rebuke stung her. "No . . . I . . . I . . . I'm sorry about what happened, Selig." Particularly because she sensed that he was nervous about coming face-to-face with his father. He needed her, perhaps more than he ever had before.

"We will not talk about it." But he was remembering. That was obvious by the way he touched the bracelet she had given back to him as he stared out to sea.

"Please try to understand . . . I—"

She didn't get a chance to say all the things she had planned, for as the ship headed inland and Roland motioned to him, Selig strode away.

Hastily, Gwyneth unwrapped the dress, remembering how Erica had also received such a gift from

Torin and had proudly worn it when arriving at Ragnar's hall. She was determined to make Selig proud of her so that perhaps some of the bitterness between them would be lessened.

The *Sea Dragon* moved up the fjord as smoothly as if it had wings. Eager to be on land again, the men had sailed during the day and into the night toward Hafrsfjord. Now, as the ship rounded a headland and Gwyneth looked at the walls of the cliffs rising around them, she realized they had reached their destination.

Several of the Viking sailors had already furled the sail and stood poised on the deck in anticipation, wondering what they would find. As for Gwyneth, she was surprised that even from a distance it was obvious how much larger the houses were here than in the settlement. There were, in fact, at least sixty dwellings visible, twice as many as in the villages in Wessex.

Gwyneth watched as Roland drew a curled horn to his lips and blew the signal that meant that theirs was a friendly ship and intended no harm. The three notes were answered by another horn high atop the hill. All the while, Gwyneth looked for Torin's ship, which had sailed ahead of them, and at last caught sight of it being unloaded. They waved as the *Sea Dragon* passed them by.

As the *Sea Dragon* stopped not more than a few feet from shore, the oarsmen stuck the oars out to form a bridge between the ship and the land. Gwyneth watched with awe as several Vikings danced daringly about on top of the oars. Each tried to outdo the other: balancing, stepping high, even jumping up in the air. Even Roland joined the festivities, nearly falling into the deep, blue waters when he got too sure of himself. Only Selig held back and once again Gwyneth sensed his uneasiness as if it were her own. For all his blustering about hating his father, he seemed somehow like a little boy, anxious to be accepted. Putting aside her own pride, she walked the length of the ship to come to his side.

"Now that I am here I hardly know what to say, or how to begin . . ." Selig said.

"Perhaps he will begin the conversation and you can react to what he says." She wondered if Torin had the chance to tell Ragnar that his son had come. It was doubtful, for Torin had been otherwise engrossed in taking care of his own ship. No doubt this first meeting was going to be awkward.

She could feel the tension in him as he encircled her waist with his arm, then helped her slide down one of the oars to the land. Clutching the silk dress in one hand and clinging to him with the other, Gwyneth looked about her at the cluster of houses huddled together. Here and there was a house balancing on the bank of the waterside, another touching the mountain slope, a third perched on a ledge high above the water. It seemed that the Vikings made use of any space to build a home. Green-and-brown fields were dotted with flocks of goats, sheep, and cattle just like in Wessex.

They walked a long distance towards a group of wooden buildings which he explained to her were outbuildings: a byre for housing animals in the cold days of the winter, barns to store their fodder, a stable, a small smithy, and a bathhouse. Oh yes, it was quite different from the settlement and she thought to herself that Selig would be foolish not to take his place as Ragnar's rightful heir here.

Though at first Selig was confused as to which direction to go, they at last made their way to the largest building, which appeared to be the central dwelling house or *skaalen*, where cooking, eating, feasting, and gaming were done.

The house was made mainly of wood with a turf

roof and a stone foundation. Around the building
was a planked wooden walkway which led up to one
of the two entranceways. Stepping inside the
wooden door, Gwyneth could see that, like the small
hut at the settlement, this large building had slats
to let in the light and a hole in the roof to allow
smoke to escape and the sun's rays to enter. Because
of the cold climate there were no windows.

Suddenly a gasp sounded behind them. Gwyneth
turned and saw an older woman with silver-threaded,
dark-blond hair and a multitude of keys hanging
from chains attached to her overdress or apron. She
clutched at one of those keys as she stared open-
mouthed at Selig.

"Who are you? I have never seen you before."

At first Selig hesitated, clutching Gwyneth's arm;
then, with all the majesty of a lord, he announced,
"I'm Ragnar's son. You can tell him that I am here."

Gwyneth's eyes were drawn to a big-boned giant
of a man who stood in the doorway. His dark blond
hair was sculpted with gray. Lines crisscrossed his
high forehead; there were crow's feet at the corner
of each eye and a ragged scar across his right cheek.
Even so, it was obvious to see from the well-chiseled
facial features that once he had been a man who
could win a woman's heart as well as a battle.

She knew in a heartbeat who he was—not because
he looked exactly like Selig because he didn't. What,
then? They were different in facial features, except
for the nose, yet there was something imperceptible
about him that was very much the same. The way
he held his head, perhaps, or the broadness of his
shoulders.

"Ragnar Longsword!"

Dressed in a reddish-brown tunic bordered with
blue-and-red embroidery at the sleeves and hem, a

brown leather corselet with shoulder straps fastened at the chest with buckles, dun-colored leggings, and silver and gold bracelets arraying his arms, he looked impressive and every inch the jarl that he was.

"So Torin found you!" Ragnar Longsword's voice was choked with emotion.

"No, *I* found *him.*" Selig clenched and unclenched his hands, wishing he were back at the settlement. Why had he come? What could he have possibly imagined might happen here?

Ragnar hesitated, then said softly, "I've imagined this moment so many times but now that you are here, I don't know what to say." Hurrying forward, he enclosed his son in a bear hug as unshed tears sparkled in his eyes. He didn't seem to notice or to care that Selig was not responding to his show of affection.

Gwyneth took advantage of the moment to look about her at the walls of the large room. Down the center of the hall was a long hearth on a raised platform. Big pots hung over the fire on chains from beams in the ceiling of the gabled roof, much the same as in the hut at the settlement. A loom and several spindle whorls for the spinning of wool stood against the farthest wall. On either side of the long hall, indoor benches lined the walls. They appeared to be used for either sitting or sleeping. Toward the far wall was a chair, much higher than the benches around it. It was heavily carved with geometric and floral designs and forms which she knew now were representations of the Vikings' gods. Several tables, which could be pushed aside to make more room, stood heavily laden with food—a welcome sight after traveling.

"And who might that beauty be?" she heard Ragnar's voice ask, breaking through her reverie.

"This is Gwyneth." Selig disentangled himself from his father's arms. "She's from Wessex."

"An Anglo-Saxon just like . . ." For some reason Ragnar did not say the name. Gwyneth wondered if it was because he had forgotten the name of Selig's mother or if the sound of her name on his lips caused him too much pain.

"Yes, an Anglo-Saxon!"

Ragnar smiled, then asked, "Is she your wife? Your woman? Which?"

A muscle in Selig's jaw ticked. "I have asked her to marry me but she doesn't like our pagan ways."

Gwyneth blushed to the roots of her hair. Although Selig had told the truth, it sounded odd and made her feel ill at ease.

Ragnar laughed. "They all say that. But it doesn't take long to change their minds once the babies come."

"And then what?" Although Selig had been holding his anger in check, it surged through him at the reminder. How could he have forgotten even for a moment how this man had deserted them? "After a woman bears a child, what is the Viking way? To leave her and forget she ever existed?"

For just a moment Ragnar looked as if Selig had struck him. Whatever reunion he had envisioned, it hadn't been like this. "I never forgot for a moment about your mother. She was in my heart then and a part of her is in my heart still."

"She's dead!" Selig rasped, in a tone that seemed to blame Ragnar for the deed.

There was so much agony in Selig's voice that Gwyneth felt tears sting her eyes. She started towards him but Ragnar held her back.

"And when she died a part of me died, too." He clutched at his heart. "Cynnefed was the first woman I loved enough to marry."

"But you didn't love her enough to take her with

you or stay with her and offer her your protection."
Selig turned his back. He'd seen his father and had
his say. Now he could just walk away and never return.

Ragnar's large hand touched Selig's shoulder as
he grabbed his son and turned him around. "And
just what do you know of it? Did you know that I
begged her to come with me but because she was
going to have a child she insisted that she stay? Did
you know that I promised to return and kept that
promise only to find out that she had been given
in marriage to another man, a hateful, vile coward?
And did you know that same man threatened the
life of my child, my son, if I even set eyes on *my*
wife again?"

He looked Selig full in the face, reading his answer in the expression clearly written there.

"No, you did not. It wasn't enough that I was
robbed of my wife and son and the days we might
have spent in happiness. He had to poison your
mind as well." Now it was Ragnar who sounded bitter.

"It seems that we have more to talk about than
I ever knew," Selig exclaimed.

"It seems that we do! Come!" Ragnar tightened
his hold on his son's arm, propelling him towards
the door.

TWENTY-SIX

It didn't take long for Selig's unannounced arrival to become the gossip of Ragnar's hall. Worse yet, while he was preoccupied with his father, catching up on all the lost years, Gwyneth was left to fend for herself with women who were openly staring at her as they moved back and forth in a seemingly ritualistic dance between the table and the cooking pots.

Realizing that she must look disheveled and grimy due to the voyage, Gwyneth brushed self-consciously at her wrinkled red gown. She was only too aware of her sea-salt-stained garments and the silver chain belt that was tarnished from days at sea. She desperately wanted to turn and leave to join the women from Selig's settlement but forced herself to stand her ground.

"Is this any way to greet a guest?" Acting in the manner of one shooing away chickens, the woman who had first greeted them frightened the women away. "Hurry, Astrid, see to the warm water and towels."

Within the blink of an eye it was done and Gwyneth washed her face and hands. "Thank you."

Immediately the woman with graying, dark-blond hair made her authority over the household known. With an iron hand she directed the actions, not only of the thralls but of the other women as well.

Gwyneth had heard about the importance and significance of the keys Viking wives wore and quickly noted that the woman was weighted down with them. The silver keys were suspended from her belt, they dangled from the brooches pinned to the shoulders of her overdress, and two small keys hung around her neck.

"My name is Nissa. I have many keys, for my husband, Ragnar, is a man of consequence," she bragged, noting the direction of Gwyneth's stare. The tone of her voice made it sound as if she were in some way responsible for his prominence.

"As is his son a man of consequence in lands that he has acquired," Gwyneth retorted, determined to protect Selig's reputation and thereby her own.

Nissa's eyes assessed Gwyneth's appearance; then she smiled in a manner of forced friendliness. "You are tired and travel-worn. You will want to freshen up. I will take you to the women's area."

She led her to a small room that was curtained off and gestured for Gwyneth to make herself at home; then she clapped her hands, summoning a young girl.

"Don't hesitate to ask her to do anything you want. That is what slaves are for." Turning her back, she was gone, leaving Gwyneth in the care of the thin slave.

"What shall I do for you?" The slave girl had large eyes and a fearful expression, undoubtedly from months of Nissa's intimidation, Gwyneth thought.

"Nothing. Just stay here and talk and tell me all that I need to know about Ragnar's wife." If she was going to be here for any length of time she needed to be able to hold her own and not let Nissa trample her as she seemingly did others.

The girl seemed to relax, watching as Gwyneth undressed. "Nissa rules the household with an iron hand, though she seldom lifts a finger to be of any help." She took Gwyneth's soiled garments. "She holds herself in high esteem, so much so that there are those who say she fancies herself to be a queen. Most importantly, she has a way of twisting the truth to further her ambitions and to blame those she considers to be her enemies."

Gwyneth slipped the blue silk dress over her head, relishing the feel of the soft, cool fabric against her body. "How will she view my . . . how will she view Selig, Ragnar's returning son?" There was enough tension between Ragnar and Selig as it was. Gwyneth wanted to ward off further trouble.

"She will be resentful, though she will not openly show it." The thrall explained that though Nissa had longed for a child, preferably a son, to follow in Ragnar's footsteps and assure her own security, she was barren.

"Does she have the power to harm him?"

The young girl shook her head. "No. Ragnar pretends to heed her words but if you ask me, he really doesn't listen."

Gwyneth hurriedly combed her long, dark hair, then put the finishing touches on her appearance. It was amazing how much better a woman felt when she knew she looked her best.

"But . . . that doesn't mean that he is safe." Peeking out from the curtains, looking over her shoulder, the thrall shuddered. "Selig's real danger comes from Ragnar's brother, Herlaug. Watch him and beware!"

The waters of the fjord were calm, much more serene than Selig's mood as he stood side by side with his father on the deck of the *Sea Dragon*.

"It's quiet here. All of my men have gone ashore.

We can talk without being overheard," Selig said, gripping the railing.

Ragnar didn't say anything for a long time but just stared into the eyes of his son. "How you must have loathed me all these years!" He took a deep breath and let it out in a sigh. "And still do, by the look in your eyes."

"Anger and hate are strong emotions, difficult to overcome, particularly when they have become a habit. Besides, how do I know that you are telling me the truth about what happened?"

"Because I do not lie and because I vow to you on my oath as a Viking that I loved your mother, that we made plans for me to return for her, and that all of the unhappiness that was suffered after that can be attributed to one man and one man only."

"My stepfather."

"He is not worthy of that name . . ."

"No, based on the personal pain he inflicted upon me and upon my mother, I agree that he is not!"

"He caused her great suffering?"

Selig nodded. "When our stronghold was invaded and my mother taken hostage, he refused to lift a hand to free her or to trade her for any of the enemy's captured soldiers. " Selig bit his lip but even so he had a difficult time controlling his emotions.

"And . . ." Ragnar braced himself.

"As you know, my mother had a gift for healing. When it became evident that she wasn't going to be useful as a pawn in the ongoing warfare, they burned her to death as a witch!"

"What?" Though he had witnessed hideous atrocities with his own eyes, Ragnar paled. "No!"

"Yes!"

"Then come, we will gather an army and march on Edgar and make him pay for what he did."

Selig grabbed his father by the arm. "I have already avenged my mother! Edgar is dead! And all that lifted even a finger to harm her have paid for their treachery in blood."

It was difficult to abridge all that had happened over the years but Selig tried. He told Ragnar about his boyhood and the treatment he had received at the hands of his mother's husband but he tempered the story by telling of her love and the joy she had given him. When he told Ragnar how she had continued to love him and always hoped in her heart to see him again, Ragnar was overcome with emotion.

"You will never know how much I wanted to see her again, if only for a moment, but I feared that her husband's jealousy and wrath would be too high a price to pay. I did what I thought best to protect her and to protect you. Perhaps I was wrong! I should have engaged that vile bastard in battle, marched into his hall, and taken you and her away . . ."

"What's done is done," Selig answered, seeing the past in a whole new light. "If blame is to be rationed out, I must accept my share. I was gone when my mother needed me the most. She paid with her life for my ambition."

Ragnar shook his head violently. "No. You could not have foreseen what was going to happen."

For a long, drawn-out moment, both men were quiet as they gazed down at the waters. Selig broke the silence.

"So, what do you think of this ship of mine? I guided every man in the building stages of her birth and carved the dragon's head with my own two hands."

Ragnar walked slowly about the deck, examining the workmanship and then grunting his approval. "It seems you are as good at building a ship as you are at picking a woman. Your Gwyneth is lovely. A rare jewel."

Selig beamed from ear to ear. "Yes, she is." As his father listened intently, he told of how she had given him his freedom and how he had then gathered together a crew, built ships to carry them over the waters, founded his settlement opposite the Isle of Man, and raided the coasts of the land that had enslaved him.

"You turned adversity into triumph, my son. I am proud of you."

"I never could have done it without her." Selig's eyes were gentle, his voice a whisper as he talked about Gwyneth and her kindness to him. "She gave me a reason to live. I looked forward to her visits more than you could ever know."

"And thus you feel a bond with her."

"It is much deeper. I love her as I have never loved anything in my life before. She is everything I have ever wanted in a woman—brave, loving, and beautiful. The only thing that stands between us is her feelings towards our beliefs. Gwyneth is a Christian."

Ragnar clucked his tongue. "The women I loved were Christian, too. Believe me, it will be no easy task changing her to our ways."

"But I must try! For I can not live without her."

TWENTY-SEVEN

In the sunken trough that ran down the center of Ragnar's hall, huge pine logs burned brightly. The smell of smoke mingled with the scent of fresh rushes and the strong odor of boiled cabbage, stewed meat, and other various foods. A long table covered with platters and bowls groaning with food, fish, game birds, butter, fruits, and long loaves of dark rye bread gave proof that Ragnar's home was a house of plenty.

Befitting his rank, Ragnar had many slaves. Several of these thralls were busily darting to and fro, bringing loaves of flatbread from their baking spot upon the rocks of the fire to the guests at the table.

The hall was thronged with men and women who had quickly gathered to help celebrate Ragnar's reunion with his son. Scanning the faces, Gwyneth remembered the slave girl's description of Herlaug, Ragnar's brother, but did not see him in the hall. She had begun to think he would not be present when the door opened with a bang and a muscular, battle-scarred man strode through the doorway.

Gwyneth didn't know if the shiver she felt up her spine was because of his fearsome presence or because of the warning that the slave girl had given her about this man. Whichever it was, she couldn't help feeling threatened as he looked her way. She knew that she would have to have eyes in the back of her head and be cautious every moment he was around.

Thinking back, Gwyneth remembered Erica mentioning that Ragnar's brother had tried to kidnap her. *Will he likewise try to abduct me? Or is it Selig who will be the target of his malice,* she wondered.

"Where is this nephew of mine?" she heard Herlaug ask. "I want to get a good look at him." It was an unnecessary question, for he quickly picked Selig out of the crowd and pushed his way forward. "Welcome to the family."

Gwyneth watched as Herlaug took Selig aside, chattering to him as if he had known him all of his life. His smiles seemed forced, his amiability phony, his back-slapping conspicuously robust. She was, however, relieved to see that Selig's reaction to his father's brother was one of caution edged with distrust. No doubt Torin had enlightened him about Herlaug's dangerous traits.

Gwyneth attuned her ears to their conversation and heard Herlaug say, "I hear you came with a woman from the land of the Anglo-Saxons." She turned her head to see him unabashedly staring.

Gwyneth was wearing the blue silk dress with her gold chain belt and the dragon's tear pendant hidden beneath her gown. She knew that she looked radiant; yet, as Herlaug's eyes touched upon her, she felt like a budding flower that suddenly withered. Even his gaze seemed to be lethal.

Determined not to let him bother her, Gwyneth sat down at the table, near Nissa. Hoping that Erica would come to the hall soon, she saved a seat beside her. As usual, the men sat at one end of the table and the women at the other; thus, she was too far away to hear clearly what Herlaug was saying to Selig, but she did notice that he was avidly engaged in conversation with his "long lost" nephew.

Nissa quickly introduced Gwyneth to the women

of Ragnar's household, which consisted of Selig's aunts and cousins. These women were attired in much finer garments than had been worn at the settlement. The under-dresses were of bright colors—yellow, blue, green, and brown, some finely pleated with short sleeves, others with no sleeves at all. None were as beautiful as the sapphire-blue dress Selig had given her.

Their garments were closed at the neck with a drawstring. Over this was a woolen tunic held in place by a matched pair of oval bronze brooches. From this oval jewelry hung chains that held knives, needles, combs, and other objects. Some wore cloaks. Instead of letting their hair flow free, it was pulled back and covered by a piece of cloth tied at the back of the neck. Gwyneth, however, had carefully braided her hair and coiled them atop her head.

"So you are from the land of the Anglo-Saxons," one of the women stated, looking her up and down.

"I'm from Wessex," Gwyneth answered proudly.

"Wessex. Isn't that where my 'cousin' was held as a slave?" The woman sitting across from Gwyneth looked at her as if she were responsible.

"It is. That's where I first met Selig."

Her gaze moved from the woman's face to Selig, who sat talking with his father on one side and Herlaug on the other. Dressed in a green tunic bordered with blue-and-red embroidery at the sleeves and hem, he looked so handsome that she felt a sudden surge of affection and longing. She wanted to be in his arms again, wanted him to desire her.

"You were a thrall, too?"

"No!"

The women waited expectantly.

"It's a long story." For just a moment she could almost imagine that she was home. She sighed, feeling a strange sense of homesickness that she hadn't felt before. "My father was a man of prominence, like Ragnar." She wondered if her father had recovered from his wounds and, if so, if he was safe from Alfred's scheming. She hoped so.

The women were intrigued. They started to rattle off a dozen questions but they quieted when Ragnar rapped sharply upon the table with his knife. It was the signal that the meal had officially begun.

"Better eat quickly," one of the cousins advised with a giggle. "Ragnar is the one who also signals when the food is to be cleared away. Anyone who has not finished will find his food removed before his eyes."

"Yes, eat quickly. Ragnar's appetite is not what it once was . . ."

Remembering that Erica had said that her father had been ill, Gwyneth looked towards Ragnar and noticed that his once sun-darkened face was pale. He looked drawn and from time to time he put his hand up to his head. What if something happened to Ragnar and Selig was chosen as his successor? Would Herlaug be an even greater danger?

Despite her misgivings, Gwyneth enjoyed the festivities. Mealtimes were always gay and noisy events but tonight it seemed that there was more laughter, boasting, and storytelling that promised to last well into the night.

She watched as the men dipped their drinking horns into the large communal mead vat. The air rang with laughter and chatter. The male guests were already elbowing each other for a seat close to Selig, the guest of honor. They were anxious to hear boasts of his exploits and of the treasures brought back from the land of the Anglo-Saxons. As they waited they amused themselves with drinking contests, board games, and trying to out-talk each other.

"Enough!" Only Ragnar's loud command stilled

their tongues. "We have other things to talk about. Such as my son's return."

There was a sudden commotion as the door flew open. Gwyneth saw with a great sense of relief that Erica and Torin had arrived. Giving their cloaks to a thrall, they separated, he to sit with the men and she to take her place at the spot on the bench that Gwyneth had saved for her.

Ragnar grinned a welcome. "I am the most fortunate of men for I have under one roof both my son and my daughter!"

Selig felt honored yet he also was pricked by melancholy as well. He had made such grand plans, had wanted to announce his impending marriage to Gwyneth before all assembled tonight, and would have had she not rejected him. As he looked at her sitting beside Erica, he wondered if his father was right. Was it only a matter of time? Could he somehow persuade her to give up her own religion and embrace Viking ways? Or would their beliefs forever form a wall between them?

Ragnar motioned to the skald, who picked up his harp. His nimble fingers moved across the instrument, plucking the muted strings as he sang about the days so long ago and the never-forgotten heroes. Proud, adventurous, with a yearning for glory, these men had excelled in battle and scorned death to venerate the very name "Viking." When he promised to devise a melodic tale about Selig the entire hall cheered, waiting expectantly. *"Sired by a man all men praise, he brought the English to their knees. Though they tried to put him in chains he rose up, braving Odin's roaring seas. The* Sea Dragon *sailed, his sword never failed. Armed with his pride and a sword at his side he laid claim to the lands of the Anglo Saxons. Praise to the conqueror . . ."*

When the skald had finished his song, Selig made his way to the keg of mead and dipped his drinking horn in the brew. He let the soothing beverage numb his senses, wondering what Gwyneth would do if he told the entire assemblage that he intended to marry her. Would she scorn him again? Or had he read remorse in her eyes?

"I know what you are thinking," Herlaug hissed in his ear. "You can not wait to strike at the English again."

"To the contrary, I have had enough of bloodshed. I want to live in peace, at least for awhile," Selig answered.

Drinking horns clanked, spoons and knives scraped across plates as the eating and drinking continued but there came a time when thirst was assuaged and hunger satisfied. In that moment the Norsemen banged their tankards upon the table in a steady rhythm.

"Selig! Selig! Selig!" they all chanted, making it known that they would wait no longer to hear his story.

Selig stood up, silencing the crowd with his outstretched hand. "I fear I am not as poetic as our beloved skald, but I think I have something to say that will interest you nonetheless." With that he began, holding them spellbound as he told them about the beauty and grace of his mother, his leaving home, his enslavement, and about the young woman who had risked her own well-being to free him from the humiliation of bondage.

As he told his story he couldn't keep his eyes from straying across the room to *her*. He could remember her kindness to him, her beauty, how passionate she had been in his arms the first night he had claimed her. He had once wanted the world; now all he wanted was her. But not at the expense of his pride and heritage. He was Viking through and through. Somehow he had to make her understand and see that he and they were not the heathens she seemed to believe they were.

"Selig is drinking more than usual," Gwyneth said to Erica.

"It's being here among so many others," Erica answered, looking towards Torin with a watchful eye. "It takes some getting used to but ye will." She explained that drinking from the ceremonial carved cattle horns was an art and that the men saw the horns as a test. "They cannot put them down until they are emptied, so a man must have a strong stomach and head to match, ere he will soon find himself the object of scorn."

"Like a game of Dare among children," Gwyneth replied, wondering if she would ever understand men, particularly Viking men.

"Aye, at times I am surprised at how like little children these strong Viking men can be. But then the men of Ulva could be just as childish."

Gwyneth saw a chance to bring up a subject that had been troubling her. "How can you, being a Christian, live among these Vikings and not tremble when they taunt God with their pagan rituals, Erica?"

"Ye must view things with an open mind. If ye do you will see that there are many ways in which the Viking beliefs are not as different as ye would suppose. They believe that one's life does not have to end when ye die and that death is just another level of existence. Likewise we Christians believe in an afterlife."

"But theirs is in Valhalla and ours is in heaven."

"Perhaps a different name for the same place."

"I hadn't thought of it that way." Gwyneth felt lighter of heart. Maybe instead of judging the Vikings so harshly she should try to learn more and understand the Viking ways.

"Ye love Selig, I know that ye do. Love can work miracles."

From across the length of the table Selig watched Erica and Gwyneth deeply engrossed in conversation. As Gwyneth looked towards him and then averted her eyes when he caught her staring, he sensed that they were talking about him. Was Erica trying to be a peacemaker? He could only hope so.

"So, my brother tells me that you carved the dragon's head on your ship and that you had a hand in overseeing every inch of the workmanship," Herlaug whispered in his ear.

"I did!" Selig replied.

"I'd like to sail with you sometime. I have enough friends to gather together a crew. You could show us the territory you conquered."

Selig shook his head. There was something about Herlaug that he didn't trust. Not just because of what Torin had told him but something he sensed for himself. "I don't think that would be a good idea. I have sailed with my men for a long time. We work together like one hand, skimming the ship across the water."

Herlaug pressed on. "I would let you command my men."

Again Selig said no. "I want my own men, my own ship."

Herlaug shrugged, laughing as one of the younger men spilled his drinking horn all over the front of his tunic. "I can understand, nephew. But at least I can persuade you to take a look at my ship and give me some advice on how I can be as successful a Viking as you!"

Though Selig had reservations about trusting Herlaug too far, he didn't see how any harm could come from taking a look at his ship.

"You can give me your expert opinion on what needs to be done to make my ship more seaworthy,"

Herlaug insisted, pushing until Selig agreed. "Tomorrow. I'll show you my ship tomorrow."

The feast lasted well into the night with drinking and storytelling. Here and there a brawl broke out as the men imbibed too much of their ale and mead. Anxious to be alone with Selig, Gwyneth waited, hoping to get a word with him but at last she had to give up. As the rest of the women retired for the night, so did she.

"Something is amiss with ye and Selig. What?" Erica walked with Gwyneth to her sleeping chamber.

"He . . . he gave me one of his arm rings and proclaimed our betrothal in front of the members of the settlement."

Erica smiled. "Then I was but imagining."

"No, you are right. Something is amiss and it is all my fault." She lapsed into the story, telling Erica about how horrified she had been because the bracelet was fashioned into a snake.

"Ye refused him."

"Yes!" Gwyneth put her fingers to her temples, massaging the pain. "And not a day passes when I do not regret it. I should never have reacted thus in front of the others. I humiliated him and tore at his pride." She had admired Erica's strength right from the first so it seemed only natural that she would ask, "What should I do to put things to right?"

"If he asked ye again would ye marry him in the Viking way?"

The question rendered Gwyneth speechless. Would she? Would she risk her soul because of her love for him? It was a question she asked herself over and over again as she lay all alone in the big bed, tucked under the eiderdown.

Built at right angles to the main hall, the bed

closet, as it was called, was tiny, big enough only for a bed and space to walk around it. As she lay on the lumpy straw mattress, she stared at the thin door waiting for Selig to walk through the portal.

"Yes! I will marry him in any ceremony that pleases him." He loved her. How could she ever doubt that? Hadn't he shown that love many times in deeds as well as words?

Hearing the sound of footsteps, Gwyneth stiffened. Someone was looking at her from the doorway. It was Selig. She longed to throw herself into his arms and tell him how much she loved him, but before she could react he had turned and walked away.

"Tomorrow . . ." Erica had asked her if she would marry Selig in the Viking way. Tomorrow she would tell Selig how much she loved him and ask him to marry *her*.

TWENTY-EIGHT

The foamy water glinted blue-green as it sucked at the rocks of the shore. The air was rank with the odor of sun-dried kelp and fish. Though it was summer, the early morning sea wind was brisk as Selig set out on foot, following his "newfound uncle" to where his dragon ship rested in the cove. Although Selig mistrusted Herlaug and in truth had little liking for the man at all, it seemed a harmless request that he should take a look at his ship.

"How much farther is it?" Selig asked, keeping a sharp eye on Baugi to make certain that he did not accost Herlaug. Though the big, black dog was friendly with most people he had taken an immediate dislike to Ragnar's brother, growling at him again and again.

"It's right around the curve of rocks, in the inlet. Right up ahead," Herlaug responded, looking daggers at the dog as he bared his teeth at him. "Vicious animal, isn't it!"

"Baugi?" Selig shook his head. "No." He scolded the dog firmly beneath his breath, then turned to his uncle. "I don't know what's gotten into him. The change of scenery perhaps. Give it time. He just needs to get to know you, that's all."

"You're sure he won't bite?" Herlaug touched the handle of his sword that rested in his belt.

"As certain as I am that *I* won't." Selig laughed, trying to lessen the tenseness of the situation.

"We could tie him to a tree . . ."

Selig was fiercely protective. "No! Since I've had him Baugi has never been tied. He is like me and needs to be free."

They trudged on ahead, speaking no more about the dog. At last they came to the inlet. Selig could see the image of the ship, like pieces of a puzzle, on the turbulent water.

"It's huge!" Larger than any other Viking ship he had ever seen. He suspected that was Herlaug's problem: a bulkier ship. Selig preferred smaller ships that were easier to handle and faster on the ocean.

"The bigger the better!" Herlaug made no pretense of modesty as he pointed towards the black-and-white sails emblazoned with a curled snake. "I call her the *Serpent's Strike.*"

As they came closer, Selig could see the painted grimace of a serpent's head on the prow, the fangs on its open jaw poised as if to bite. Remembering Gwyneth's aversion to snakes, he stared at the figurehead noting that in truth it did have the appearance of something evil.

"Come, take a look and give me your advice." Herlaug made a grandiose sweep with his hand.

Selig scrambled aboard, walking the length of the vessel as he appraised it with his eyes and his hands, taking note of the overlapped planking, the way the ends were hammered flat over a rove, or washer, to hold them, and the caulking of tarred animal hair between the planks that kept the hull watertight.

All ships had certain distinctive characteristics in common. The hull was symmetrical at the ends, with a slightly curved keep blending into a curved fore-stem and after-stem at the bow and stern. The evenly spaced floor timbers were attached to the planking but not to the keel, producing a flexible structure. Though some ships were fastened with treenails, or wooden pegs, this ship was fastened with iron nails.

"The shipbuilder did a good job—I won't argue with that but . . ."

Herlaug waited expectantly. "But what . . . ?"

Selig eyed the oarports, cut the full length of the ship. He decided to be truthful. "This ship was built for looks and not for seaworthiness." He forced a smile. "No doubt you hoped to frighten your enemies into surrender."

It was obvious that Herlaug was less than pleased by his reaction. "It cost me a great deal to have *Serpent's Strike* built. There are lands far to the west that have not yet been conquered. I have made great plans."

"Take my advice. Build another ship. Lighter and faster. This ship will be cumbersome upon the seas!"

There was a long, uncomfortable silence, and then Herlaug laughed. "I wanted honesty and by Thor's hammer, that is what I got." He started to approach Selig but stepped back when Baugi growled. "But do not judge this ship too hastily. At least let me demonstrate that even a big ship can be graceful."

Selig had been so absorbed with examining the ship that he hadn't noticed the approaching men. As they climbed aboard to take their places at the oars, he tensed, but Herlaug put him at ease.

"We'll be back in time for *dagveror,* our morning meal." He clapped his hands, signaling his men to begin rowing. "See my snake? She is straining to chew at the waves."

Herlaug's men strained and sweated at the oars and at last the monstrous ship was out to sea. The sail was up, whipping at the gusts that struck at it as if blown by Odin himself. Soon the ship dipped and pitched in the waves of the North Sea as a flock of seagulls circled and screamed overhead.

Selig was surprised that such a large ship could move so fast and he said so. "Perhaps your shipbuilder knew some secret."

"He did. I forced the secret out of him!" Herlaug answered, scanning the horizon as the ship moved farther and farther from shore.

"I think you proved your point. If we are going to get back before the others sit down to *dagveror*, we had best head back to shore," Selig suggested, anxious to set foot on land again. There was something about Herlaug's crew that bothered him, though he couldn't say what. Just a feeling he had in the pit of his stomach.

"At the helm of the *Sea Dragon* your word is law but the *Serpent's Strike* is mine to command," Herlaug answered with grin. "The morning is young. The others will be so blurry-eyed from the drinking last night, they will not even notice we are not there. Besides, I doubt if all the food will be gone. Their stomachs will be in turmoil and their heads will be pounding as if Thor's hammer were inside."

Against his better judgment, Selig ceased to protest, trying to fight against his apprehension. As his uncle had said, the crew of the *Serpent's Strike* was his to command. Even so, trust was a delicate thing. As the ship headed westward, Selig's emotions snapped. There was no doubt in his mind that something was terribly wrong. He knew it and Baugi knew it.

"Fool that I was, I did not listen to my dog's warning," he mumbled beneath his breath. Now what was he going to do about it? "Turn back!" he shouted, determined to have his say, even if it was Herlaug's crew.

"They won't listen to you, 'Nephew.' They will do as I command."

"And just what was your command, 'Uncle'?"

Herlaug's cheerful demeanor changed. He glowered at Selig. "To get rid of you!"

The answer chilled Selig's blood. "Why? I have not harmed you in any way."

"Why?" Herlaug's voice was scathing. "I want to be jarl—it is as simple as that."

"You? Jarl? What about my father?"

"Ragnar! You think I will always be content to be in his shadow?"

Herlaug's treachery hit Selig like a physical blow. He knew his father's fate. "You're going to kill him."

Herlaug didn't deny it. "As soon as I take care of a few unplanned-for disturbances."

"Me! And Erica!"

"And a third wolf cub out there somewhere . . ." Herlaug squinted, as if by so doing he could see where the other threat to his "jarldom" might be.

"How could you? You grew up together at your father's knee. You are brothers!"

"And opponents, though my fool of a brother can not see that. Nor does he realize how long I have hated him for being born a year before I."

Selig felt the need to defend his father's honor even in such dire circumstances. "Ragnar didn't inherit all that he has. He fought long and hard for it."

"As did I. Right by his side. And how does he reward me? By deciding to put one of the sons that he has never seen in my place as successor." He spat on the deck. "That is gratitude for you."

"He means well. Ragnar is a good man."

Herlaug shrugged. "Good men die."

Selig clenched his jaw, controlling his temper as best he could. He had never realized how cruel and traitorous any man could be. "My father's illness. The headaches. Your doing."

Herlaug didn't deny it. "With the help of a *sejd-*woman."

"They are supposed to be healers."

"Enough gold and amber . . ."

Selig glanced uneasily out to sea, wondering how he was going to save himself. Now that Herlaug had told him what he planned—he couldn't allow Selig to stay alive.

"What do you plan to do to me?"

"Sell you as a slave!"

Selig would have preferred death. His temper exploded. "Never! If that is what you plan you had best kill me right now, for I will never live one moment again as a slave!" With that he leaped upon Herlaug, pushing him to the ground as Baugi barked frantically. Over and over they rolled on the deck as havoc erupted among the men.

"Grab him! Get him off of me," Herlaug shouted. "And slit the throat of that dog!"

Four men moved toward Baugi but the dog's furious barking and snarling held them at bay. Selig was not as fortunate. He winced in pain as he was grabbed from behind. Pretending to collapse, he waited, then took advantage as his captor's grip loosened. Turning around, he brought both arms up to break the man's hold, then threw a blow to the man's jaw that sent him sprawling.

"Fools! Get him!"

Selig looked left, then right, then behind him. There were too many of them to fight. Even so, he had to do something before he was bound and gagged and rendered helpless.

"Baugi!" Before Herlaug could react, Selig ran to the side of the ship and jumped over the side.

The ice-cold sea took his breath away as he hit the waters. He heard a roaring in his ears as the ocean closed about his head. He felt as if his lungs would burst, but he refused to let the seawater fill his lungs.

The burning in his chest was unbearable. He felt as if he would die at that moment but the imagined sight of Gwyneth's face in front of his eyes gave him courage. Pushing with all his might against his watery grave, he broke the surface. Air filled his lungs again and he gasped at the breath of life, wondering if it was the ocean mist he felt spring to his eyes—or his tears.

He looked up. Through a veil of moisture he saw the figurehead of the *Serpent's Strike* bobbing up and down like an evil sea serpent. Despite his aversion for the beast, he reached up.

Suddenly he felt something tugging at him and knew what it was. Baugi. The dog had followed him and jumped over the side of the Viking ship to rescue him. "Good dog!" Somehow the dog's presence gave him added courage. Together they could make it to the shore. Or could they?

A thick cloud of smoke hung over the hall from the large hearth fire as the women prepared the morning meal. They chattered away about all that must be done for the day. Gwyneth held on to the wooden pail with one hand as she wiped her eyes with the other. Early this morning Erica had showed her how to milk a goat and she felt a sense of self-satisfaction that she had so easily managed the task.

"I *am* becoming a Viking." She had come a long way from being the sheltered daughter of her land-owning parents.

"Just in time for the barley porridge," Erica said, taking the pail from her. "Are ye going to speak with Selig?"

Erica nodded. "If I can find him!" She looked

…erlaug's story credence in he…

…he realm of Niflheim itself if …
…him," Ragnar insisted. Together…
…organized a search party.

towards the tables, scanning the chairs for Selig. She didn't see him. "It's not like him to sleep late."

"This morning may be different. All of the men drank more than they should. Torin got out of bed a few moments ago, but only because I tugged him by his hair!" She smiled impishly but her smile vanished as she spoke with one of the thralls. "Gwyn . . ."

"What's wrong?" Somehow, without even asking, Gwyneth knew. "Selig?"

"Astrid says she saw him this morning with Herlaug."

"Herlaug?" They looked at each other.

"Hurry!" With Gwyneth only one step behind, Erica scurried around the room, asking each person in the hall if they knew where Herlaug and Selig had gone, piecing together the story. "Selig went with Herlaug to see his ship."

"To see his ship?" Gwyneth tried hard not to panic, despite all that she had heard about Ragnar's brother.

"I do not like it! Herlaug can not be trusted. He kidnapped my poor Geordie, burnt Torin's and my house to the ground, and tried to abduct me. He will do mischief to Selig as well."

Gwyneth had a premonition that Erica was right. "We have to go after them! There is no telling what Herlaug might do."

Gwyneth had good intentions but in the end there was nothing she could do. Herlaug had not told anyone where he was going nor was it common knowledge where he kept his ship. Thus, all that could be done was to wait and look towards the door in hopes that Selig would soon appear. Selig never appeared, despite Gwyneth's hopes and prayers, but Herlaug did.

"What's happened? Where is Selig?"

Herlaug slammed the door behind him, then

slumped in the nearest chair and put his head in his hands. "There has been a terrible accident!"

"Accident!" Gwyneth put her hands up to her mouth to stifle her hysteria. It was Selig. Something had happened. Something that was no accident.

In a tone of forced bereavement, Herlaug told the story that he and Selig had decided to take his ship, the *Serpent's Strike*, out to sea so Selig could assess the ship's seaworthiness.

"We were hit!"

"Hit?" Ragnar stood in the doorway. "By who?"

"By what, don't you mean?" Herlaug wove his deceitful tale skillfully. "It was a whale. The largest one I have ever seen." He spread his arms. "Nearly as large as the ship."

"What about Selig?" Gwyneth inquired, trying to maintain some semblance of calm.

"He is a true, selfless hero, that one," Herlaug praised. "He took it upon himself to see if there had been any damage done to the ship. We lowered him over the side with a rope to take a look when alas . . ."

"What happened? In God's name tell me!" Gwyneth demanded.

"We were hit again by the whale. The rope broke and Selig tumbled into the sea. Though we searched for him, he was lost . . ."

"Lost?" Ragnar paled. He grabbed hold of the door for support.

"It was as if the sea swallowed him, or perhaps the whale . . ."

"No!" Ragnar was devastated.

Gwyneth could not speak. Her eyes merely stared at Herlaug's face. It was as if at that moment she could not utter a sound, but her mouth formed the word "no."

"My son! It can't be. He was just returned to me . . ."

TWENTY-NINE

Gwyneth spent the next few days in a haze of grief. She had no awareness of time nor of those about her. She tried to eat but the food choked her, so she pushed her plate aside. All she could think about was the bracelet and the night Selig had proudly announced to everyone on board the *Sea Dragon* that he wanted her to be his wife.

"And I rejected him." It didn't matter why she had done it. She had humiliated a proud man. How she wanted to tell him that she had changed her mind, that she would marry him in any ceremony under the sky, but it was too late. Ragnar had gone out in his own ship with Torin and Erica to search for any sign of his son, but he had found no trace of him or of Baugi.

"There is no place they could have gone," Erica told her.

"No islands to swim to," Torin rasped. "Selig was not as fortunate as Erica and I. When our boat capsized off Ulva, we were washed ashore on the Isle of Staffa."

"Poor Selig. There was no place to swim to. Only the endless ocean."

"There is no way he could have survived. I'm sorry . . ." Torin hung his head.

Gwyneth knew that she had to accept the truth—Selig was gone—but she could not still the voice deep inside her heart that whispered that he lived. "No. He's not dead. Somehow Baugi got him back to shore." She wanted so desperately to believe that!

"It was too far. Ye must accept the truth, hinny." Erica dashed away her own tears away with the back of her hand. "If only he had listened to Torin. He told him not to trust Herlaug."

"I think he was wary, but Herlaug is a convincing man and he is Selig's uncle," Gwyneth said softly. "I know what it is like to trust someone evil." Like a ghost, the memory of Alfred's treachery came back to haunt her. "If only I had had a chance to talk with him about it. If only I could have pleaded . . ."

"Even if ye had, the consequences might hae been the same." Erica laid a sisterly hand on Gwyneth's shoulder. "Herlaug is crafty and dangerous, more so because my father is blind to his treachery. How then could Selig have not been tricked?"

"But I should have foreseen. I should have known danger was afoot by Herlaug's pretense of camaraderie. I . . ."

"Hush!" Erica sighed. "There are many things I wish *I* had done but we only torture ourselves with those thoughts." She said gently, "We cannot change the past, though we might well wish to do so."

"No, we can not," Gwyenth cried softly. "And I have something precious to treasure. His love. I will always have that." Still, she knew it would be a long time before her tears were dried and the ache in her heart was just a memory.

Selig thrashed at the thin linen that covered him. He had to break the surface. He had to breathe! Struggling with all his strength, he fought against Herlaug, against the ocean. He didn't want to drown. He wouldn't!

"The serpent. The symbol of evil!" It was staring at him as it bobbed up and down in the ocean. Herlaug's snake. The *Serpent Strike*. It was going to gobble him up.

"Easy. Easy," he heard a man's voice say. "Herlaug won't be able to touch you here."

"Gwyn . . ." He felt a hand touch his forehead. Not the soft hand of a woman but the strong, callused hand of a man.

"It's all right. You're safe here . . ." The voice was a deep rumble.

Selig's eyes flew open. "Who . . . ?"

At first the shape of the man was hazy, merely the huge shape and silhouette of a bearded man. Then as his vision cleared, Selig saw the scarred, thickly bearded face of a man. A Viking.

"Who . . . are . . ."

"I'm the man who fished you from the sea like a soaked sack of meal," the man answered.

"You saved my life!"

"Not I! Your big, black bear kept you from sinking. I only dragged you out of the water and aboard my ship."

"Baugi. Where is he?"

The Viking laughed. "Not far. That one is as loyal as they come." He pointed to where Baugi stood guard just a few feet away.

"I remember him diving in after me." Selig put his hand up to his head. "The rest is a haze."

The Viking told Selig how his ship had been hiding behind the rocks in the cove, determined to avoid Herlaug and his men. From a distance they had witnessed Selig's struggle and had watched as he dove over the side of the ship.

"Herlaug and I are old enemies. Any foe of his

is a friend of mine." The Viking told Selig that once Herlaug and his men had left the area, his ship had sailed in for the rescue.

"Ragnar's brother is no stranger to you then." Selig sat up, curious about his rescuer. "What is your name?"

"Roland. Roland Thorvalsson. " A look of pain creased the bearded man's face. "It is a name you must forget . . ."

To the contrary. Selig was determined to remember. Roland Thorvalsson! He whispered it to himself.

"I talked it over with my men. If it is your desire you may join with us," Roland Thorvalsson invited.

Selig visually examined Roland's crew. Like their leader they were heavily bearded; some wore scars and most of them were ragged. He sensed that they were outlaws, banished from Viking society for one or many transgressions or crimes. It was not the kind of life a sane man wanted.

"I must go back. There's a woman there . . ."

The shaggy-bearded Roland shook his head. "You can not go back! If you do, Herlaug will make an attempt on your life again and this time he may succeed."

"You don't understand! I have to expose Herlaug for what he did and what he is. I have to warn my . . ."

"No matter what you say, Herlaug will think of a way to appear innocent. He will claim that you suffered an accident, then when your guard is down he will find a way to wound you."

Selig looked towards the shore. Beyond the waters, past the rocks, his heart rested in the hands of a dark-haired Englishwoman who had given him her love. Somehow he had to find a way to return to her without bringing danger with him.

"How can I beat Herlaug?"

"Accuse him openly before everyone at the gathering of the *Thing*. That is the only way to settle this matter once and for all."

THIRTY

The roar of the ocean, the cry of seagulls as they circled overhead, slowly awakened Selig from a deep slumber. Taking in a deep breath of the salty sea air, he sat up expecting to be on the *Sea Dragon* but, as his eyes touched on Roland Thorvalsson, he remembered.

"So, at last you are awake. You slept so soundly I feared that you were dead," the outlawed Viking proclaimed.

"I won't die. I have too much to live for. The love of a beautiful woman and my lust for revenge."

Long into the night he and Roland had carefully constructed a plan to make Herlaug pay for what he had done, not just to Selig but to many. The plan hinged on taking Herlaug by surprise so he didn't have time to conjure up an alibi. With that thought in mind Selig was going to wait until the Thing to reveal that he was still alive. At that gathering he would denounce Herlaug publicly and take great pleasure in listening as the lawgiver declared the punishment. In the meantime he had to content himself with being on board a rickety old ship filled with scarred, sweaty, bearded dregs of the Viking community.

Selig had tried to learn of why Roland had been outlawed and then banished, but the man had refused to talk about himself, preferring to talk about

Selig. The only thing Roland had revealed was that he had a son, taken from him long ago and that now this son was a grown man.

Roland Thorvalsson had also told Selig about his ship. He had salvaged a funeral ship by swimming out as it floated on the ocean, beating at the flames with his cloak until the fires were out. Making use of the tools put on board to aid the dead Viking in the afterlife, he had made enough repairs to make the ship sailable. As to his crew who, like himself, were outlaws banished from the Viking community, he had acquired them one by one. Selig had a feeling that each of them had quite a story to tell.

"I'm afraid that all we have for the morning meal is dried barley bread and water spiked with ale. There has been too much activity in this area from ships searching for *you*. We can't take a chance on going ashore in case we need to escape detection quickly." He held out a basket. "But we do have a few berries . . ."

Selig shrugged. "I'm not really very hungry. I'll satisfy myself with a few berries and a piece of bread." His expression was bitter and intent as he reached for a knife to slice the bread.

How he longed to be back among his friends where he could enjoy food cooked over the fire. And where he could hold Gwyneth in his arms again. This time he wouldn't let his pride separate them. He'd hold her and never let her go.

"Your impatience shows upon your face."

Selig clenched his fists in frustration. "I want to go back."

"You can't!" Roland clutched at his arm as if fearing he might act rashly. "To venture out now would mean your death, for Herlaug is not a man to be thwarted. Better for him to think that you have died. That is the only way that I have survived all these years," he added.

Selig walked to the side of the ship and looked towards the land. Beyond the waters was the woman he loved yet he could not even tell her that he was alive. It seemed to be an impossible situation. He turned towards Roland.

"Why don't you and the others come with me and clear your names at the Thing?"

Roland shook his head, averting his eyes so Selig would not see the pain so clearly written there. "Because we can not."

He reminded Selig about the law and what happened to a man found guilty. His children became illegitimate. He became a fugitive, ejected from the boundaries of the Norsemen, a man who had lost all rights and could be killed without any legal redress.

"To draw attention to ourselves would mean instant death for all of us."

"Then you are guilty."

"Not of everything we are said to have done, but guilty of enough crimes to insure our banishment for all the days of our miserable lives . . ."

He sounded so desolate, so desperately unhappy that Selig pitied him. "You are a survivor! That is something to be admired."

"We have all eked out a living, but there isn't a moment that passes by when we do not regret doing that which has separated us from the homes and families we once had."

Selig knew that he would rather die than find himself outlawed and banished. "Tell me what happened to you."

At first it seemed that Roland was going to be evasive once again, but then all at once he seemed to relax. "What harm is there in telling you?"

He told Selig how murderously unruly he had been as a young man. "I disobeyed the law by killing a fellow Viking for a very small offense. Worse yet,

I beat my wife while in a jealous rage. Though she did not die immediately, it was the injuries I inflicted that eventually took her life and left my son without a mother."

"You must miss your son."

"Very much. Worst of all, I cheated myself out of seeing him grow up to become a man."

He told Selig that Ragnar had scorned his son as was his right by law, then had taken the motherless boy from his hearth, with the intent of bringing further humiliation upon the entire family.

"In retaliation, I contested Ragnar's right to rule and openly challenged him. For that reason I was a dangerous man to have around, so Ragnar banished me." The rogue Viking hung his head. "What I would not give to see my son again."

"Perhaps you will one day."

"No, and it is better that I do not. Torin has made a new life for himself. At least I can take satisfaction in knowing that he is Ragnar's right hand man."

"Torin?" Selig was certain he must have heard wrong.

"Yes, Torin."

Excitement surged through Selig's veins. "I know your son! He is married to my half-sister."

"You know my son?" Roland asked Selig more than a dozen questions, savoring the answers like a great delicacy.

"When I get back I'll tell him that I saw you. Perhaps . . ."

Roland grabbed Selig by the hair, pulling his head back. "You will do no such thing. I do not want him to know I am alive. I want him to think I have died."

Gwyneth had wondered why the Northland was often referred to as the land of the midnight sun.

Now, as summer was at its full peak and the days
were filled with an endless light, she knew.

"The long days mean all the more time to
mourn," she said to Erica as they dipped their
wooden buckets into the well.

"Selig wouldn't want ye to be miserable."

"Nor would he want me to forget him." She
tugged so hard at the rope on the bucket that it
tore loose and the bucket tumbled into the water
below. "Oh, no!" Somehow it seemed to be a por-
tent of misfortune in the days to come. All she knew
was that she had to retrieve it. With that in mind
she leaned precariously over the edge.

"Leave it!" Dropping her own bucket to the
ground, Erica was beside her in an instant, grabbing
her around the waist to keep her from falling in.
"One of the men can get it out. They have longer
arms."

Whether it was because of all that had happened
or the stern, scolding tone of Erica's voice, she
didn't know, but suddenly Gwyneth was sobbing so
hard that she feared she couldn't stop.

"Hush . . . !" Just as she had done many times
with Geordie, Erica took Gwyneth by the hand, sat
her down on a rock, and stroked her hair. "It will
be all right. Ye will see."

"It will never be all right again. Selig is gone. I'll
never see him again . . ."

"Not in this life perhaps, but if ye believe in
heaven . . ."

"I don't want to wait. Besides, in heaven all the
righteous do is float around in the air playing harps.
It wouldn't be the same thing. There's no . . ."

"Lovemaking?"

Gwyneth blushed. "Yes."

Erica squeezed her hand. "Ye don't know that."

"Selig didn't . . . didn't believe and so . . ."

"He won't go to heaven." Erica smiled. "Ye don't

know that for sure, either." She tugged on her hand. "Come . . ."

Erica led Gwyneth on a long walk through the surrounding meadows and forest land, only stopping when they came to a small stream. The water was clear and cool, with a tangy, refreshing taste from the thyme and mint that grew along its banks.

"Whenever I was upset at home in Alba I visited a small lake. It was beautiful there just as it is here. Just looking around, I was reminded of what a precious gift life is."

"Precious, but lonely for me now." Gwyneth knew what Erica was trying to do and she was deeply touched. "You and Torin have been more than kind and I appreciate your friendship but without Selig I realize that I don't belong here."

"Ye want to go home . . ."

With Selig gone it had become an obsession. She missed her mother, her father, and all the others. Besides, she was woefully out of place here in the Northland. "Would Torin take me?"

Erica nodded. "After the Thing he's planned a journey to Eire. Though I canna speak for him I think he would sail the extra distance."

Though they spoke no more about it, the journey home was on Gwyneth's mind as they took off their shoes and waded in the water. She watched the little whirlpools created as they took each step, but the water soon returned to normal as they moved farther along. Life wasn't like that. She knew in her heart that she would always be affected by having known Selig.

"Did you ever wonder how different your life would have been if you hadn't met Torin?"

"My life would have been boring, I fear. I would have remained unmarried and . . ." Erica winced as she stubbed her toe. She picked up the offending stone and it was then that she noticed they were

not alone. "Do not look now, but Herlaug has followed us."

The breeze carried a multitude of sounds: birds
singing, water gushing over the rocks, and the snap
of a dead branch. Gwyneth sensed the noise had
been made by Herlaug's big foot as he took a step.

"He is over by the trees."

"Herlaug!" How she hated Ragnar's brother! She
blamed him for Selig's death, but she also feared
him. "What does he want?"

"I don't know. Me perhaps!" Turning towards
him, Erica put her hands on her hips in a show of
defiance. "But I am not afraid of him."

"You should be!"

"Nae, he should be afraid of me for I intend to
denounce him at the Thing for all that he has
done!"

"Erica . . . hush!"

"Why? I dunna care if he knows it!"

"You will come up missing like Selig!" Gwyneth
stiffened as she saw Herlaug take one step closer
and then another. He bent over to scoop up a hand-
ful of water, then sat down on a large rock. All the
while he was watching them.

"He wouldn't dare! There have been enough
questions raised already concerning Selig. He will
have to wait!" She put her hand on Gwyneth's arm.
"But just in case he is so dull-witted as to come after
me, I want ye to run at the first inkling that ye have
that he is going to do me harm."

"Run?" She didn't want Erica to think she was
too much of a coward or too fragile to help. "No,
I'd stay and help you."

"If he poses a danger ye must run and fetch the
others."

As Gwyneth watched, Herlaug came to the very
edge of the water. "The forest can be dangerous for

young women, especially when they are unarmed," he called out.

Erica reached down and picked up the largest rock she could find in the stream. "Who said I was unarmed?" She brandished the rock. Gwyneth reached down, grabbed a huge stone, and mimicked Erica's stance.

"I've seen bears and wolves out here. I come to offer my protection."

"I can take care of myself as ye should know," Erica reminded him. "As for the bears and the wolves, I much prefer their company to yours!"

Though Herlaug laughed, Gwyneth didn't like the sound of it. It was too obvious that he had been stalking them like an animal seeking its prey.

"I'll leave but this won't be the last time you will see me near you, Gwyneth. I feel the need to protect you now that Selig is . . ."

"I would as soon keep company with a snake," Gwyneth retorted, surprised by her own show of defiance.

"We'll see . . ." He smiled, an action more frightening than if he had brandished his sword; then, with a grunt he turned and walked away.

"We hae won a victory," Erica proclaimed.

"Have we?" Or had they just targeted themselves for an early death?

THIRTY-ONE

The longer he was among the rogue Vikings the more Selig came to admire Roland Thorvalsson. Although he had faced a harsh punishment that would have beaten most men, Roland had faced adversity head-on and had survived. In that way they were alike.

"Sometimes I think this life is not so bad," Roland was saying as he started a cooking fire on the shore. Though they had to be extremely careful not to be seen, Roland had decided it was safe to make camp for the night on land.

"We do not have to answer to any man," Knut Ormsson exclaimed as he proudly displayed the deer he had killed.

"There are plenty of streams, an ocean full of fish, birds in the sky, rabbits to snare, and juicy, wild berries to supplement what we can not steal," Alf the Stout interjected.

"Food, ale, water, and freedom. What more does a man need," Knut boasted.

"A woman's softness . . ." Selig replied, seeing Gwyneth's face and voluptuous silhouette in his mind's eye. He had always known that he would miss her but he had not realized how much.

"Bah, women are as plentiful as fish in the ocean. Like the fish we have only to catch them and use them for our needs," Alf the Stout grumbled.

"And have them crying and fighting all the while." Knut sighed. "I have to admit that there are times when I long to cradle my head on a woman's breasts while I sleep and know that she will be there in the morning just because she wants to be."

Roland turned his back on the others, asking Selig, "Torin . . . is he content with the woman he has chosen? Is she docile?"

"Docile?" Selig grinned, knowing that the word did not describe his half-sister. "Erica is a strong-willed woman whose red hair matches her temperament. She is adventuresome, brave, and has a zest for living. Your son will never be bored."

"He loves her."

"Completely."

"Ragnar . . . is he treating him well?"

"Torin has everything he could ever want or need except his father." Knowing firsthand how healing it had been to be reunited with his own father, Selig asked, "Are you certain that you do not want to see Torin? I could bring him to the cove. You could meet him in secret. No one would ever have to know . . ."

"No! I have wronged him enough already. Torin assumes that I am dead and it is better that way. I would only be a stone around his neck. He is content. Let him stay that way." He threw several small branches upon the fire. "Promise me that you will not reveal the truth to him." When Selig hesitated, he insisted, "Promise me!"

"I promise!"

Roland put several seagull eggs wrapped in wet leaves in the fire. "Roast eggs, a delicacy you will enjoy if you have never tried them before," he exclaimed, hastily changing the subject. Selig knew that the subject of Torin would not be addressed again.

A cool, silvery light lay over the water. It was a

tranquil evening that gave lie to the tumult that
would result when Selig openly charged his uncle
of attempted murder at the Thing. Was it any wonder that Selig decided to take advantage of the calm
before the storm and just sit back and relax as the
evening meal cooked in the fire? As always, his
thoughts turned to Gwyneth, wondering what she
was doing at the moment, if she was safe, and if her
thoughts were on him.

"Surely she must think I drowned, Baugi," he
whispered to himself as the dog lay down beside
him. "Well, she will find out very soon that I am
very much alive." Tomorrow at the first crack of
dawn he would set out for the yearly gathering of
all free men and there he would seek his vengeance
upon the man who tried to take his life.

"Gwyneth! Gwyneth . . . wake up . . . !" The
voice of Erica seemed to call to her from afar but
as she opened her eyes Gwyneth remembered that
she had spent last night in Erica and Torin's room,
curled up on a blanket at the foot of their large
bed. After their confrontation with Herlaug near the
edge of the forest, Erica had insisted that she not
sleep alone.

"Please . . . let me sleep a little longer . . ." Since
Selig had drowned, Gwyneth had been spending
more time abed than usual, but Erica was having
none of that.

"Ye must get up and collect your belongings. Lest
ye have forgotten, hinny, we leave for the Thing this
morn."

Gwyneth was rebellious. "I don't want to go! Herlaug will be gone. I'll be safe." She didn't want to
remind Erica that she was *not* a Viking and thus
cared little what happened at their foolish meeting.

"Ye must go!" Grabbing her by the ankle, Erica

laughed softly as she tugged her from the bed. Gwyneth tumbled to the floor.

"No! Selig is dead. Punishing Herlaug will not bring him back! I shall stay here."

"Och, what a stubborn lass! Ye leave us little choice but to carry ye kicking and yelling if need be for ye *will* go!"

Realizing that it was going to be a battle of wills, Torin raised his hands in a gesture of compromise. "Please, Gwyneth. Erica and I have many grievances against Herlaug, including Selig's death. The more voices that speak up declaring his foul deeds the better. To put it in so many words, we need you."

When voiced like that, how could Gwyneth refuse? She remembered hearing them talk about the assembly of free men. The Thing, it was commonly called. It was there that people would gather to hear the lawgiver review laws, where they made new laws, set fines and punishments. At the Thing they lodged suits against transgressors, worshipped their gods, displayed skills, and even bought and sold various items.

"I'll go and hope with all my heart that Herlaug will pay the ultimate penalty for what he did to Selig."

Hurrying to wash her face and hands, eat a bowl of cold cereal sweetened with honey and drenched in goat's milk with a few berries, she gathered her traveling sack together. She would take her gowns, brooches, two pairs of shoes—one of thick leather in case the days held rain—and two cloaks, one made of fur in case the nights were chilly.

Nissa, Gerda, Erica, Gwyneth, and the household thralls gathered together the baking pans, wooden bowls and spoons, buckets, and several iron cauldrons which would be suspended over fires by a tripod. Even far away from the hall there was cooking that must be done.

Gwyneth could see several litters harnessed between two horses and three ornately decorated and carved wagons that would take them to their destination. She could also see that the wagons were carved with faces and images of the Viking deities and other ugly heads she thought must be trolls.

"Come, I'll help you into the wagon," Ragnar invited, putting his arms around her waist. His eyes were kind as he smiled. "I keep hoping in my heart that I will see your body thickening with Selig's child for I would desire more than anything to have a grandchild! In that way he would stay alive!"

His words gripped Gwyneth's heart. How she wished now that she had not taken Ingunn's potions, for she knew that Ragnar was right. If only she were with child, Selig would live on for both of them.

Feeling a sudden prickling in her spine, Gwyneth looked over her shoulder and saw Herlaug staring at her. As their eyes met he looked away. She saw him join Ragnar and the other men who would ride on horseback beside the wagons. Gwyneth would ride in a wagon with Erica, Nissa, and Gerda. The other wagons would be shared by the other women of importance in the household, including Herlaug's wives. The female and male thralls would have to walk the entire distance. Gwyneth pitied them for she knew it was a hard life to be a slave.

When the preparations had been completed, they set out upon their journey. Gwyneth could see that the men of the household were decked out in their finery: cloaks billowing out behind them as they rode, bright ribbons, or *hlads*, worn tied around their foreheads, arms bedecked with bracelets as they held their weapons.

Gwyneth wondered if it would be uncomfortable to have to carry spear, shield, battle-ax, and sword while riding. She supposed that indeed it would be, but had learned how important it was to the men of Ragnar's household to arrive in style at the gathering.

Looking over at Nissa, she was not surprised to see the woman adorned in all her finest jewelry, bracelets covering every inch of her arms. Nissa had chosen a brightly colored gown of scarlet and rode with her nose in the air as if she, and not Ragnar, were the jarl.

Gwyneth had chosen a plain, dun-colored gown to wear over her beige, pleated chemise, and a cloak of dark brown. Two brooches and her beloved pendant were her only jewelry. She had chosen to dress in dull colors to show that she was mourning Selig.

"I wish he were here! I can almost imagine him riding tall and proud beside Ragnar!" she whispered to Erica.

"If ye conjure him up in thought, then he is here in spirit," Erica replied.

More people joined the party as they traveled along. From impoverished peasants to tradesmen and artisans, from wealthy Viking raiders to heavily burdened thralls, all joined in to go to the Thing. Through dense forests and low-lying fields and meadows they rode through the daylight hours.

When Gwyneth thought that her aching bottom could stand the wagon no more, they finally arrived at their journey's end. Ragnar, Herlaug, Torin, and the others erected rough tents of wool and laid down piles of fur for sleeping pallets. Men took up their drinking horns, toasting each other boldly with their mead and ale, the women also sharing in the drinking. Stories abounded as the sagas were told and retold.

Gwyneth heard again of Yggdrasill, the gigantic ash tree which the Vikings thought supported the nine worlds. It was said that its branches reached the sky; its roots touched Asgard, the home of the gods; Midgard, the home of mortals; and even the darkness of Hel.

Erica told a story she had recently learned about how Freyja was once the wife of Odin. A very vain goddess, he deserted her for the goddess Grigga because Freyja loved finery more than her husband. As she told the tale, she looked at Nissa and Gwyneth had to suppress a giggle or two as the others in the party looked Nissa's way also. Gwyneth knew that from now on she wouldn't be able to look Ragnar's wife in the eye without thinking of the story.

The night was bright with a rosy glow from the sun, which would not set completely until midnight. Meanwhile it remained low in the sky, just barely touching the horizon. Fires were lit as the company filled their stomachs with mutton and various vegetables which bubbled from the cauldrons over the fire. Fish and meat were baked in holes in the ground covered with heated stones; the aroma made Gwyneth realize she was famished. She ate a goodly share of the mutton and vegetables which Erica had brought to her.

"I don't think I can sleep tonight," she confided to Erica. In Ragnar's large house there were shutters to block out the eternal light of the summer sky, but here there would be no such shelter. Besides, she was nervous about Erica's condemnation of her uncle. What if Herlaug found a way to make it look as if he were innocent just as he had done so many times in the past? What would happen to Erica and Torin then?

Erica seemed to read her mind. "Herlaug will not escape punishment this time! Somehow, someway Torin and I will see that he pays for the heartache he has caused us all." She pointed to Gwyneth's sleeping pallet and motioned for her to lie down.

"Try to get at least a little sleep. Ye would not want to fall asleep during the assembly."

"Oh, I don't know about that. Perhaps I do," Gwyneth teased. "These gatherings must certainly be tedious."

"This one will not be once Torin and I have a chance to speak. Just wait and you will see . . ." Having spoken, Erica followed Torin to their pallet; Gwyneth was shamed to feel a surge of envy at their togetherness. It made her all the more conscious of how empty she felt without Selig, more so as the night wore on and she could hear the soft sounds of pleasure that escaped Erica as she and Torin made love.

Gwyneth tossed and turned upon her pallet for what seemed to be an eternity. When at last she fell asleep, it was with Selig's name upon her lips.

Selig had only the clothes on his back to wear to the Thing, thus he accepted Roland's gifts of a tunic, belt, leather shoes, and cloak with the greatest appreciation and made ready for his journey. As he lay on his back and looked up at the pink glow of the sky, trying to discern the faint marks of the stars and moon which were just barely visible, he cautioned himself not to be too rash in his actions at the Thing. Herlaug had proven that he could be treacherous.

Hearing the cry of a wolf, Selig looked in the direction of the sound. He was certain he could see several pairs of eyes upon him, watching. Getting up, he built four fires that surrounded him. He had heard that the meat of humans was not a favorite with carnivorous creatures because it was too stringy, but he wasn't taking any chances.

Although Selig would have felt much more at ease traveling in a ship, and though he knew the journey would be longer by land, he intended to ride a horse that one of the outlaws had miraculously "found" for him. Another gift from Roland. He knew the workings of Herlaug's mind, which was what forced his choice. Undoubtedly his uncle would have lookouts stationed to spy upon all comings and goings from the ocean in fear that he might have survived, but the land route was too vast and would be left unguarded.

He was anxious to have this matter of Herlaug settled once and for all, to have his say at the Thing, and then hurry back to the comfort of Gwyneth's arms. It seemed an eternity since they had made love—his flesh hungered for her. Even now the very thought of her beautiful breasts, her slim waist, the curve of her hips, the softness of her hair, aroused him to a painful physical longing as well as one of the heart.

Looking back at his life, he realized how wrong he had been. It wasn't glory he had hungered for but a sense of purpose. Loving Gwyneth had opened his heart to the beauty of the world. Despite all that had happened, despite what Herlaug had done, Selig was not as vengeful as he was anxious to return to his old life. Love was an all-consuming emotion that seemed to leave little room for baser emotions.

"It won't be long, my love," he murmured.

THIRTY-TWO

Gwyneth woke the next morning to the sound of laughter. Looking outside the confines of the large tent, she saw that during the night many others had arrived, their small camps sprinkled about the hillside like the leaves of autumn. She could see the familiar forms of Ingunn, Kadlin, and the others from the settlement and she felt excitement surge through her. She hadn't seen them since they were on the ship together.

Jumping up from her pallet to dress and comb her hair, she hurried outside. Greeting Ingunn first, she noted that she was big with child, her ample form proof of her husband's virility, or so Ingunn said.

"I heard about Selig!" Ingunn exclaimed. "How tragic that after all the storms he survived he should drown in an accident!"

"It was no accident." As quickly as she could, Gwyneth revealed her strong suspicions of what had really happened. "Selig was ambushed and killed by Herlaug."

Ingunn felt saddened by what had happened to Selig but she cautioned Gwyneth to keep her distance from Ragnar's brother. "If he has killed once, he will kill again. Make certain you are not the target."

"He has no reason to kill me. I pose no threat

to him, but I'm worried about Erica." She did not see her in the crowd. She started to go in search of her when the sound of a horn rent the air. The jarls and their bondi had begun to assemble. Had Erica and Torin been able to find any witnesses who would testify against Herlaug? Gwyneth could only wonder.

"It will be a long time before the meeting is over," Ingunn murmured. "Did you eat, Gwyneth?"

Gwyneth shook her head, wishing now that she hadn't slept so long and had taken time for *dagveror*. She was hungry already. By tonight she would be starving. As if reading her thoughts, Ingunn pulled a slice of bread and a piece of cheese from a small pouch at her side.

"There is too much food here for me. We'll divide it."

"No! You need it for your baby."

"I insist." Ingunn would not take no for an answer.

Gwyneth ate in a hurry, then she and Ingunn joined the throng. A large tent had been erected at the foot of the hill where the thegns and jarls sat in wooden chairs brought from their halls. Even among men of his own stature, Ragnar stood out and was clearly visible.

On the hillside, the bondi gathered together, arranging themselves according to which jarl they served. Some were as finely dressed as their leaders, others wore garments that were threadbare. Nevertheless, each freeman's vote was equal to that of another. Behind them in their ragged garments, their heads closely cropped to identify them as slaves, stood the thralls.

As a gray-haired old man stepped forward, Ingunn said that he was the lawgiver. After he finished reciting the Viking law and traditions as was customary, a rumbling undercurrent of voices blew in the wind from the hillside where the onlookers stood. Giving them a stern look, the lawgiver motioned to a tall man who again raised a horn to his lips, after which there was silence once more.

Ingunn told Gwyneth that under Viking law, a jarl or bondi charged with a crime such as theft or murder would be brought before a court of judges made up of his peers. The accused could either plead innocent or guilty. If he pleaded innocent he could call witnesses to testify to the facts of his honesty and good character as well as to his innocence, or he could demand a trial by ordeal.

Gwyneth wondered how wrongdoers were dealt with here. Would the punishments be more lenient than those meted out in Wessex, or would they be more barbaric?

The meeting began. Minor crimes were first. A bondi was charged with cutting down a tree. His punishment was to help the landowner plant a new orchard of trees. The assembly was reminded that only landowners could cut down trees, but chastised landowners to do so sparingly because trees were more important than gold in the Northland.

Another bondi was charged with killing a thrall, a minor offense among the Vikings, who considered these slaves to be little more than farm animals, fit mostly to spread dung in the field or toil over the hot fires in the kitchen and bathhouses. Under Viking law, a master could put an aged slave to death as one would an old dog, but to kill another man's property was a crime. The bondi was ordered to take the thrall's place for a time not to exceed one month.

As each sentence was passed and each decision made, the assembled peoples showed their agreement with the decision by striking their shields or rattling their spears. Ingunn called this "grasping of weapons." Gwyneth found the noise unpleasant and put her hands over her ears to block out the sound.

The baser crimes were judged next. Ingunn whispered in Gwyneth's ear that harsh punishments were used to keep order and peace among men who were hardened by their struggle with nature. Only upon the sea did the Northmen take the law into their own hands. Upon the ocean there was no law but victory and no punishment but defeat. On land the Vikings faced a stricter structure of laws.

Indeed, many of the punishments seemed severe to Gwyneth. A woman found to have committed thievery was sentenced to slavery as was a man who was a debtor. Several insurrectionists were ordered to have their hands struck from their arms and this penalty was carried out before the throng. Gwyneth cringed as the second man lay his arm across a large tree stump waiting for the axe to come down. She couldn't bear to look. As her stomach tightened she feared that she would be sick.

"Are you all right?" Ingunn put her hand on Gwyneth's forehead.

Though Gwyneth knew that punishment meted out in Wessex could be just as severe as in the Northland, she had never witnessed a public punishment at home. Her mother had wanted to shelter her from the cruelty of the world. Regretting her show of weakness, she resolved to stand bravely by to watch the other proceedings.

A woman and man were brought before the crowd and charged with adultery. The woman's husband had found the two together in his bed when he had returned unexpectedly from a voyage. Although it was within his rights to kill a man found with his wife, the man had elected to have the matter settled before the assembly. The guilty pair were ordered to be hanged from the nearest tree so that both would be punished equally.

Gwyneth heard whispers about the wergild, the monetary levy imposed on wrongdoers to compensate those whom they had wronged. It was something that she intended to mention to her father when she saw him again, for it seemed an interesting and fair way to stop men from killing a man for a small transgression.

When a man found guilty of stealing another man's sheep was ordered to pay a wergild but another man guilty of the same offense who had no wealth was commanded to lose his hand, Gwyneth had second thoughts about the Viking way of doing things. It seemed that the wealthy felt no pain and that the punishment lasted no longer than it took to pay out an amount of gold whereas those who had no money suffered the loss of a hand, a punishment that lasted all their lives.

"Surely Herlaug will be punished more severely than just paying a wergild," she said to Ingunn. "No amount of money can bring Selig back to us."

"Payment of wergild is for wrongful killing or bodily injury but you must remember that Selig was the son of a jarl."

The proceeding took up most of the morning. It looked as if they would continue well into the early evening hours. As Ingunn spread her cloak upon the ground and offered Gwyneth a seat, she accepted.

A forest of bodies hid the goings-on from Gwyneth's eyes, but she did not care. This matter of punishments was not to her liking, though she had to admit that most of the judgments seemed to be moderately fair.

Wishing she could find some shade, Gwyneth closed her eyes to the bright noon sun. She could hear the murmur of the crowd as three murderers stood before the judges. They were ordered to pay the victim's family a wergild, the estimated value of the dead person's worth. Since one of the victims had been a poor bondi, the payment was minimal, but a rich bondi had brought a wergild of several pieces of silver, two pigs, four sheep, and three cows. A man found guilty of wounding another man in a brawl was ordered to make "bone payment" to the victim in the form of enough silver to make amends for his wounds.

Lying back upon Ingunn's cloak and looking up at the sky, Gwyneth tried to put all thoughts of the Thing far from her mind. No matter what happened, no matter what the verdict was, it would not, could not, bring Selig back.

A blood-red sun smoldered on the horizon as Selig moved steadily towards his destination. They were nearly there and just in time he thought, rubbing at his aching bottom. Now he knew why he much preferred traveling by ship rather than on horseback.

It had been a long, tiring journey for him and Baugi through dense forests and over hard, rocky ground. As they crossed meadows that dazzled the eye with wildflowers he was in high spirits, anxious to be reunited with Gwyneth.

As he traveled, Selig joined a tiny caravan of those making their way to the Thing. It was an assembly of men whose ranks varied from impoverished peasants to landowners, shipbuilders, artisans, and a few wealthy Viking raiders. Some rode on horseback, many in broken-down carts, while there were still others who straggled along behind with only their legs to carry them. Despite the difference in their stations, however, all would speak with an equal voice at the Thing.

Selig arrived at his destination none too soon. He was stiff and sore, tired and hungry. As he got down

off his horse he looked around, admiring the place
his father had chosen for the gathering. It was a
perfect meeting place, a natural arena of open,
grassy space surrounded by rocky ledges and trees.

"You look hungry and thirsty," one of the men
in the caravan said to Selig. Unpacking one of his
large, leather bags filled with food, cooking ware,
and a few worthless trinkets, he proved himself to
be a crafty merchant by selling his goods to several
women in the camp who either sought to quench
their boredom or supply themselves with items they
had forgotten to bring.

Selig had a few coins that Roland had given to
him, enough to buy water and dried meat for him
and Baugi. As he ate he walked about, stretching
his legs, familiarizing himself with the camp. Newly
erected wooden huts had been set up, but Selig decided to sleep out in the open and save the shelters
for the women and children.

Selig wanted to stay hidden so as not to alert Herlaug to his presence; thus he stayed towards the back
of the crowd. Squinting he searched the assembly
for his father and Erica, but there were too many
people for him to be able to find them right away.
He just listened to the proceedings, wanting to wait
until just the right moment to tell his story.

The afternoon events seemed to move rather
quickly. A bondi had been charged with killing a
thrall. The bondi was ordered to take the thrall's
place for a time not to exceed one month. A man
found guilty of stealing a goat was ordered to make
payment in silver. Another, found guilty of stealing
a sheep, was given the penalty of working for the
wronged owner of the lamb until the payment was
made.

The next two thralls, judged guilty of murdering
a brutal owner, knew no mercy. They were told to
lay their heads on the stump of a tree and were

quickly beheaded. In the Viking world it was usually an eye for an eye and a tooth for a tooth, though there were times when a murderer's family had to pay to the victim's family a wergild in the value of the man murdered. If there was no money, another form of restitution had to be made. In some cases that meant one of the murderer's family members being forced to serve as a thrall. A victim's family always had to be recompensed for their loss, though the punishment did not always fit the crime. And yet at least there was some sort of justice, Selig thought.

As the proceedings continued, Selig got tired of standing. Lolling on the ground, he closed his ears and eyes to what was going on and went over and over again in his mind all that he planned to say.

Suddenly a loud scream rent the air, a tormented cry so grief-stricken that it pierced through Selig's self-imposed barrier. Bolting to his feet, he saw a young boy down on his knees, crying as he held on to his father's leg.

"No! You can't take him away! You can't! You can't! I won't let you. He is the only family I have!"

Selig nudged the man next to him in the ribs. "What has happened here?"

The man shrugged. "The boy's father has been judged guilty of stealing from one of his betters. The man wants restitution as is his right, but the guilty man has no money."

"What has been judged as the penalty then?" Selig asked, feeling the necessity to help.

"He is being taken away, forced to serve as a thrall. Not an unusual sentence . . ."

Something about the boy reminded him of himself and though he had been determined to stay hidden, he elbowed his way toward the platform. Though it was hot, he pulled up the hood on his cloak. Finding out how much the debt was for the stolen property, he offered to pay from his own pouch. The sight of the smile on the boy's face as he was reunited with his father was worth a hundred times what Selig had promised in silver.

As he moved towards the back of the crowd, Selig looked first to the left, then to the right, trying to catch sight of Herlaug. He was relieved to see his uncle so engrossed in conversation with another man that he had not even glanced his way. He was safe. He had not been seen.

"Gwyneth . . . look at that man. There is something about him that is strangely familiar, don't you agree . . . ?"

Gwyneth turned her head in the direction of Ingunn's stare and thought for a moment that she was seeing things. "He . . . he looks . . . looks like Selig." The man was the same height, had the same muscular build, walked with the same bold stride. Wisps of blond hair the same color as Selig's jutted out from the hood of the cloak. As if in a trance, she started after him.

"It can not be!" For a moment Ingunn feared she had been unkind to remind Gwyneth of her dead lover. She started to tell her so, but as she turned her head she realized that Gwyneth was gone.

THIRTY-THREE

Selig kept his head down as he moved through the crowd. Though he was quite certain he hadn't been seen, he had a strange feeling that he was being followed. Gathering his cloak tightly around him, he looked over his shoulder but saw only a shadow.

"It's my imagination." Or was it? As he walked along he sensed a presence behind him. Was it Herlaug? No. As he climbed the hill and looked down, he could see his uncle from a distance, ingratiating himself with anyone who came near him. Selig clenched his jaw as he thought about his uncle's treachery.

He walked at a brisk pace, then stopped and turned around as he sensed once again that he was being followed. This time he saw enough of his "shadow" to realize who it was.

"Gwyneth!" For a moment he wanted to wait for her, gather her in his arms, and tell her how glad he was to be alive, but he realized that were they seen together Herlaug might be forewarned. Therefore, he ran as fast as his feet would carry him.

Gwyneth tried to catch up with the man but he was fleet of foot and after a moment or two she was easily outdistanced. Even so, the fact that he had run away from her made her all the more curious.

Perhaps he knew I would recognize him if I got closer.

That was it—she knew it in her heart. Her mind whirled with foolish flights of fantasy, but she pushed them from her mind. It couldn't be Selig. Selig had drowned! And yet . . .

"Could it be? Was it possible? If it was, why would he run away? Why wouldn't he seek her out, or his father, or Erica? Why come to the Thing hidden beneath a hooded cloak? Why not confront Herlaug openly?

Puzzled, she walked up and down through the crowd, searching for any sight of him. She had begun to give up hope when her eyes were drawn to a small group of children. They had formed a circle and were chattering excitedly. In the middle of that circle was a black, long-haired animal Gwyneth recognized only too well.

"Baugi!"

Selig was alive! He was alive! She had thought that she had lost him but he was there. Though myriad questions pulsed through her brain as to how, when, and why, she made no further attempt to find him. She had to trust that Selig had his reasons for staying hidden.

Gwyneth felt light of heart as she made her way back to Ingunn. Though the afternoon dragged on and on until there were two remaining cases to be heard, she was in a peaceful mood.

"You haven't stopped smiling since you came back," Ingunn noted. "It was Selig, wasn't it?"

Though Gwyneth refused to answer, determined to honor Selig's apparent wish to keep his identity a secret, her eyes gave her away.

"Oh, Gwyneth, I know it was!" Ingunn gave Gwyneth's hand a squeeze just as the lawgiver struck a bronze gong.

The sound reverberated in Selig's ears. The moment he had waited for was quickly approaching.

The next two cases involved accusations of murder. Though the men pleaded their innocence, the judgment was carried out quickly. As the executioner brought out his battle-ax, testing it on the leg bone of a cow, Selig envisioned his uncle's head on the body of one of the murderers. He saw the look of anger quickly change to fear and then horror as the ax came down upon his head.

"No!" The second guilty man became hysterical at the sight of the severed head. Pulling free of the men who held him, he ran down the hillside, screaming his innocence until he was caught and a piece of cloth stuffed in his mouth. He was dragged to the tree stump and his head held down by the hair.

For just a moment Selig wondered if there had really been a mistake. What if the man was telling the truth? What if he was innocent? He took a step closer, feeling a twinge of doubt about the system of justice. That was, until he recognized the guilty man.

"Jokel!"

Ironically, it was the man whom Selig had banished from the settlement. The same man who had led the Danes against them and set fire to their houses. In deference to Gwyneth's beliefs he had shown the man more mercy than he deserved and had ordered him set adrift in a small boat out in the ocean but Jokel had survived. He had come all the way to Norway only to face death once again because of his evil deeds.

It was as if Viking law had been justified in Selig's mind. If the Viking laws were harsh at times, it was because they had to be. Only so could they survive in a world where bloodshed reigned.

Selig listened as the lawgiver asked if there were any remaining judgments to be made. Taking a deep breath, he started to raise his hand to make his announcement when he heard a familiar voice.

It was Erica, accusing Herlaug not only of kidnapping her younger brother but murdering her older brother as well.

"He took him out to sea in a ship, threw him overboard, and left him in the ocean to die!"

"I am innocent of this wrongful charge," Herlaug growled, his eyes roaming to where Torin stood. No doubt he thought that Erica and Torin had conspired together to bring him down.

As he walked down the hill with Baugi following at his heels, Selig focused his eyes on Herlaug's face. He could see the anger in his eyes, but that was tempered with an insolent grin. The treacherous villain was certain he was going to get away with his crime, but then why not? No doubt he had come away unscathed by his misdeeds many times before.

Herlaug stepped forward so that the assembled throng could look upon his face. "I demand a trial by combat," he said. "Let it be proven before all this assembly that I am innocent of this accusation." His eyes looked into those of Ragnar as if to proclaim that he was being humiliated before the gathering.

"And would you fight a woman?" The lawgiver's eyes touched upon Erica, who stood with her feet apart, a sword in her upraised hand.

"Of course not!" Herlaug guffawed, then winked at those who by their actions proved to be his supporters. "That is, unless I am forced to do so."

"I want to fight him!" Erica was determined, fighting against Torin, who tried to hold her back. "I know that God will be on my side!"

"Then so be it."

Within sight of the sea was a natural arena of open, grassy land. The lawgiver began to pace off the battleground, setting down boundaries. Whoever stepped beyond the line was considered to have fled.

There was an uproar as Erica moved across the grass, her head held high. Several men placed wagers upon this strange battle and not all of those wagers were put in Herlaug's favor.

"Choose your weapons . . ." the lawgiver said.

Herlaug started to make a grab at one of the sturdiest-looking swords but before he could reach out, Baugi lunged. Growling, he jumped on Herlaug and knocked him to the ground.

"That's my son's dog. I'm sure of it!" Ragnar was stunned. A look of hope gleamed in his eyes as he scanned the area for any sight of Selig. Then he saw him. "Selig!"

"Selig!" Erica was so happy that she cried.

Selig ran forward to pull Baugi off Herlaug. "Easy . . . easy. Don't eat him up. You will spoil all my fun." Grabbing his uncle by the shirt, he pulled him off the ground. "What my sister says is true, only I jumped and I didn't die. But your intent was that I would."

"Nephew. You are alive. By Odin's teeth, I never meant you any harm."

"Liar."

"May the goddess Hel freeze your blood," Herlaug whispered beneath his breath. His fingers clenched on the amber buckle of his belt.

"I spit on you," Selig answered. "You are no kin of mine!"

Mayhem ruled as those in the crowd took sides. The lawgiver took up the bronze gong and struck it to bring silence.

Selig took advantage of the quiet to speak. "I will take my sister's place and thus make my own charges against this man who is my father's brother. He did lie to me and attempt to take my life. Had it not been for the dog and my good fortune that a ship passed by, I would have been food for the fish."

If Herlaug had viewed Selig as a rival before, he

loathed him now. His eyes blazed with hatred, but Selig answered his glare with an even fiercer fury.

Gwyneth stood watching as the two men chose their swords. Though she had seen Selig fight before, had faith in his prowess, and believed that right would win out over wrong, she nonetheless whispered a frantic prayer. Removing the dragon's tear pendant from her neck, she moved quickly to his side, slipped it over his head, and kissed him gently on the lips.

"My heart is with you," she said, clasping her hands together to keep them from trembling. "May my God and your gods protect you and keep you from harm!"

Gwyneth's gesture gave Selig a feeling of invincibility as he turned to face Herlaug.

"I may have failed to kill you once but I will not fail again," Herlaug whispered so that only Selig could hear.

The lawgiver's voice was not as hushed. He spoke loud and clear, setting forth the terms of the combat. The fight was to last only until one of the two men was wounded.

Gwyneth gave a gasp of relief, but the crowd roared their disapproval loudly, thirsting for the sight of more blood. All commotion ceased, however, as the lawgiver raised his hand.

"Almighty Thor, we call upon you to witness this combat and for all assembled to bear witness as to the final judgment." He struck the bronze gong again.

Herlaug and Selig stripped off their outer clothing and wore only their trousers. Both were well-muscled men, although Herlaug was stouter and Selig taller.

Gwyneth's hands were cold, her throat dry and her eyes moist as she watched Herlaug circling Selig like a skulking wolf.

Selig moved with silent grace, like a hunter. The Viking throng elbowed each other to get a better view, the crowd becoming silent as Herlaug lunged swiftly like a striking snake. Selig easily danced aside, unscathed by his uncle's sword.

"I won't let you ruin everything for me! I want you gone!" Herlaug said between clenched teeth. He struck again, this blow parried by Selig's blade. Again and again the sound of iron on iron reverberated through the hillside along with the voices of the Vikings calling loudly to the fighter they favored.

"If only you had realized," Selig taunted. "I didn't even want to be jarl. I would have turned it down. All of this could have been avoided." His thrust missed Herlaug by the breadth of a finger.

As the sun rose high in the sky, the two men strained together, each holding his own. Gwyneth stood as still as a statue, afraid to look yet afraid not to see what was happening.

The veins swelled in Herlaug's throat as he made a sudden lunge for Selig, who felt the blade just touch his ear. He leaped forward, aiming a blow to Herlaug's arm, but as he moved his foot struck a rock and he fell to the earth with a thud.

The air was silent as Herlaug moved in to take quick advantage of his good fortune. Too quick. Selig was only changing his sword from hand to hand, but as Herlaug threw himself forward, the sword connected with his arm.

Herlaug howled. Though the terms of the judgment had been met, though he had been wounded and should have ceased fighting, he revealed his blood lust. His face was dark with the urge to spill his opponent's blood.

"Hold . . ." Moving forward, the lawgiver tried to stand between Herlaug and Selig, but Herlaug pushed him out of the way.

"Get back, old man!" He lunged at Selig again and again, at last connecting with his blade.

Gwyneth gasped, covering her eyes. When she looked up again, Selig's arm dripped blood. Herlaug's sword had hit its target.

Once again, the lawgiver stepped between the two men. "The decision has been made." He pointed to Herlaug. "You have defied our law. You have scorned the judgment of the Thing. For that you will be punished."

The angry roar of the crowd proved that they thought so, too. Herlaug had lost and by the rules of the Thing that meant he was guilty and should therefore have to pay the penalty.

To Selig's relief, it was decided that Herlaug was to leave the Northland for a year. If Selig would have preferred the sentence to be for a lifetime, well, it was better than nothing.

"He shall be outcast and received nowhere among men from this day until the time of the Thing next year. Like a wolf, he shall be driven away by all men. He shall be shunned wherever fires are tended, wherever men and women gather, wherever ships sail, wherever the wind blows. He is welcome nowhere except for the darkened halls of Hel."

Out of habit, Herlaug turned towards his brother. "They are wrong, Ragnar. I didn't try to kill Selig. He is my own flesh and blood. You must believe me!"

Ragnar shook his head. "I can not! The look in your eyes when you gazed at my son, the violence in your actions, shout louder than your words. Though you are my brother, though I have believed your lies many times, I can not believe you now!" With a sigh, Ragnar turned his back on his brother.

"No!" Like a man under a spell, Herlaug slowly moved past the group of Vikings, motioning to those who had followed him in the past to join with him now. None accepted his invitation. He was alone and suddenly he knew it. "I'll remember all of you who turned on me. I'll remember and exact my revenge."

It was a threat that chilled Gwyneth to the core. She felt a hand on her arm and jumped, but it was Erica.

"And so the matter is laid to rest, at least for the moment. For a year we will all be safe."

"Will we?" Gwyneth was not so sure. She looked up at Erica in awe. "Weren't you scared at the thought of fighting Herlaug?"

Erica confessed. "I was so scared I was shaking in my shoes, but I was determined to see Herlaug punished for what he did to me, to Geordie, to Torin, and to Selig."

"Have you ever seen such a stubborn, foolhardy woman?" Torin came up behind Erica and put his arm around her. "I think she is trying to give me gray hair." He nuzzled her neck. "Even so, I have never been so proud." Seeing Gwyneth's apprehension written clearly in her eyes he added, "Selig is all right. The wound is not deep. The healing woman is caring for him now."

"I have to see him!" There was so much she wanted to say.

Lying on the ground, Selig was aware of all the turmoil and the people hovering over him. He dimly perceived that the fight was over, that he had won, and that Herlaug had been meted out at least the convenience of human companionship for the next year. Touching his arm, feeling the sticky wet of his own blood, he could smile. The pain had been worth it.

"Selig . . . !"

Hearing Gwyneth's voice, he pushed himself up

on one elbow, grimacing in pain as it started the bleeding in his arm anew. As she leaned down to touch his face, however, it was as if all the pain went away.

"I thought you were dead. I thought I had lost you. But just like a miracle, you are here and words can never tell you how I feel. All I can say is that I love you. I know now that I always will . . ."

Selig had dreamed of her so often that for just a moment he feared she was a mirage. He reached out tentatively and, feeling her soft skin, he knew she was real. He gathered her close in his arms; she clung to him as he cradled her to his chest. "I have been a foolish, selfish, stubborn fool."

"You?" She pulled away just enough to be able to look into his eyes. "What do you mean? I would say it was I who should make that statement."

"I should have understood how you felt being away from your people and how important your faith is to you. I do now, Gwyneth. I learned many things after I jumped overboard." He repeated, "Many things."

His hands caressed her in a manner that spoke of his yearning, burning her where he touched her. It had been so long since they had made love. Too long. She wanted to heal him with her touch, wanted to blend herself with his body until they were fused so tightly together they could never be separated again.

"You are like my heart, Gwyneth. I have never loved anything as much as I love you." Forgetful of his pain, he sat up. "And because of that love, I am asking you once again to marry me."

She didn't hesitate. "I will! Erica told me about the Viking ceremony and I . . ."

"No!" While he was with Roland Thorvalsson he had done a great deal of thinking and had come to a decision. "We will be married by a priest!"

"A priest . . ." For a moment she was confused. There were no priests here.

"I'm taking you back to our home in Wessex to be reunited with your family. We can be married while we are there. That is, if they can forgive and forget what happened."

"Back home!" How could he have realized how very much she wanted to go back there. So much so that she suddenly felt close to tears.

"You're crying. Have I said something to hurt you?"

She shook her head. "They are tears of happiness, not of sorrow." Was there a chance for happiness for them? Surely at the moment it seemed so.

"We have so much time to make up for. So much time. Shall we begin right now?" Selig's eyes gleamed with mischief and desire.

"Not now. Later." She silenced him with a kiss that made him impatient for the night to come.

THIRTY-FOUR

A copper-colored sun hid behind the clouds as it set on the horizon, only to be replaced by a big, silver moon. The air smelled fresh with the scent of wildflowers and greenery. Campfires danced across the meadow as all those who had been at the Thing made camp for the night.

Side by side, Gwyneth and Selig joined in the night's festivities, sharing a horn of mead. Realizing that his arm pained him, Gwyneth helped him eat despite his protestations that he could manage on his own. Once the evening meal was over, they settled in for the night. This time when Gwyneth retired to her shelter, she was not alone.

There on her pallet, concealed from all those around them, she lay in Selig's arms, content just to be with him. Then, when he kissed her, there was a familiarity that sent a tingling warmth through her. Her senses were full of him. Strange how, after all they had been through, she could be shy, but suddenly she was.

"Is something wrong?" he asked, sensing her reticence.

"No, everything is right. It's just that . . ." To her mortification, she blushed.

He pulled her closer. With strong, deft fingers he undressed her, running his warm hand over the graceful curve of her waist and hips. For a long moment he just looked at her, exploring every inch of her with visual hunger.

The fires had blended with the summer heat. It was hot inside the tent, but instead of deterring Selig, it merely inspired him. Reaching for an earthenware jug, he moistened his fingers. Motioning for her to turn over, he ran his hand over her back, sliding down to her hips, then her legs.

Once again, he awakened passions within her. His hand was making her dizzy. She was drowning. Drifting away.

"I want to touch you all over. Every part of you." More than anything, he wanted to commit her body to memory, to savor her softness.

Turning her over on her back, he traced a moist finger across the peaks of her breasts—first one, then the other—making gentle, erotic circles. Wetting his fingers again, he gently trailed a path from the cleavage between her breasts to the indentation of her navel. Gwyneth's breath caught in her throat. Her eyes were deep blue pools of desire, beckoning him, enticing him.

Selig stretched out beside her again. Every muscle in his body was taut, including the pulsating hardness of his manhood. His tongue edged along his lower lip, then he bent to kiss her. Not on the mouth but on her abdomen, tracing the indentation there with his tongue. Licking. Stroking. Gwyneth let out a sigh, closing her eyes.

"I want to cool you off, too," she whispered.

"Cool me off?" Selig let out his breath in a long, ragged sigh. "Impossible." Still he complied as she reached for the jug of water.

Moistening her hands, Gwyneth slid her hands beneath his tunic, tenderly caressing his chest. Strange how touching him was just as stimulating as being touched. As she heard him suck in a shuddering breath, she felt a burning deep inside her.

Drawing the moment out just as he had done with her, she moved lower, unfastening his trousers. Moving her hand inside, she traced his hipbone. "I ache for you inside me," she breathed. How quickly the meek can become daring, she thought.

Selig aided her, tugging at his clothing. Entangling himself for just a moment, he swore an oath, then kicked the garments away.

Suddenly she remembered. "Your wound!"

He grinned. "I've had worse wounds than this. I will survive. But I can't survive one more night without you!"

She could feel his pulsating hardness straining against her as he cradled her against him."Oh . . . G-w-y-n . . . !"

Skin against skin. Was there anything that could compare with that? Selig doubted it. Particularly when it was her soft, fragrant skin.

She entwined her arms around his muscled neck and lifted her mouth to his. As they kissed, their bodies writhed together in a slow, delicate dance. She was alive, soaring. He was losing control.

"Slow. I want to take it slow," he said. As she moaned and arched her hips, he gasped again and again.

Gwyneth sighed, opening her mouth to his exploration. His tongue plunged, rhythmically stroking like the waves of the sea. He could sense the pent-up passion in her that rivaled his own, but still he didn't want to hurry. He was leisurely in his exploration, gentle, taking incredible care to make certain that she was coming as close to readiness as he.

"You're beautiful . . . ! So beautiful . . . I saw your face, even when I was drifting in the sea. I was determined that we would be together again."

Watching her face, he massaged her with all the artistry that he had used when he sculpted her face and figure in wood. He ran his hands over the contours of her breasts, her stomach, her thighs. He parted her, sliding his fingers into her warm dampness. It caused him to tighten inside. He felt himself harden even more.

"*Now*, Selig . . ." She was trembling. In his arms she wasn't shy any longer, she was demanding. A wild thing. Her body was liquid with agonizing sensations. If this was the way Eve had acted when she had tempted Adam, if it was sinful to feel this way, she didn't care.

Selig hovered over her, staring down at her for just a moment, whispering words of endearment, both in the Viking tongue and in her language.

Selig was not a particularly sentimental man. He had always thought sentimentality was foreign to his nature but it wasn't tonight. Somehow being apart had changed him, made him realize what he really treasured.

Gwyneth opened up her legs, her hands moving frantically across the muscles of his buttocks. As his mouth found hers, she reached between their bodies and guided him into her. She had never realized how incomplete she had felt but now she did. As if for the first time in her life, she was truly alive!

She called out his name as he moved. Slowly at first, then harder, faster. He moved deeper, so far within her that it was as if she blended with his flesh. Their separateness faded as she absorbed him into herself. With her hands, body, and mouth, she tried to show him how much she loved him, wanted to give him everything there was to give in declaration of her feelings.

Selig heard himself whispering her name, felt her legs tighten around him. He pulled back, then slowly brought himself deep inside her again, plunging, sliding. She was making sounds that drove him over the edge. He groaned as a kaleidoscope of swirling sensations engulfed him, rendered him thoughtless for just a moment in time. Then he shut his eyes. His breath was warm against the hollow of her neck.

"Gwyneth . . . !" Call it Valhalla, call it heaven, he had just found out that it really existed. For the moment he wanted nothing more.

It was an emotional journey back from the assembly. Everyone from Ragnar's household was overjoyed that Selig was alive and well, but an air of sadness hovered over the caravan also. Despite all the difficulty Herlaug had caused, Ragnar had a deep affection for his younger brother and he was obviously troubled.

"It's my fault. I should have listened to the warnings but I thought . . . I hoped . . ." Riding up beside Selig, he reached out and touched his uninjured arm. "My foolishness nearly cost me the life of my eldest son."

Selig shook his head. He wouldn't let his father take the blame for his own mistake. "I should never have set foot on that ship no matter how much Herlaug pleaded. Erica and Torin had warned me." He tried to lighten his father's mood. "But all turned out well in the end. Let's hope that Herlaug will learn a lesson and that when he comes back we can be a real family."

Selig's eyes met Gwyneth's as she rode in the wagon and he couldn't keep from smiling. The look that passed between the two did not go unnoticed by Ragnar. "You speak of family in a manner that tells me that you have something to say besides any talk of my brother."

"Gwyneth and I . . ." Selig motioned for his father to ride with him beside the wagon.

"She is going to have a child. My grandson!" It was obvious that Ragnar was elated by the very thought of another generation beneath his roof. "That is good. My hall is too quiet. There should be the sound that babies make."

"I'm not . . . !" Gwyneth looked down at her hands. At least she didn't think that she was with child. She had, however, stopped taking Ingunn's herbs so anything could happen.

"You are not? Then what . . . ?" Ragnar queried.

"Gwyneth and I are going to be married."

"They are going to be married," Ragnar repeated, so loud that nearly everyone could hear. "And such a wedding it will be! We will invite every friend and relative that I can remember. Since it is still summer you will be married in the sacred grove." He laughed joyfully. "And such a feast we will have!"

"Father . . ." Selig tried to get Ragnar's attention but he was babbling on and on about the details of his son's wedding.

"My family is growing right before my eyes just as I had hoped." He turned to Torin. "You have been responsible for bringing me two of my children. Only one is left. The son I sired in Eire. Kodran. Kodran Ragnarsson! Oh, that he could be at this wedding, too." He shrugged. "But that is too much to ask." He laughed again. "You are fortunate that I already have a wife to nag me and that I did not see your Gwyneth first. She is quite a beauty. Quite a beauty indeed."

"Father . . ."

"I wish the wedding were tomorrow. I can hardly wait to escort you to the *skuldelev*, Gwyneth and I . . ."

"We are not going to be married here!" Selig exclaimed, determined to straighten out the misunderstanding.

"Not married here?" Ragnar's smile faded. He looked so crestfallen that Gwyneth felt guilty. "At the settlement then." He shrugged. "I was hoping to host the festivities but I can just as well sail with you to the western coast of the Anglo-Saxons. I'll take three ships. Enough for the relatives!"

"We aren't getting married at my settlement, either."

Ragnar's heavy brows drew together in a worried frown. "What are you trying to tell me?"

"I am taking Gwyneth back to Wessex. Back to her family. We are going to be married by a priest."

The silence that met Selig's disclosure was deafening. It was obvious that Ragnar was thunderstruck. "It is a mistake!"

"It is the only way."

"Bah!" The look that Ragnar gave Gwyneth clearly showed that she had suddenly earned his disfavor. "I say again that it is a mistake. One that I made myself once long ago. I wanted to make my dear Colleen happy, thus I married her according to her beliefs and ways. In the end I was most vilely betrayed by one who swore to serve her God."

"For that I am sorry, but you must admit that there are betrayals even among us Vikings." Though Selig didn't speak Herlaug's name, the inference was unmistakable. "Besides, I am beginning to think that we might be able to learn from the Christians."

"Bite your tongue!"

Selig struggled to make his father understand the importance of the issue. "I love Gwyneth. I will not give her up. If that means giving in to her wishes, so be it." He hoped that she, like Erica, would eventually marry by Viking law.

Ragnar sat astride his horse like a pillar of iron, strong in his determination. He raised his hand to command his son's attention. "Don't! Do not give in on this matter. If she loves you enough she will try to understand our ways."

"And if I love her enough I will do everything in

my power to learn about hers." Selig didn't want to argue. "I have made a promise. One I do not want to break. Therefore, in a week's time I am sailing for Wessex."

A steady parade of women moved towards the already crowded wooden bathhouse. After the dust and grime of the journey to the Thing, the water would be especially precious, Gwyneth thought, clutching her thick linen towel. She smiled as she remembered how her father and the priests had always called the Norsemen unwashed heathens. How false that statement was. Among the Vikings, she had found cleanliness was expected.

"May I walk with ye to the bathhouse?" Erica asked, coming up behind her.

"Yes, I would like that."

"We can talk of the wedding. Will ye hae flowers?" Erica asked, then said wistfully, "Were ye marrying in Alba, ye could hae a bouquet of heather."

"There will be lots of flowers. My mother will make certain that I have a bridal garland woven of wheat, rosemary, and myrtle for good fortune and . . . fertility." That was, if her mother accepted in her heart that her grandchildren would be sired by a Viking, Gwyneth thought.

Now that she realized that she would truly be going back to Wessex, she was nervous about her parents' reaction to Selig. Could they find it in their hearts to forgive him for leading a Viking raid that fateful day? She pushed her doubts from her mind. They must. She would have to find a way to make them understand that she was only happy when she was with him.

"And . . . and I imagine my bouquet will be made of magenta corn roses, white shepherd's purse, and violet and blue delphiniums, my mother's favorite flowers," she continued softly.

"Ye are troubled. I feel it." Erica grasped her wrist. "If ye think that there is any danger in going back, dunna go!"

"I must! As much as I love Selig, I can not shut my family out of my life. I will not!" Suddenly she felt a surge of excitement. "Oh, Erica, if I can only make them see what a good man Selig is, perhaps my father will give us a large tract of land. Perhaps Selig could even see to the building of a castle and . . ."

"Nae." Erica stopped walking. "That will never be. If ye really think that will come to pass then ye do not know Selig at all and my heart aches for what will come of this journey."

Suddenly there was a wall of tension between the two women. They walked silently past the outhouses, past the fire pit where refuse was burned, and came at last to the bathhouse. Before they entered, however, Erica took Gwyneth aside, asking her the question that troubled her.

"I know that ye love Selig, Gwyneth, but if ye are faced with a choice of him or yer old ways and family, what will it be?"

Gwyneth was offended by the question. "Why . . . why, Selig, of course!"

"And ye truly think that ye can do as I have and live the Viking way?"

I won't have to, Gwyneth thought. *Somehow I can make Selig see that we can have a much better life in Wessex*. A long time had passed since he had spent time there as a slave. A time of healing.

All the way back from the Thing that thought had been on her mind. She would have the priest talk with Selig and make him understand the teachings of the Church. Once he truly grasped the idea and his faith blossomed, he wouldn't want to go back to the Northland.

"Of course I can do as you have done, Erica," she said convincingly. "You will see. Selig and I will have a good life!"

Together they stepped inside the bathhouse, where the cauldrons of water boiled over the fire to create a sauna. The men had already had their baths and were now out and about beyond the confines of the steaming room.

Tugging off her clothes and pinning her red hair atop her head, Erica quickly made her way to one of the three giant tubs in the middle of the room.

"Come on, Gwyneth! Hurry, before all the space is taken." Erica relaxed in the waist-high water.

The smoke and steam merged together to sting Gwyneth's eyes, but even so, she pulled off her garments and laid them in a neat pile. It was hot inside. For a long moment she closed her eyes, dreaming about her wedding. This time would be different. This time she was marrying for love.

Suddenly a shrill cry startled her. "Fool, you have nearly scalded me," Nissa hissed.

Gwyneth tried hard to see what was going on, but the smoke and steam merged together to sting her eyes and make clear vision difficult. No doubt the slave girl had accidently poured some of the water meant to refresh the bath upon Nissa's sensitive skin. She, too, must have been blinded by the smoke and the steam. Gwyneth felt a twinge of pity for the thrall and anger at Nissa. Oh, if only her mother were here, she would soon take Nissa to task for her unkind treatment of her thralls. Her mother knew how to discipline them with kindness.

Ignoring Nissa's harshness with the slave girl, the other women chatted on about womanly things— children, baking bread, chores that needed to be done, and wifely duties. Gwyneth had learned that to the Vikings a woman was not, like Eve, the mother of sin, as the priests taught, but the mother of strong, brave men brought forth from their loins. A woman had one-third right to her husband's wealth and after twenty years of marriage, one-half of his wealth, which she shared among his other wives if there were more than one. She was consulted by the husband in business arrangements and was the hostess in the home, mingling freely with the men.

"His other wives," she scoffed, troubled once again by pagan ways. Polygamy was practiced openly by those who could afford it. She wondered why Ragnar had only one wife now and supposed it was because Nissa would frighten off any other prospects. Well, so would she!

Gwyneth took her place among the other women, groaning in pleasure as the hot water surrounded her. As if by magic, the water soothed her sore muscles and relaxed her so much that she could hardly keep her eyes open.

"Are you really going back, Gwyneth?" Ingunn asked.

"Yes. Selig has agreed that we will be married by a priest in a Christian ceremony."

"Why?" Ingunn was puzzled. "When two people feel love in their hearts what does it matter who says the words over them?"

"It matters to me!"

Ingunn's smile faded and in its place was a scowl. "Then perhaps you do not love Selig as much as you suppose."

"I do. I love him very much. It's just that . . ."

"What does love have to do with marriage?" asked Nissa. "Marriage is nothing more than a contract between two families." She smiled at Gwyneth as if suddenly her worth had risen in her eyes. "Ragnar is giving Selig a large sum of gold and silver to pay your bride-price."

"Bride-price?" Gwyneth laughed softly. "In Wessex my father would be handing over my dowry to Selig."

"Perhaps there are more advantages to being a Viking woman than you have ever supposed," Erica answered, getting into the conversation. "Here the bride-price or dowry remain the property of the bride after the wedding."

"You mean I can keep it?"

"Perhaps Vikings are not as pagan as you think, hinny," she whispered in her ear.

The steamy room buzzed with talk of marriage as each woman there spoke of how large or small her bride-price had been. The women talked about the beginning stages of a marriage and also about its end if the need arose. If a marriage was an unhappy one it could be ended by a divorce, though they said it did not happen very often. All that was required of the party seeking a divorce was that they summon witnesses and declare himself or herself divorced.

"How is that done in your land?" Ingunn asked.

"There is no divorce," Gwyneth answered.

"No divorce? You mean if a man is horrible, drinks too much, beats his wife too often, grunts, picks his teeth with his fingernails, is lazy, or too fond of other women you can not leave him?"

"Not unless the Holy Father gives his consent."

Ingunn grinned. "And you say that we are pagan."

Gwyneth felt the need to defend her people. "In earlier times the husband could divorce his wife at will and remarry but the Synod of Hertford denounced this custom and little by little the influence of the church promoted the stability of unions. That is the way it should be."

"If I were married to Selig I would be glad that there is no divorce," Ingunn replied good-naturedly. The matter was quickly dropped as a piece of juicy gossip surfaced. "Helga, the daughter of Einar the Walker who lives but a few miles from here, stowed away on Leif Jorunnsson's ship."

"No!" The gasp of several women was clearly audible.

"Yes." Ingunn continued. "You see, she was in love with Leif and didn't want him to leave her behind, so she dressed up like a lad and joined the Viking crew."

"Hmmmm. As skinny and plain-faced as she is, she most likely made a far better-looking young man than girl anyway," Nissa offered jealously.

"From what I've heard of Leif, it wouldn't matter if she was as homely as a goose. He's not particular," Kadlin added. "But I wish her well. And hope they can sail quickly away before her father catches up with her." She turned to Gwyneth. "And I wish you well, too. May you have every happiness."

There were more than twenty women in the room and they all offered Gwyneth their best wishes, each promising to give her a gift to wear on her wedding day. Her favorite gift of all, however, was a pair of earrings which dangled from chains looped over the ear, promised to her by Erica.

"May ye be as happy as Torin and I hae been and always love each other," she whispered, "whether ye are here or far away."

PART THREE

Dragonfire

Wessex

THIRTY-FIVE

It was a clear evening. The moon rose out of the darkening sea, watching over them like God's eye, Gwyneth thought. It was peaceful. Never in all her life had she felt so content. She was with Selig and they were here. Home! The shores of Wessex lay just ahead of them, caressed by the darkness. Once the sun rose, however, she would be able to see the sands and rocks and trees of the land where she had been born.

Waves lapped against the side of the ship, but she hardly noticed. She was too excited to think of anything but seeing her family again and telling them her news—that she had fallen deeply in love and was going to be married.

"If I can forgive him for what happened then, so can they," she whispered to herself.

In her thoughts she had it all planned. Selig had sent a messenger to Chester with a note that she had written to the priest briefly explaining that the Vikings who had brought her back home were friends. She had requested that he bring her father, mother, and brothers to an assigned meeting place where she could tell them all that had happened, including her plans to marry Selig. From there on, her father could make all the arrangements, much as he had done with Alfred.

Alfred! The only thing that ruined her happiness was the thought of the man who had been her betrothed. Alfred, the traitor. Alfred, the betrayer. That was one more thing that had to be done. She had to denounce Alfred and tell her father what he had done. Then at last she could feel that everything that had happened had come full circle.

Gwyneth sighed. How strange that as excited as she was about seeing her family, she also missed some of those she had left behind in the Northland. Erica, of course. She reached up to touch the earrings that had been her dear friend's gift. The gold rings dangled from chains looped over each ear and matched the arm rings that Torin had given to her and Selig.

"Torin . . ." She smiled as she thought about her soon-to-be brother-in-law. He had promised to teach her the game of *hneftafl* when they returned, then had quickly issued her a challenge to try and learn so well that she could beat him at the game.

"Ingunn." She had given her a linen head cloth that she had embroidered, explaining that once Gwyneth was married, she must wear it over her hair to keep it out of her eyes while she was going about her wifely household duties.

"Ragnar . . ." Last but not least was Selig's father, who, despite his disappointment that the wedding would not take place in the sacred grove, had gifted her with two items she would treasure: a russet-colored woolen cloak trimmed in ermine and an intricately carved silver brooch fashioned as a small box that could hold tiny treasures. Ragnar had also told her to rummage through his storehouses and take with her anything that her heart desired.

Gwyneth smiled as she remembered how like a little child she was, taking the greatest pleasure in carrying out his generous invitation. She had searched greedily through each chest, appraising every piece of cloth, every bauble, every fancy household item, and stashed them in a wooden trunk to carry on board the ship. Each piece would be a reminder of the Northland and of the fact that not all Vikings were heathens.

Walking to the middle of the ship, she put her hand on the trunk and then another that was its twin. Inside the other trunk were gifts from Selig—finely pleated chemises of sheer linen, gowns of honey yellow, azure blue, sea green, and her favorite color of red.

Gwyneth thought she was alone and the others were asleep. Then, she saw that a tall figure paced the deck. Selig. She recognized his muscular silhouette. They had spoken only briefly during the voyage because he had been too busy; now she found the need to communicate with him. There was so much to talk about.

"So you can not sleep, either," she whispered, coming to his side.

"No. I feel anxious. On edge. Something doesn't feel right. It's much too silent."

She laughed. "Since when is silence ominous?"

"When a man is in enemy territory," he answered unsmiling.

She put her hand on his arm. "It will not be enemy territory for long. Once my father, brother, and the priest realize that it was Alfred who is the greatest evildoer, once I tell them all that has happened to us and how I can not live without you, then all will work out well. You will see!"

Selig wished he could believe her but there was something that bothered him. Even Baugi felt it. Though the dog usually slept like a baby at night aboard the gently rolling ship, he too was on guard.

"What if your family does not see kindly to our marriage? What of that? What if the only way they feel that the past can be forgotten is by shedding my blood? What then?"

She looked at him with wide eyes. "You act as if my family are heathens."

"But of course they are not," he answered dryly. He couldn't help but be angered by her arrogant attitude, more noticeable now that she knew she was returning to Wessex. "Only we Vikings are that!"

His face was in shadow, but she could see that his mouth was set in a grim line. She moved very close to him. "Selig, I'm sorry!" She had hurt his feelings and she had never meant to do that. "I do love you."

"Even if I am a heathen?" he asked bitterly.

"You are no heathen. You are the finest man I have ever known. And the man I love."

"And will you love me just as much if I am scorned by your family?"

"I would love you if the whole world scorned you! When I say that I can not live without you, I do not lie! The most miserable I have ever been in my life is when I thought that you had died." The very reminder of that ordeal made her cry and her soft sobbing broke his heart.

"Hush . . . We will speak no more about it. I do not want to quarrel with you." He smiled. "I will have enough quarreling when I come face-to-face with your father."

He could not help himself. He took her into his arms. She felt his hard body pressing against hers. She put her arms around his neck, yearning for his kiss.

Strangely, Selig did not kiss her on the mouth. Instead he kissed her on the forehead, then gently pushed her away. "I need my strength for tomorrow and you are far too tempting. Best go to your pallet, my love. I bid you good night." He strode away, leaving her there.

THIRTY-SEVEN

The thunder of hooves against the hard ground echoed through the quiet of the courtyard as Gwyneth, on a red-gold mare, rode behind Alfred's dark brown stallion. Her horse was tied bridle to bridle to the man once her betrothed and now her abductor. He wanted to insure that she would not ride away.

How strange it was, she thought, that she was now the prisoner of a man she was once supposed to have married. How ironic. And now he planned to force her to go through with a ceremony that would tie her to him forever.

"Far better to have married Selig in the grove." At least then she would have sworn to a man she truly loved and not a man she loathed. Now the uncertainty of her fate was like a sore, festering as she rode along.

Alfred looked straight ahead as they rode in silence. The landscape looked familiar to Gwyneth and with surprise she noted that it was toward her father's hall that they traveled. Her heart leapt with joy at the thought of going home. Would her mother be sitting at the hearth overseeing the spinning? Would her father be out hunting, her brothers out hawking? Or would they be supervising the work of the slaves? Whatever they were doing, she knew they would stop in their tracks and welcome her. Then, somehow, she would enlist their help in freeing Selig and the others.

Her heart fell, however, when Alfred led his mount down the right-hand fork in the road. Her sigh was audible.

"Where are you going? I thought you were taking me home . . ."

"We are merely passing through your father's land on our way to my lands to the east," he answered curtly.

"Your lands?"

"When you disappeared, your father took pity on my loneliness and turned over a few acres to appease my bereavement and to tie us together ere the Vikings return," he explained.

"Those were my lands," she hissed. Since they had not spoken the vows they still belonged to her. "My father had no right!"

"He had every right. You are naught but a woman, after all!"

Gwyneth seethed inwardly. Looking up at the sky, she could see the sun directly overhead. They had been riding a long while. Her backside attested to the many miles they had traveled. Still, she held hope that somehow she could get the best of Alfred and find a way to aid Selig. After all, they were all alone. In his smug manliness Alfred no doubt thought she would be little threat. After all, she was, as he had put it, naught but a woman.

"You have me at your mercy, Alfred," she called out sweetly. "I will not resist any plans that you have made, but do tell me what you have done with the Vikings for I fear them."

He looked daggers at her. "Fear them? From what the priest told me, you wanted to marry one of them. You wanted to arrange a meeting."

She shook her head. "Clearly there has been a misunderstanding here." She knew that Alfred had not read the message for he could not read. "I hate the man who held me prisoner. I wanted to bring about revenge, that is all," she lied. "But it appears that you have taken measures to do that for me."

Alfred wasn't so easily fooled. "I don't believe you hate him at all. Your first words were to ask what I had done with the savage bastards!"

"Because I was afraid and wanted to make certain I would be safe from any further harm." She looked behind her again, wondering if she could outdistance Alfred and reach her father's hall.

Yes, she told herself. She was much lighter of build than he and had often ridden horseback. She could make it—that is, if she could get free of him. The problem was, how could she loosen the ropes which bound them together? She tugged at one of the knots but it was tied too tightly. She would have to find a way to trick Alfred into untying them.

"Perhaps you do not have the Vikings in captivity after all. Maybe you are lying to me. What assurance do I have that I will not be captured again?"

"They are being guarded at Chester by your brothers and several of their men." He clenched his jaw as if realizing that he had foolishly told her too much. "Don't worry about them ever assaulting you again. Where they are going they won't get the chance."

His voice sounded so ominous that Gwyneth felt a flash of fear, but just as quickly she talked herself into being optimistic. Her brothers were guarding them. Surely she could make them understand that they had to free Selig right away. If she could talk to them, that is. As they rode onward, escape was foremost on her mind.

"Ohhhhhh, Alfred . . ." she called out at last in a voice meant to sound weak with fatigue. "Can we rest? I am so hungry and thirsty. I swear to you that

I can go no further." Putting a hand to her head, she made as if to swoon.

"Women!" Dismounting from his horse, he yanked her down from her mare none too gently. "We have to eat and quench our thirst as quickly as possible. There are many miles yet to travel." His eyes seemed to search the road behind them. Of what or whom was he afraid?

Taking advantage of Alfred's lack of attention to her, Gwyneth slipped away from his watchful eyes. Making her way through the underbrush, she came to a place where the woodland met the river. How many times, as a child, had she sat on this very bank and watched Pengwyrn and Edwin frolic in the rough waters? She knew every rock and blade of grass near the river.

I'll soon be home again, she thought with a smile. She could see Alfred frantically searching for her and felt a surge of triumph as she slipped behind a bush. She would get free of him and ride frantically to Chester. All was not lost after all.

"I've got you! Running away?"

Turning around, she found herself face-to-face with Alfred. Somehow he had taken a shortcut and intercepted her.

Forcing a smile, Gwyneth looked upon him with eyes wide with innocence. "Why . . . no . . . I . . . I was just wishing to go for a swim. I could not abide the filth from the road one moment longer. Surely you cannot begrudge me a dip in the waters?"

He searched her face for the truth of her words and seemed to find no guile there. With a shove, he pushed her up the hill. "Dirt is healthy. It's water that can be dangerous." He shuddered. "Baths . . . ugh! Once every five years is enough for me."

She wondered what he would say if she told him the Vikings bathed every week, but thought better of it. Still, she was reminded once again of how the Vikings were always called filthy.

Alfred thrust a piece of undercooked rabbit into Gwyneth's hands. She ate slowly, hoping that perhaps he would leave her again, but he stayed right by her side. Once he had finished his own portion, he grabbed her by the arm.

"Hurry, we can tarry no longer here."

They took to the road again, riding just as swiftly as before. Gwyneth gazed about her at the greens and browns of the hillside as they passed by. The gently rolling hills were covered in lush green grass and dotted with gnarled trees whose leaves had the first hint of autumn colors. They were getting farther and farther away from Chester. She had to find a way to get free. Quickly.

Gwyneth cursed the rope which bound her horse to Alfred's. She had nothing with which to cut it but she had an idea.

"Alfred, I fear my horse has gone lame. May I ride with you?"

Issuing a curse, Alfred reined in the horses and climbed down from his horse. "Women. God curse them all. They are a bother and a nuisance."

Untying the rope which joined her horse to his, he reached for his sword to put the animal out of its misery.

"Wait. Help me down first."

"Are you helpless?" He cursed again, roughly pulling her from the mare."

"I do not want to witness the kill. I faint at the sight of blood."

As Alfred moved towards the horse, Gwyneth picked up a big rock and brought it crashing down on his head.

"If you knew me better you would know that knocking evil men senseless is my specialty," she exclaimed. "Even if I am only a woman."

Hurriedly, she tied him up with the ropes used to tie the horses together, then gave his stallion a slap on the rump. It would be quite a while before Alfred gave her any trouble. In the meantime she hoped that everything would be resolved.

Gwyneth hurried back to her mare. The wind tore at her face as she rode onward, but she didn't notice. All that mattered was that she was free. She had won a small victory. Now all she needed was to seek the safety of her father's hall and do her utmost to convince him to ride with her to Chester.

Selig, Roland, and the other Vikings who were able to walk could see the stone walls in the distance. They were coming closer and closer to the church and Selig couldn't help but wonder what would happen next. Would they kill him right away and give him a chance to die with a sword in his hand to enter Valhalla, or would they make him suffer?

"What shall we do with them?" two of their captors taunted as they walked along.

"Feed them to the wolves," said one large man.

"Hang them from the trees and let the birds pick out their eyes," said another.

"Let's chop off their heads and watch their headless bodies jerk about," cried out a third.

"Ha! Child's play. I tell you we should give them the blood eagle. That is how my father died by Viking hands when I was just a child. His entrails were cut and spread out before him as he lay helpless."

And Gwyneth called the *Vikings* heathens, Selig said to Roland in their own language.

"What did you say, you Viking pig!" The heavyset man pushed Selig violently to the ground, laughing as he tried to get up but couldn't. "Say *please*."

From his place on the ground, Selig looked up

and was met by eyes as familiar to him as his own. Gwyneth's brother. Despite his auburn hair he knew it had to be. He read compassion in those eyes and kindness.

"Leave him alone, Geofyr. We do not have to act like brutes." He gave Selig his hand and pulled him up.

"If it was my sister who was so ruthlessly vanquished and disgraced, then carried off, Pengwyrn, I wouldn't help him to his feet. I'd grind his head in the dirt."

"That's not my way. I leave it for God to judge."

"And us to punish," the big man answered.

"Pengwyrn," Selig whispered. He had often heard Gwyneth speak of her brothers. They were close—he knew that. This one was the gentle sibling, Edwin the headstrong one, and Aidan the youngest.

"He's mumbling again. Shall I cut out his tongue?"

"No. Leave him be. He'll suffer enough later." He started to walk away but Selig stepped in the way.

"Please. We must talk," he said in Pengwyrn's language. "Help me."

If he was surprised that the Viking captive knew their tongue, he didn't show it. "Help you? Why should I after what you did?"

"Because of your sister and what we mean to each other and . . . and because she has always told me that you Christians are taught to forgive."

"My sister?" Another muscular young man elbowed his way to Selig's side. His facial structure and the color of his hair proclaimed him to be the other brother. "You have defiled her and taken her from her family. For this and many other things you will be punished."

"I did not defile her. I love her and she loves me.

I'm the one who gave her the pendant. You must be . . ."

Selig was hit from behind with such force that he cried out in pain, but this time Pengwyrn didn't intercede. Even so, there was something in his expression that said he was torn between listening and joining the others who called for this Selig's blood.

"Where is she?" Selig pressed, ignoring the threat to his person. "Where?"

"She is safe," Pengwyrn answered. "She is with our sister, Ethelin."

"Ah, Ethelin. From what she has told me about her older sister I know that she will protect her." He was relieved. "Perhaps she has already explained our story."

"What story?" Pengwyrn and Edwin spoke at the same time.

"The reason we are here is because Gwyneth wanted to be married by a priest in the Christian manner. She sent a note to the priest here requesting a meeting between us all."

"Sent a message to the priest? Gwyneth?" Pengwyrn looked puzzled. "I didn't hear of this. Did she?"

"You have only to ask her," Selig said.

"He's a lying pile of cow dung!" the man named Geofyr shouted, pushing Selig to the ground once again.

Selig struggled to his feet, his eyes riveted upon Gwyneth's blue-eyed brother, whom he perceived to be his only hope.

Pengwyrn was deep in thought. "What he says makes sense. Surely we should listen to Gwyneth on this matter and find out how she was treated."

"He is only stalling in hopes that he can make an escape. I can read it in his eyes," Geofyr grumbled. "Throw them in the storeroom and keep close guard over them. If they escape you will take their place."

Once again, Selig was struck by the irony of it all as he, Roland, and several of the others were thrust inside the cramped storeroom from which they had taken the church's treasures. It was a windowless structure with thick walls and only one small door which was now being locked. He could hear the rattle of the key.

"I don't think we will get out anytime soon," Roland said, cursing their ill luck.

Selig thought about Gwyneth's brother. "There is one hope, that the blue-eyed one will keep us safe until Torin comes."

"*If* he comes," Roland said dejectedly, lying down on the floor.

"He will come." Or it was possible he would never lay eyes on his beloved Gwyneth again.

THIRTY-EIGHT

Gwyneth tethered her horse and ran towards the door of her father's hall. Though she had tied Alfred securely, she had been fearful all the way here that somehow he would get free and follow her; thus she was out of breath as she pushed the door open.

Aenella was the first person she laid eyes on as she ran inside. Her mother was noticeably thinner but still maintained her regal bearing. She looked up from her embroidery, her eyes wide with amazement as she saw who stood before her.

"Gwyneth! God has answered my prayers. He has sent you safely back to us after your horrid ordeal."

"It wasn't an ordeal, Mother. At least not until we came to these shores."

Rising from her weaving, Aenella stretched out her arms and gathered her daughter safe within the warmth of her embrace. "How? When? Are you all right?"

Gwyneth explained everything to her mother, her words tumbling so quickly that she was soon out of breath again. She told her mother about Alfred's betrayal, about her blossoming love for Selig, about Erica, Torin, and Ragnar. Lastly she told her about her message to the priest and about his seeming betrayal.

"You came here to marry that . . . that Viking?"

The shocked look upon her mother's face was nearly more than Gwyneth could bear. She broke free of her mother's embrace. "I thought that at least you would understand and be on my side."

"But . . . but marriage to a . . . a Viking. A . . . a heathen."

"Heathen? You dare mention that word to me after I have told you about Alfred and all that has happened since I came home?"

Aenella started to speak but Gwyneth silenced her.

"I held myself so aloof, just like you. I loved Selig but perhaps not enough to accept him the way he was. I thought to bring him home and change him. To turn him into a . . . a respectable Englishman. Well now I know the truth and to me the word 'heathen' will always conjure up memories of the other night." She slowly closed her eyes, then opened them. "I trusted that my message would be honored, but I was wrong and now Selig and the others are in danger."

"I'm sorry . . ."

"Then help me. Talk to Father. He must do something!"

Aenella shook her head. "A wise woman does not interfere in man things."

"Then I am not wise, for I will, the moment that Father takes one step inside that door!" Though she had been strong up until now, Gwyneth couldn't help crying. Her mother's attitude made her feel isolated. She realized she truly was all alone, more so than she had ever been among the Vikings.

"Gwyn . . ." Her daughter's tears upset Aenella. She tried to put her arms around Gwyneth but she pushed her away.

"Selig took me in love. Never did he force himself upon me. He wanted to marry me in a Viking ceremony but I refused. So, because of his love he came with me here to stand before a priest and marry me in the manner that would make me happy. Is that the way of a heathen? Is it, Mother?"

Her mother thought the matter over, then said softly, "No."

"Alfred never cared about me. He wanted land and power. To get it he enlisted the help of the Vikings. I know. I heard him talking to them. Then when he realized that I had overheard, he tried to strangle me."

Aenella put her hand up to her throat. "I find it so hard to believe that he would try to kill you. I know him. He seems to be a good man."

"Well, he isn't."

There was a long, drawn-out silence; then Gwyneth's mother said, "You can not blame Alfred because you were kidnapped by Vikings."

"I can and I do."

She was suddenly ravenously hungry. She had been too upset to eat Alfred's offering. Spying a loaf of bread and some fruit left over from breakfast, she broke off a piece of bread, sliced the apple, and crammed them into her mouth. She washed it down with milk.

"Alfred didn't even put up a fight. He wanted that oafish Viking to take me. But Selig . . . he fought for me more times than I can count and now I must fight for him. Will you help me, Mother?"

Taking her mother's hand and kneeling before her, Gwyneth pleaded with the woman who had borne her.

Aenella gently lifted her daughter up. She would not have her humble herself. "I will do what I can, but you know how stubborn Cedd can be."

No sooner had she made the promise than they heard a pounding on the door. Looking out the

large keyhole, Gwyneth saw in horror that it was
Alfred. Somehow he had managed to get free, catch
his horse, and gather a few of his men.

"He has come after me, Mother, but not in the
name of love. He wants to punish me and keep me
from telling what I know. Don't be weak like
Ethelin. Don't let him take me."

"I won't!" She turned to one of the slaves. "Bar
the door." She watched as the man lowered a large
log into place. "Gwyneth, stand behind me. Alfred
has no power here. I am the lady of this hall and
as such will have my say who comes and goes."

Gwyneth could hear the pounding as Alfred tried
to break down the door, furious that it should be
locked against him. When at last he realized the
door was strong, he beseeched those inside to let
him in.

"Aenella! Open up. I need to talk to your daughter."

"And you bring an armed guard to do so?" She
looked at Gwyneth. "Now I truly do believe you! He
will not touch you. Never again."

"Open up!"

Gwyneth could hear the sound of swords hacking
at the wood. She clutched her mother's hand.

"Put down your swords at once," Aenella demanded loudly, incensed that the men outside the
door should seek forcible entry. "You are no better
than the Norsemen or our other enemies who arm
themselves against us." Turning to the few guards
who stood nearby, she bid them take up arms.

"I came here to protect you, Aenella. Let me in.
Your husband would be angered that you should
shut me out."

"Husband or no husband, you will not enter
here. My daughter seeks safety under my roof and
she shall have it."

The hacking sound ceased. "Woman, you interfere where you have no business! Gwyneth is my be-trothed.''

"Not anymore! She has suffered at your hands. That to my mind is sufficient reason to break any agreement you might have had in the past.''

Aenella looked at her daughter and smiled. There had always been a bond between them but never was it stronger than at this moment.

"Go, Alfred, before there is bloodshed, for Gwyneth will stay here as long as she wishes.''

There was silence outside the door and for a moment Gwyneth and her mother thought that Alfred had left, but once again he spoke, this time with renewed fury.

"I will seek Cedd. He will see to it that my demands are satisfied. I will not leave this land until Gwyneth goes with me. She was promised to me by his word.''

This time Alfred ordered his men away from the door, as if he had no doubt in his mind that Cedd would give in to his demands. Cedd had always been afraid of him and this fact made him over-confident.

After he had gone, Gwyneth sat down upon one of the wooden benches. It had been a trying day and she was exhausted. "Will Father do as he says, Mother? Will he make me go with a man I detest? Am I then just chattel?''

Aenella gently stroked her daughter's hair. "I care not what your father says. As long as you want to stay here you shall do so. It is just as I told Alfred.''

"But I don't want to cause a rift between you and Father.''

Aenella smiled. "I know how to handle Cedd. Somehow I will convince him to intercede on your Viking's behalf. You will see.''

* * *

It was dark, cold, and depressing. Though each of the Vikings in turn had tried to escape from their storehouse prison they had been unsuccessful.

"We have to face the truth. Whether we like it or not we are at the mercy of our captors unless Torin comes to our aid, and I doubt that he would be able to find us here even if he does. We are doomed," Roland complained.

"No. I won't give up. I am going to keep trying to find a way out of here until I get out or I die!" Selig exclaimed. "There has to be a way."

Roland seemed to take hope from Selig's steadfast determination. "Maybe we can overpower the guard. Surely they will feed us and then . . ."

A grinding noise alerted them to the presence of someone outside the door. Hunched down, each Viking waited eagerly, but only a small slot in the door, little bigger than the size of a fist, opened. Through the slot a shower of cheese, vegetables, and fruit poured through.

"Your food, you stinking Viking dogs!"

Selig recognized the voice of Geofyr, the hostile one. As always, he was filled with anger and Selig wondered if perhaps it was because of the raid upon these shores. Had he lost a loved one? Or was he just by nature a very angry man?

"At least you feed us," Roland shouted out.

"Not for long. I won't have to. In two risings of the sun you will be taken out to the rocks of the cliff, all of you, and tied securely. As you wait for the tide to come in you will know that the same waters you have sailed over in your terrible ships will be the very waters which will bring your death."

"You will drown us without a chance to fight?" Roland was indignant. With a growl he surged forward, trying to get his hand through the opening before it shut. He was too late. "I'd like to break your neck."

"Easy, Roland," Selig counseled. "We must save our strength."

"Two days, Vikings," a mumbled voice threatened. "Two days. Think about it and remember the lives you took that day."

"And what about your own man? The traitor."

Although there was silence, it was obvious someone outside the door was listening. Then a voice asked, "What traitor?"

"How do you think we knew that your coast would be unguarded because everyone would be at the wedding? Did you think it was by accident that we stumbled into your hall? No. It was one of your own kind who led us there and told us of the feast. He told us that we would take you unaware and for his services he was given silver and gold."

"You are lying."

"There is no reason to do such a thing. You will kill us anyway," Selig shouted out. "And when you do you will forever still the voice that could reveal the name of the man who betrayed you."

There was silence, then a voice whispered, "You are just trying to trick us so that you can stay alive."

"Am I? Or is there a traitor in your midst? Think about it."

"And you think about this. In two days' time you will die." The clomping of feet told them the man had left.

"Two days. Two risings of the sun. That's all we have," one of the other Vikings whispered.

"Let's hope that it is enough time," Selig proclaimed.

THIRTY-NINE

The joyful barking of the large hounds in the hall announced that Gwyneth's father had returned. She could hear his booming voice as he greeted the animals; then he strode into the hall with the lymers close behind him. He did not see Gwyneth sitting in the corner of the room—his eyes were only for his wife. Even after all these years, it was obvious that she held his heart.

"I just got back from Chester. We have them locked in one of the large storehouses, but we must move quickly before something terrible happens."

Gwyneth was shocked by her father's appearance. His hair was almost completely gray. His usually clean-shaven face showed the shadow of a beard. He is getting old before his time, she thought, regretful for any part she might have played in his early aging. Had his worry about her been to blame?

"Cedd . . ." Aenella began, glancing behind her at Gwyneth.

"Damn the Viking, I say. I hope the whole lot of them burn in hell . . ." Still blustering, he walked towards his favorite chair. Seeing Gwyneth for the first time, he frowned. "What are you doing here? I thought you were with Ethelin."

"Alfred came to take me away but I escaped and came here."

"Escaped!" He shook his head. "For the love of

God, woman, he is the man I have promised that you will marry. Had it not been for the Viking attack, you would have been married already. How then can you speak of leaving him as an escape?"

"Because that is exactly what it was. He is cruel, Father. And worse than that, he betrayed us all. He led the Vikings here."

He reached out and patted her cheek. "Alfred told us that being amidst the Vikings had addled your mind. My poor little lamb. But all has been put to right now, thanks to Alfred. He has put those heathens in a place where they will never trouble us again."

"Where? Where are they?"

"Locked securely in the church's storehouses, at least for the moment."

"Then they are still alive!" She had worried that perhaps Alfred's plan included killing them.

He nodded. "Ah, but it is good to have you home again, even if it is only for a short time."

"And it is good to be home again, but only if you listen to me and listen to me well."

When it appeared that his concentration was wavering, Aenella nudged him in the ribs. "Listen," was all she said.

"That day . . . the day of the attack, I was trying to find you and my brothers when I happened upon Alfred talking to a group of Norsemen. As I moved closer to hear what they were talking about, I overheard enough to know that Alfred had betrayed us. He planned for him and me to be married and for the Vikings to kill you and my brothers so he could lay claim to all of your lands."

"What?" It was obvious by his expression that he did not believe her.

"Alfred is ambitious and greedy. His own lands are not enough for him. He wanted your lands as well and that was how he intended to get his hands on everything!" She repeated, "Everything, Father!"

"Bah! It was the Vikings who were to blame. Alfred would not . . ." He thought for a moment. "None of our own would sink to such treachery. What's more, I refuse even to talk about it."

Aenella stepped forward. "Listen to the child, Cedd. Listen to her well and ask yourself how the Vikings were able to so easily fall upon us."

Gwyneth told him the whole story in as few words as possible. She told him that Alfred had tried to strangle her, then had given her over to a brutish Viking without a qualm. "He didn't even lift a finger to save me because he wanted me gone!"

"And so you were abducted?" He reached for her hands, holding them palm up as if to look for blisters and calluses. Seeing no traces of hard work, he dropped her hands and looked her in the eye. "It does not appear that you have suffered. Why?"

"Because the Viking on whose ship I found myself was known to me. Thus I was not a slave, Father, but an honored member of the household."

Cedd raised his eyebrows. "And . . . and did this Viking force you to his bed?"

"No!"

He sighed in relief. "Good. Our blessed Lord shielded you after all. Now you can marry Alfred just as we had planned."

"Never!" Gwyneth tugged at the skirt of her dress in outrage. "You didn't listen to a thing I said! Alfred tried to strangle me. He told me openly that he planned for all of the family males to be killed. He brought the Vikings here, Father. I am not talking out of my head. It is true!"

He shrugged. "Then I will marry you to another. Athelstan, perhaps. His lands border ours to the south and . . ."

"A thousand times no! I love someone else."

"The Viking!" He spat the words.

"Yes!"

"Then you will find yourself a widow long before you can wed."

"And you will find yourself without a daughter!"

Hurriedly, Aenella stepped between them. "Cedd! There has to be some way to avert a tragedy here. Perhaps if you got to know this young man you might see that he isn't as bad as you believe him to be."

Cedd turned on her, his face drained of all color. "Not as bad! Not as bad! Vikings have no laws. They are heathens. They worship false gods. How could we ever accept him with our daughter?"

"Their laws are just, Father. You do not understand them as I do. I lived among them. I learned that there are good and bad among all people." She clutched his arm. "Please help me to help him! I asked him to bring me here so we could sort this out together. Out of love for me he did! He brought me back to Wessex only to find that his ship was attacked and his crew locked up like animals."

"Because they *are* animals!"

"And what are we? If you allow them to be murdered, then we are not better than heathens ourselves!"

"And you are nothing but a Viking's harlot who does not know her place. Women are to do as they are told."

"Cedd!" Aenella gasped. "Hold your tongue."

"She should have killed herself rather than allow that Viking to touch her." He touched Gwyneth's stomach. "How do I know that even now some Viking bastard isn't growing inside her?"

"And if there is a child it will be part of us," Aenella said softly. "I will love it with all my heart and if you have any sense, so will you."

Gwyneth fought to keep her temper in check. Anger would not do her any good. It would only spur her father on to do something rash. "Alfred was cruel to me but the Viking showed me kindness. He saved my life several times. At first I thought as you do but then my heart was joined to his heart and became as one. Our love was strong, so strong that it has survived every test."

"Love . . ." he said scathingly.

"Yes, love!"

Gwyneth remembered all the days of her childhood when she had sat upon her father's knee, listening to his every word. She had respected his wisdom. Now she was determined that he would respect her.

"Alfred will come for you."

"He has already come here. Mother sent him away."

"What?"

Aenella put her arm around her daughter's waist. "I have given Gwyneth my word that we will give her shelter here."

"Here?"

"After what she has told me, I will not allow Alfred to take her. I have made a vow. And a vow is a vow! Gwyneth has a right to happiness."

Cedd snorted. "Women and their talk of happiness will cause trouble for us all."

"And men and their constant battling will be our very deaths!" Gwyneth's mother answered.

Gwyneth tried one more time. "Please, Father. Please use your influence to save him! Set him free. Set all of them free."

"No!" His eyes were cold as he looked upon mother and daughter standing in defiance. "I tell you, woman. From now on it is your daughter that she will be. If she persists in this foolish talk, if she brings disaster down on our heads, then she will be dead to me."

"No!" Gwyneth fought against the tides of sorrow his words brought forth.

"Cedd, you do not know what you are doing," Aenella choked. "Gwyneth has been through so much. How can you turn your back upon her? How?" Tears rolled down her cheeks, not for herself but for her daughter.

"Close your mouth, woman. I will hear no more. It is enough that I will not turn the harlot out of doors where she belongs. She may stay here, but I refuse to have anything to do with her. If you are wise you will pray that her coming here will not bring hardship to us all and that Alfred will not seek retaliation for your stubbornness." With that, Cedd left the sobbing women in the hall.

It was dark in the storehouse. There wasn't even a crack in the door big enough to see any sunlight. What time of day was it? Time seemed to pass by so slowly that Selig wasn't really certain. The ugly Viking had said that they had two days to live but how was he going to measure time when they couldn't see outside?

Selig felt like a caged animal. It was cramped inside. Taking a head count he had found out that there were thirty of his crewmen inside, including Arni, Agaut, Bork, Gunnar, and Mord from the settlement, who were severely wounded. The rest were bruised and cut up but ready to fight if necessary. If only they would get the chance.

"I'm thirsty!" Sigurd, one of Ragnar's followers, rasped.

"There's no water. They didn't see fit to give us any. Not even a drop," Roland grumbled.

"From what they tell us we will have more than enough water in two days," Selig answered wryly.

"Ocean water. It's deadly to drink."

"What I wouldn't give for even a sip of spring water . . ." Selig said wistfully. Even now, his tongue felt dry and swollen. In frustration, he pounded on the door.

Suddenly the small slip opened, revealing a partial view of a face. Selig looked down and realized that a blue eye was staring into the darkness. "Viking. You, the one who abducted my sister. Where are you?"

"I'm right here by the door!"

"I want to hear more about you and my sister. Were you good to her?"

"As good as a man can be to the woman he loves," Selig whispered. "I brought her back because I knew that it was important for her to marry in your Christian way. And I wanted her to be happy." He hunkered down so that his face was near the slit. "I know you are more compassionate than your brother. Please take her a message for me. Tell her that I will always love her."

"I don't think I should tell her anything at all. Soon she will be another man's wife."

"Alfred?"

"Yes."

"Would you have her married to a traitor?" Selig asked. He could not bear to think of Gwyneth in the arms of another man, particularly a cruel man. "If you love her, you must save her!"

"Save her?" Pengwyrn pulled away.

"Please, before you turn her over to him . . . her . . . her . . . betrothed . . . please talk with Gwyneth and listen to what she has to say. She will tell you that it was not by accident that you were attacked that day. It had been carefully planned with Alfred's help."

"I don't believe you."

"You don't believe me or do not want to. There is a difference." Selig reached into the pouch he carried beneath his tunic and caressed the wooden carving he had made of Gwyneth those first few days at the settlement. Slowly he pushed it through the opening. "Take this to your sister. I made it for her. While you are with her be patient enough to learn the truth."

Selig could feel a tug on the carving, then it was yanked out of his hand. He saw a flash of light as the wooden carving was held up to a torch. "Dear God, it's beautiful workmanship and it . . . it looks just like her. She looks so peaceful."

"Will you take it to her?"

"I might and then again I might not." Though the words were taunting, Pengwyrn's tone of voice gave Selig reason to be hopeful.

FORTY

Gwyneth tossed and turned in bed all night. Her father's unforgiving attitude and her apprehension of what was going to happen to Selig made it impossible to sleep even a wink. She was wide awake when she heard one of the household servants running through the hall, waking the household with his shouts.

"Riders! Riders! To arms!"

Gwyneth ran her fingers through her thick, dark hair, then bolted out of bed. Running down the hall, she ran headlong into her father.

"What's wrong?"

"There is a band of riders approaching. My instincts tell me it is Alfred. So you see what you have done?"

"I meant no harm in coming here. I came because it is my home . . ." Strange, the moment she had said the words she realized it wasn't true. It wasn't her home. Not anymore. Her home had been in the settlement with Selig or anyplace where they were together.

"If any blood is spilled this day it will be upon your head." He brushed past her. Gwyneth followed him through the hall to the large double doors and looked out. Even from a distance she could that it was Alfred and his followers.

Looking at her father, she was surprised to see

that he was afraid, he who had always seemed so strong and authoritative. "Trouble can be avoided if you will only go back to *him,*" he said.

For a moment Gwyneth was tempted. She knew she would do almost anything to avoid a disaster. Aenella, however, was determined that her daughter would stay inside.

"If we don't stand up to him now he will forever be a thorn in our side and your sacrifice will be all for naught. I want you to be happy, not miserable." She looked daggers at Gwyneth's father. "And Cedd wants your happiness, too."

Cedd mumbled an oath beneath his breath, watching as Alfred rode forward like a conquering lord. With a gesture of peace, he dismounted and strode forward.

"I've come for Gwyneth."

Gwyneth hardly dared to breathe. Would her father give in? Would he force her to go? As her father paced up and down, she feared the worst. Then at least he spoke.

"I can not and will not let you take Gwyneth from these walls."

"You spineless old man." The words exploded from Alfred's mouth. "You let your wife be the lord here. Well, so be it. I do not care about that but I do care about being compensated for the humiliation I have suffered. Gold and silver will suffice or I can be paid in land."

Cedd turned pale. "I will not give you anything! So you can go back to where you came from." He turned to look at Gwyneth. "For I am prepared to do anything to protect my daughter."

"Then prepare to fight, old man, for I will get what I want!" Turning his back, Alfred strode towards his horse, mounted up, and rode up the hill towards his men.

"Where are Pengwyrn and Edwin and the others? We are going to need them here."

"They are in Chester," Aenella answered, "as well he knows."

"Then I will have to fight with what men I have."

Gwyneth watched as her father hurriedly rounded up the men. Could she allow this to continue? Was her own happiness and well-being worth the price? How could she watch men die for her? If the sacrifice of her own contentment would stop this carnage, then she had to offer herself after all.

"Wait. Father!" She ran after him. "Wait!" Grabbing the sleeve of his tunic, she tugged at him, then held on for dear life. "I'll go with him . . ."

Cedd shrugged her from his arms. "No. I have been wrong. I can see that now. You are not something to be bartered, but someone to be cherished." He shook his head. "How could I have been so blind as to have promised you to a man like that?"

"We are all blind at times . . ." she whispered.

He reached out to touch her face. "I'm sorry. Sorry for what I said and for not believing you."

"You believe me now?"

"Yes, Alfred's actions speak for themselves. He is a greedy man!" He mounted his horse, lifted his sword, and prepared to fight.

Gwyneth watched from afar as the two bands of armed men came face-to-face upon the hillside, hacking and thrusting at each other. The clang of sword against sword echoed down the hill as she and her mother stood holding each other's hands.

"Gwyneth. . . ." Shading her eyes against the sun, Aenella gasped. "Look! It's Pengwyrn!" Gwyneth's brother was not alone. The men that he had brought with him made a great difference in the odds of the battle. Alfred was wise enough to shout out orders to retreat.

From her place at the doorway, Gwyneth watched

as Alfred's mounted men galloped back in the direction from which they had come. In that moment she knew that they had been saved.

Ever since she was a little girl, Gwyneth had always liked to walk in the gardens right outside the kitchen of the manor. Then she had always walked alone. Now she walked arm in arm with her brother.

"You were a hero today," she told him. "I was proud of you and proud of Father for standing up to Alfred."

"I didn't really believe the story the Viking told me, but now I know it is true." Pengwyrn paused and reached for his belt, loosening an object there. He handed it to Gwyneth.

"The carving! Selig made this." She stared at it. "He . . . he's not dead, is he?"

"Not yet, but he soon will be."

She felt the world spin about her. Foolishly she had hoped that she had some time to win his freedom, but Pengwyrn's story of the Vikings' capture, their incarceration, and their planned execution brought reality back to her with a thud.

"They're going to drown him?" The very idea was cruel and perverse. "When?"

"Tomorrow!"

She fought against her hysteria. "We must stop them! We must move heaven and earth if we have to but we can't let this happen." She turned her anger on Pengwyrn. "If he dies, if this horrible punishment is meted out to him, I swear I will never forgive you. Any of you!"

"Gwyn . . ." He reached out but hesitated as he saw that her face was streaked with tears. "You love him."

"More than I ever thought it possible to love another human being!" She dabbed at her eyes with the end of her sleeve. "Can you stop it?"

"I don't know. You know Edwin. He never listens."

"He will to me." Suddenly she was angry. "I'll make him listen."

Hurrying to the stables, she readied her horse for the long ride. Pengwyrn gave her a hand up and swung himself onto his own saddle. For an instant she knew fear. Then, clinging to the saddle, she felt only a sense of exultation. She would find a way to free Selig and the others. She must!

Selig was startled by the bright light that suddenly flooded the room. As his eyes grew accustomed to the light he realized that there was a throng of men outside the door, all of them jeering at him.

"What is it? You can not tell me that two days have passed . . . ?"

Gwyneth's brother, Edwin, shook his head. "No. Just one. But there has been a change in plans. Alfred insists that we carry out your sentence today."

"Today?" Selig stared at Gwyneth's brother. Was he imagining it or was there something in his eyes that said that he was not exactly anxious to witness the scene?

"Just you and him!" He pointed toward Roland. "The others are going to be put aboard the ship tomorrow right before it is set afire."

"What is the hurry with my friend and me? Why today?"

One of the other men spoke up. "Because Alfred has arranged it."

"He wants to silence me. He fears I will reveal the truth."

Selig looked at the crowd of men, trying to see Pengwyrn's face. When he didn't, he felt a small shred of hope. It wasn't too late. If only Pengwyrn hurried.

"Come, Viking!" He and Roland were pushed and prodded forward, then led across the meadow, down a long pathway to the sea. As they walked, the men were chanting, intoning some kind of prayer.

Selig gloried in the rustling and twittering of the birds as they flew about. To hear their chirping removed some of the burden from his heart. It was strange how one took so many things for granted. How he would miss those things now, but most of all he would miss Gwyneth and her love.

"Gwyneth . . ." He whispered her name like a prayer.

As they walked along, Selig looked down at the rocks as the sea foamed and thrashed. He thought about how easy it would be to end it all now by leaping to those rocks below, but his pride would not let him do such a cowardly thing. He would be brave and show his captors how to die.

At the foot of the cliff the sea pounded, slowly receding bit by bit, but it would return, bringing death with it. Seeing two large rocks, slim and smooth, he knew at once that this was to be his final resting place.

"You will be tied to those rocks to think about the evil you have done and to ask your many gods to help you," the man named Geofyr said with a snarl. "Your kind sold my daughter into slavery and she killed herself rather than be dishonored. Think of that as you listen to the rhythm of the water."

"Maybe they will call out to their gods for help," one man shouted out, giving Selig a shove.

The feel of ropes sliced into Selig's arms and legs as they bound him to the rock. He looked out at the ocean, imagining how it would be as the tide crept ever closer, choking him. First it would come to his knees, then to his chest, finally to his nose and mouth.

The Englishmen jostled each other to watch. All the while the sea moved back and forth, pounding the rocks with greater and greater strength as the tide rose higher and higher.

"Untie me. Let me die with a sword in my hand so I can go to Valhalla," Selig pleaded.

"Give you a sword so that you can attack us? Do we look like fools?" Geofyr asked.

Roland was bound beside Selig. "Where is Torin? I had hoped that by now he would have come to our aid."

"So did I. So did I." Selig feared for Baugi. Perhaps the dog had been killed or had not been able to reach his destination.

"There is nothing we can do."

Both looked out at the ocean, their thoughts on those they would leave behind.

The waters sloshed and whistled at Selig's feet, rising ever higher as he closed his eyes in silent farewell to the woman he loved more than anything on earth and in that moment it seemed that the very wind whispered the name, "Gwyneth!"

FORTY-ONE

Gwyneth was weary as she rode back towards Chester beside Pengwyrn. All sorts of thoughts were tumbling through her brain. Was Selig alive? Could she convince those who held him captive to set him free? If so, would she be allowed to go back to the Northland with him or would she have to run away and leave her family behind forever?

At last they reached the church and dismounted. It was then that her brother at last said to her that which had tormented him all along the way. "Forgive me, Gwyn. I never meant to hurt you. None of us did. It's just that we hated the Northmen for what they did during the raid and Alfred was very persuasive. We should not have done what we did, Edwin and I and the others. But all can be put to right, you will see."

"At least if Edwin will not listen to you, he will listen to me."Together they made their way to the storehouse. Opening the gate, Pengwyrn was surprised to see that except for the guards, it was virtually abandoned. Gwyneth watched as her brother spoke first with one guard, then with another. As she looked at the expressions moving over his face, she knew the news boded ill.

"What is it?" she asked when he returned to her side. "What has happened?" She took hold of her brother's shoulders, confused by his babbling. At last the cruel truth struck her full force. She was too late!

"They killed him. This morning." His head hung in remorse.

"No! No!" She was screaming the word as she came perilously close to losing all control of her emotions. "My fault. Mine! If only we had come sooner . . ."

"Don't blame yourself. If it will make you feel better, blame me. If only I had known, I would have stayed and tried to do something . . ."

"I'm too late!" Selig was dead. Her eyes were like the eyes of a wounded animal. "Alfred's doing?" She could well imagine that he had hurried up the execution in retaliation for the beating he had received at the battle.

"He told the others that a Viking ship had been spotted on the horizon and that if Selig and the other Viking leader were not killed immediately they would be freed."

"And the ploy worked." Oh, if only there really had been a Viking ship! If only somehow Selig had been rescued.

"Tell me how he died again." She closed her eyes, knowing that she would feel his pain. At least in that way she could feel as if she were with him at the end.

"I told you," he said, refreshing her memory. "They were to be secured to the large cliff stones, there to await the incoming tide. Alfred said that it was only fitting that they should die by drowning since it is the sea which brought them here." Pengwyrn hung his head again.

"The tide!" Sudden hope came to Gwyneth.

"Come with me, Pengwyrn. It can't be too late. Oh, God, please. Don't let it be too late."

Without another thought about her own well-being, driven by the necessity of saving Selig from the ocean, she mounted her horse. As she looked westward, however, she was amazed at what she saw. It was a band of Vikings and if her eyes did not deceive her, they were Torin's men.

"Alfred wasn't lying this time. The Vikings are here!" Undoubtedly it was something that Selig and Torin had worked out between them, that Torin would be there in case of trouble. Now Torin had arrived in time to save all the others, but had he come in time to save Selig and Roland?

"Vikings!" came the shout as the men guarding the Norse prisoners caught sight of the approaching men. Total pandemonium reigned as the Viking band came closer, their swords raised.

Gwyneth nudged her horse into a gallop. "Aren't you going to wait?" Pengwyrn asked.

"No. There is no time. Torin can take care of Selig's men. It's up to me to take care of Selig."

"But how?"

"I don't know. Not yet." But as she caught sight of Baugi with Torin's band she had an idea. "Pengwyrn, I'm going to ride ahead. You get the dog and bring him to the rocks. We may have need of him."

"The dog?" He hesitated, staring at her as if she had lost her mind.

"Just do as I say."

Gwyneth rode at breakneck speed. Even so, it seemed to take forever to reach the cliffs. At last, however, she could smell the distinct, salty, air of the sea. Cresting a hill, she jumped from her horse and ran down the path to the sharp rocks below.

The sight which met her eyes made her cry out. Selig was still alive, though she could see the water was up to his chin. He was coughing and sputtering as the waves assaulted him. Roland, the taller of the two, was not in as deadly a peril, though his life, too, hung in the balance.

There were no guards around. No doubt having learned somehow that the Vikings were approaching, they must have gone back to Chester, she thought. The rocks were deserted except for the gulls circling overhead and the crabs clinging to the banks as the tide pressed inward.

"Selig!" she shouted, running towards him. Ripping off her shoes in order to have better footing on the slippery rocks, she frantically struggled to reach the man she loved.

Selig heard his name being called and thought at first that his mind was playing tricks on him. He had longed to hear Gwyneth's voice so much that now he was imagining things. Or had he already died and was listening to the angels Gwyneth had once told him about? He choked as the water got into his mouth, and felt a surge of relief to know that he was still alive.

"Selig!" Again the voice called to him. He fought to turn his head, but the chill of the water had numbed and weakened him. "Selig, I'm coming."

Gwyneth was only a short distance away. She was in time, if only she acted fast enough. Her assessment of the quickest way to rescue him was to swim toward him, untie him, and then help him get up on the rocks and out of danger. Heedless of her own safety, she eased herself into the water to save Selig's life—or die trying.

Gwyneth felt the icy cold ocean engulf her as

she fought against the waves. Every nerve in her body was on alert. As a wave closed over her head, she knew a moment of panic but talked herself out of her fear. It was the only thing she could do if she was going to save Selig. There was no other way, no one else.

Shivers ran up her spine. From the chill of the water? No. She sensed that someone was watching her. Turning her head, she gasped for breath as she saw Alfred standing on the rocks where she had been just a short time ago. His grin was evil personified as he plunged into the icy depths.

Frantically she moved her arms and legs. She had to get to Selig before Alfred overpowered her. "Hurry . . . hurry . . ." she thought. "Untie him and then he can handle Alfred."

Something beneath the water touched her leg. She screamed, kicking out with her foot, but a hand grasped her tightly. She felt herself being tugged under, but she somehow managed to struggle free. Gasping for air, she pushed her way to the surface.

"No!"

She struck out at Alfred, hitting him again and again with her fists and her feet. All the while the thought kept reeling through her brain that Selig would die if she did not free herself.

"You'll both die. First I'll drown you and then the ocean will take him," Alfred called out as he pulled her under again.

Although Gwyneth was losing strength, she lashed out, connecting her foot with Alfred's nose. As she gasped to the surface she cried out in glee as she saw that blood was pouring from his nostrils. In that moment she felt a blood lust and knew how a man must feel in battle. Kill or be killed!

She looked towards Selig. The water was past his mouth. Only by holding his head as high as possible was he able to keep from drowning. "Selig . . . !" She yelled. He had to hang on. She only needed a little more time.

"Gwyneth . . . !" Through the crashing of the waves she heard her brother's voice, echoed by a bark. "Baugi!"

Her joy was short-lived. Recovering from his injury, Alfred was upon her again. "Bitch! I won't let you save him! I want the sea to take him."

"Why? Why?" She couldn't understand Alfred's motives. "Why do you hate him so?"

"Hate him?" He laughed, a terrifying sound. "I don't hate him, I hate you. You have ruined all my plans. My only satisfaction is knowing that I will do the same to . . ."

A sudden look of pain contorted his face. A black, furry head bobbed up and down in the waves and Gwyneth realized with a surge of relief that Baugi had come to her rescue. She started to call out to him, to send him towards Selig, but Baugi was already on his way, and so was she!

Gwyneth could hear him choking. The water was well past his mouth. She swam to his side, pulling at his bonds frantically as Baugi caught hold of the neck of his tunic, trying to tug him to safety.

It was no use. The ropes were engorged with water from the sea. "Selig. Hold your hands closer together so that I can get you loose," she exclaimed.

Selig heard her pleas as if through a tunnel. He held his breath. His chest burned with the pain of needing air yet with all the strength left to him he pushed his wrists together.

Baugi bit at the ropes with his teeth; Gwyneth grabbed a loose rock and used it like a knife to work against Selig's bonds. From time to time she paused to lift his head gently so he could catch a breath of air through his nose.

At last she and the dog had him free. Selig breathed the sweet elixir of air into his lungs. "Roland," he choked.

Baugi and Gwyneth worked together to free Roland as Selig struggled to keep his head above the water. To her sudden horror she felt a hand grasp her by the waist and she knew that Alfred was back. But not for long. Jumping into the water, Pengwyrn swam towards the rocks. Pulling Alfred's hands away from his sister, he wrestled with him until they were both under the water.

"Pengwyrn!" Gwyneth watched out of the corner of her eye as she worked at the ropes that held Roland.

At last Roland, too, was free. But what of Pengwyrn? For a moment she feared the worst as she saw Alfred's head bob up from the water. Pengwyrn was strong but he was not as cunning as Alfred. She sensed Alfred's ploy. He would pretend weakness only to take her brother unaware.

"Pengwyrn, watch out!"

Her warning came too late. Alfred kicked with his feet, lashing out at Pengwyrn. Grabbing him around the neck, he gouged at his eyes with his fingers. Gwyneth watched in agony as Pengwyrn was tugged under.

"No!" She tried to come to her brother's aid, but Selig held her securely, knowing that there was nothing that she could do. Then, suddenly, Pengwyrn's head shot out of the water.

The battle moved out of the water and to the rocks. They all watched in terrified fascination as the two men fought. Alfred was tall and thin with the grace of a deer; Pengwyrn was also tall but he was more muscular and not as quick as his opponent.

As if moving in some kind of pagan dance high above the sea, they moved back and forth, crouching and bending, colliding with each other from time to time.

Selig pulled Gwyneth with him towards the shore. "Let me rest a moment and then I will help him."

Alas, there wasn't time. Gwyneth shrieked as Pengwyrn fell. Alfred moved in for the death blow, jumping at Pengwyrn with a loud shout of victory. She closed her eyes, but opened them as she heard a blood-curdling scream. At first she thought it was her brother who had fallen to the jagged stones below but as she looked again she saw Pengwyrn get to his knees. In that moment she realized that Alfred had somehow slipped on the wet rocks and plunged downward to the very rocks which had held Selig and Roland only a short time before.

Though she had loathed Alfred, Gwyneth turned her head away from the gruesome scene of Alfred lying shattered, bloody and broken on the rocks. She clung to Selig.

"Is he dead?"

Selig gently stroked her wet hair. "Yes. It's over!"

She shuddered. "Oh, Selig . . . I thought . . . I feared . . ."

"Hush . . . oh, my love we're together! That's all that's important."

"Together!" At that moment it was the most precious word in the world.

Soaking wet but happy, Pengwyrn, Gwyneth, Selig, Roland, and Baugi returned to the hall. Stepping inside the doorway, they headed at once to the roaring hearth fire, shivering as they sought to dry off.

"Gwyneth . . . !"

Turning, she saw her mother standing in the doorway. "You're drenched! Oh, my dear one, what happened?"

"Alfred tied Selig to a rock out in the ocean. He tried to drown him . . . and Roland also. But Pengwyrn and I saved him."

Selig cleared his throat.

"Oh, and Baugi, too. He helped."

Seeing the huge, black dog, Aenella stepped back. "What is that? Is it a bear?"

Gwyneth patted Baugi's head. "I think he must be at least part bear and part dog, but whatever he is, he is a godsend. Remind me to tell you about him some day."

Aenella's attentions quickly turned to Selig. "So this is your Viking!" She smoothed back several flyaway hairs, then brushed at her gown. "You have grown into a very handsome man, Selig. Very handsome. Is it any wonder that you so easily stole the heart of my daughter?"

Gwyneth smiled. "He didn't steal my heart, Mother—it was very freely given." Taking her mother's hand in her left hand and Selig's hand in her right, Gwyneth told Aenella all that had happened. "Alfred is dead. Killed by his own evil doing."

"God have mercy on his soul," Aenella whispered, crossing herself. She moved back towards the fire, taking Gwyneth and Selig with her. "My daughter tells me that you came all this way so that she could be married to you by our priest."

He nodded. "It's true!"

"And would you then agree to be married to my Gwyneth by Christian vows?"

He nodded. "I have much respect for your God and His Son."

Aenella pressed the matter. "But can you put aside your own beliefs?"

"For love of Gwyneth I am willing to try." He squeezed her hand.

"I can not ask for more than that," Aenella said softly.

Gwyneth leaned against Selig. It was as if her nightmare had turned to a dream. What more could she wish for? Selig was alive and soon she would be wed to him by Christian vows. In her heart, however, she was prepared to try and understand Selig's beliefs. It would take time.

FORTY-TWO

A fire blazed in the small fireplace, filling the sleeping chamber with warmth. Gwyneth let her long, dark hair caress her shoulders as she brushed her hair. She was totally relaxed as she gave in to her dreams. Soon she would marry Selig with the blessing of her family, including Edwin, who upon hearing of Alfred's treachery, had been meek as a lamb.

Aenella mixed a potion of herbs and flowers to perfume Gwyneth's and stood back to gaze upon her daughter. "Your contentment is obvious to everyone around you," she said.

"Yes, I am happy, Mother. I've loved Selig since I was barely out of my girlhood. I guess you could say I've loved him from the first moment I saw him. And if God wills it and we both live into old age, I shall love him even when we are wrinkled and toothless."

"You are lucky, child, for true love is rare."

"I can tell that you love Father."

Aenella smiled. "Even after so many years I feel dizzy and breathless when he returns after having been away a long time. I think perhaps all women in love feel the same."

Aenella helped her daughter dry her dark hair with a soft woolen cloth. When Gwyneth's hair was dry she wrapped the wool around her daughter's body. Gently she brushed Gwyneth's shining locks, braiding the crown and sides but letting the back hang free.

Gwyneth felt the cool linen of her chemise as her mother slipped it over her head. The wedding gown followed, a pale blue embroidered with flowers stitched by Aenella's own hand. It had been Ethelin's wedding gown, too; thus it had a sentimental value. The draped sleeves hung to the floor, exposing the undertunic.

Upon Gwyneth's head was placed a bridal garland woven of wheat, rosemary, myrtle, and late-blooming flowers. Magenta corn roses, white shepherd's purse, and violet and blue delphiniums made a colorful bouquet, just as she had told Erica that they would.

"The wheat is a symbol of fertility," Aenella reminded her daughter. "Let us hope that you will bring forth many children. My grandchildren!" She seemed almost as excited as she must have been at her own wedding.

Aenella took a step back to appraise her daughter's appearance. "Pinch your cheeks a bit and lick your lips. Ah. Perfect!"

Walking solemnly through the hall, Gwyneth tried to control her excitement but it was nearly impossible. After so many misunderstandings and partings, she and Selig were at last going to be married.

Edwin, Aidan, and Pengwyrn, who usually ignored their sister's beauty, looked at her in awe. Ethelin could barely hide her envy.

"You have never looked more beautiful," Selig whispered in her ear as he took her hand. He was dressed in one of her father's best tunics and looked magnificent in a sapphire-blue tunic trimmed in fur.

"Love makes all women beautiful," she answered, giving his hand a squeeze.

"The bridal cup," Cedd exclaimed, handing it to Gwyneth. With its sprig of rosemary and trailing colored ribbons, it looked like a pagan offering. Perhaps, she thought, they were not so different from pagans as she had once thought.

Because the church in Chester brought back hurtful memories, Gwyneth had elected to be married in the chapel in the courtyard, despite the fact that it would be crowded with all the guests who had come for the festivities. Guests that included Torin, Roland, and several of the other Vikings.

Though Gwyneth's mother had scolded her for her lack of a forgiving heart, Gwyneth had nonetheless refused to have the usual priest witness the vows. Wittingly or unwittingly, he had been a pawn in Alfred's hands and had contributed to their ordeal. The new priest, from a neighboring village, was plump, ruddy-faced, and jovial. He beckoned to Selig and Gwyneth with a smile.

As the priest began the familiar Latin words in his rich voice, Selig looked bewildered, not being familiar with that tongue. He took Gwyneth's hand firmly in his own as she whispered the words. When it was his turn, she whispered in his ear and he repeated what she had said. As the ceremony progressed, Gwyneth felt peace and love in her heart.

The priest bid her sink to her knees to show her homage to the man who would be her husband. Except for women who had the vocation for life as a nun, all women lived dependent on their male kin—father, husband, and, one day, her son or sons. Now that she was marrying, Gwyneth passed from the protection and authority of her father to that of her husband. To symbolize this were the gold rings given and received.

The priest motioned for Selig to take his place upon his knees at Gwyneth's side. Marriage was a willing partnership, a union essential for survival. The ceremony celebrated the change in status for the couple and the promise of their sexuality.

The blessing came and they were wed. Selig kissed her then, his lips caressing hers. "Come, wife," he whispered. "It is time we tasted of each other again." As they ran from the chapel and through the hall, Edwin, Pengwyrn, and the other male guests bid the couple a "lusty wedding night."

Arriving in Gwyneth's bedchamber, Selig smiled. This time the candles and new linen sheets scented with sweet herbs were for him. Closing the door behind them, he took Gwyneth in his arms.

He kissed her long and hard, savoring the soft sweetness of her mouth. Her hand lay flat against him, twining in the golden hair of his chest.

"I'm anxious to go home," she whispered.

"Home?" For a moment he was taken aback. He had thought that she considered Wessex home.

"Back to the settlement. That's where we really belong! And that is where we were our happiest."

"The settlement!" Selig couldn't believe his ears. He had been prepared to sacrifice his own happiness and stay in Wessex if that was what she wanted.

"I was thinking that perhaps we could visit your father every summer . . ." she whispered, thinking fondly of Ragnar.

"And your family . . . ?"

"Just before winter sets in. Father has said that he would be more than happy to help us gather our supplies for the cold weather. After all, the settlement isn't that far away—we are nearly neighbors."

For just a moment, Selig stiffened. "Only if we come to some arrangement where we can benefit him, for I will not take charity."

"Well . . . Father has hinted that he would like to borrow Baugi from time to time to mate with several of his finest dogs."

"Baugi?" He laughed. "I can not believe the bear would have any objections. So it seems the matter has been settled."

Stepping away from him, Gwyneth stripped off her gown and tunic and stood naked before him. The breath caught in his throat as he beheld her beauty again. He ran his hand over the softness of her shoulders, down to the peaks of her full breasts. A blazing fire consumed them both as their bodies touched and caressed.

"Come . . ." she invited, helping him cast away his garments. He followed Gwyneth to the bed.

With hands and lips and words they gave vent to their love, reaching a shattering ecstasy much like the crashing of the waves of the sea. Dragonfire, Gwyneth called it.

"I'll always love you, Gwyneth. You are the treasure of my heart."

"Just as you are mine." Gwyneth nestled in the warmth of his arms, her fingers touching the dragon's tear pendant. "You don't suppose . . ."

Selig covered her hand with his. "Suppose what?"

"The raven's eye brought Torin and Erica together and now the dragon's tear has . . ."

He brushed a kiss against her lips. "Are you getting superstitious, wife?"

"It was just a thought . . ."

"One that I have had as well."

He looked into her eyes, feeling an overwhelming sense of peace and happiness. He had everything he had ever hoped and dreamed of. More importantly, they had their entire lifetime to be together—many sunsets, many dawns, rain and sunshine. Love truly had conquered all.

Look for the next book in
The Vikings series
—EXPLORER—
coming from Zebra Ballad
in September 2002.

Embrace the Romances of

Shannon Drake

Discover The Magic Of
Romance With

Janis Reams Hudson

Celebrate Romance With One of Today's Hottest Authors

Amanda Scott

Put a Little Romance in Your Life With

Betina Krahn